Brian W. Aldiss

THE BOOK OF
BRIAN ALDISS

DAW BOOKS, INC.

DONALD A. WOLLHEIM, PUBLISHER

1301 Avenue of the Americas
New York, N. Y.   10019

COVER ART BY KAREL THOLE.

ACKNOWLEDGMENTS

My thanks go to the editors of the magazines and
anthologies in which the stories concerned first ap-
peared: COMIC INFERNO in *Galaxy*, CARDIAC
ARREST in *Fantastic*, IN THE ARENA in *If*, ALL
THE WORLD'S TEARS in *Nebula*, THE UNDER-
PRIVILEGED and AMEN AND OUT in *New
Worlds*, AS FOR OUR FATAL CONTINUITY in
New Worlds Quarterly, THE SOFT PREDICA-
MENT in *Fantasy & Science Fiction*, SEND HER
VICTORIOUS in *Amazing*.

—B.W.A.

This book is dedicated to
THE SPIRIT OF CAPTAIN JUSTICE

FIRST PRINTING, 1972

PRINTED IN U.S.A.

CONTENTS

Introduction

A mixed feeling of mirth and horror steals over me when recalling the way Mozart, one of the boy wonders of the musical world, picked up a violin for the first time and discovered that he could play it. Perhaps he is the originator of all those jokes that go, "Can you play the piano?"—"I don't know, I've never tried." In Mozart's case, it was no joke.

Mozarts are born, not made. Writers are different; in our profession, it seems it's never too late to learn. To encourage late comers, there is the notable case of William de Morgan, a somewhat Pre-Raphaelite sort of Victorian who spent most of his life designing pottery and glass. He retired from work in his mid-sixties, and only then took up writing. His first novel, *Joseph Vance*, was published when he was sixty-seven, in 1906. It was a great success, and he went on to write several more.

By contrast, I embarked upon the perilous seas of authorship early in life, and am still trying to learn. As soon as I was able to write, I was able to write little stories. It came naturally to me. What prompted me to it I do not know, nor do I find the question particularly rewarding, although it is one that often gets asked.

As to what moved me to write science fiction, that is a different matter. It happens that as this book is being compiled I am drawing toward the end of a larger and much longer-term operation, the writing of a history of science fiction. This history, to be callled *The Billion Year Spree*, has led me on some strange and interesting quests.

One of the most curious of its byways is represented by a small book which lies on my desk now, amid stacks of other work. A book dealer had just produced it for me. The volume is one in a long series published in England between world wars by the old Amalgamated Press. The series is the Boys' Friend Library.

This particular volume is No. 505 and, since four titles in the series were issued every month, it is dated precisely: 5—12—35. Its title is *The World in Darkness*, and it was written by Murray Roberts. I bought my first copy in Webster's Bookshop, in East Dereham, Norfolk. And the sight and touch of this second copy, arriving out of time so many years later, is enough to have the effect on my memory of Proust's petite madeleine, so that I can recall vividly how it felt to be ten years old and to search through the narrow shelves behind Webster's glass door, where the Boys' Friend Library titles were kept. I was wearing—I have to face the fact—blue serge shorts; and in that same month I bought another title, also science fiction, called *When the Great Apes Came*.

On these two volumes I blew money which should have gone toward my mother's Christmas present: Can any science fiction reader boast greater dedication than that?!

The World in Darkness was my prime choice. The source of my excitement was made clear in a little box on the cover which proclaimed "CAPTAIN JUSTICE'S greatest adventure." But the cognoscenti needed no such nudge. The author's name alone was enough to alert us that this story would be about Captain Justice; for he was Murray Robert's hero. Besides, the Gentleman Adventurer was portrayed on the cover, clad as usual in white ducks and wearing his nautical cap at a rakish angle.

With Justice were his loyal companions, the bald O'Malley, red-haired Len Connor, and snub-nose young Midge. They are staring out appalled (people on Amalgamated covers were always being appalled) at a motor yacht passing them on the sea, gleaming an eerie white. All the rest of the world has been plunged into darkness impenetrable.

Useless to tell me that that inert light-absorbing gas in which Murray Roberts' solar system found itself was derived from Conan Doyle's gas in *The Poison Belt*. Roberts' gas was much more terrible, much more fun. And as a child I could not perceive, as I do now, that Roberts' style was atrocious enough to make the teeth ache and the retinas detach themselves.

When I bought *World in Darkness* the first time, I had long been a fan of Captain Justice. He appeared in serial form in my favorite magazine, *Modern Boy,* every Saturday, price 2d., and these adventures were later gathered into the fragile book form of the Boys' Friend Library, in their paper covers.

It was Captain Justice, I am convinced, who gave me my baptism in science fiction. I have now been working in the field for many years myself, and have come to see that it has a lot more to offer than simple catastrophes, wonder adventures, and inversions of the natural order (although these eternally have their place). My simple thought is that those writers so moved should go out and break new ground and find new subject matter, or otherwise the field will become rigid and formalized to the extent where eventual fossilization will take over. In my own fashion, I am generally interested in finding something fresh to talk about, or in talking about traditional matters in ways that emphasize their relevance to the present. Since I do not credit the existence of telepathy in anything except perhaps a rudimentary form, and do not believe that the immensity and mystery of space should be cheapened by spaceship forays made generally for the sake of little more than astonishment, I am naturally a difficult case who has to go his own way.

But in the stories collected here, written over several years, I am not endeavoring to present myself as a difficult case. I am telling stories—a pleasurable and generally harmless occupation. Some astonishment goes on. There may even be a spaceship here or there, or a sudden splutter of something akin to telepathy. Most of the stories are genial, in telling if not in mood, because bad news about other people is by no means displeasing to read.

What is more, there is a general scattering of inversions of the natural order, a bit of Conan Doyle's responsibilities are still not at an end. Which is why I have dedicated the volume with such tender care.

—Brian W. Aldiss

Heath House,
Southmoor.

March 1972

COMIC INFERNO

January Birdlip spread his hands in a characteristic gesture.

"Well, I'm a liberal man, and that was a very liberal party," he exclaimed, sinking further back into the car seat. "How say you, my dear Freud? Are you suitably satiated?"

His partner, the egregious Freddie Freud, took some time to reply, mainly because of the bulky brunette who pinned him against the side of the car in a festive embrace. "Vershoye's parties are better than his books," he finally agreed.

"There isn't a publisher in Paris does it more stylishly," Birdlip pursued. "And his new Twenty Second Century Studies is a series well worth a stylish launching, think you not, friend Freddie?"

"This is no time for intellectual discussion. Don't forget we're only taking this babe as far as Calais." And with that, Freud burrowed back under his brunette with the avidity of a sexton beetle.

Not without envy, Birdlip looked over at his younger partner. Although he tried to fix his thoughts on the absent Mrs. Birdlip, a sense of loneliness overcame him. With tipsy Solemnity he sang to himself, "There was a young man in December, Who sighed, "Oh I hardly remember, How the girls in July Used to kiss me and tie—"

Moistening his lips, he peeped through the dividing glass at Bucket and Hippo, Freud's and his personal romen sitting in the front seats, at the dark French countryside slinking past, and then again at the brunette (how good was her English?), before softly intoning the rest of his song, "Daisy-chains round my sun-dappled member."

11

Then he started talking aloud, indifferent to whether Fred answered or not. It was the privilege of slightly aging cultural publishers to be eccentric.

"I found it consoling that Paris too has its robot and roman troubles. You heard Vershoye talking about a casino that was flooded because the robot fire engine turned up and extinguished a conflagration that did not exist. . . ? Always a crumb of comfort somewhere, my dear Freud; nice to think of our French brothers sharing our sorrows! And your ample lady friend: her robot driver drove her car through a newsvendor's stall—through stationary stationery, you almost might say—so that she had to beg a lift home from us, thus transforming her misfortune into your bonchance. . . ."

But the word "misfortune" reminded him of his brother, Rainbow Birdlip, and he sank into silence, the loneliness returning on heavy Burgundian feet.

Ah yes, ten—even five—years ago, Birdlip Brothers had been one of the most respected imprints in London. And then . . . it had been just after he had seen the first four titles of the Prescience Library through the press—Rainbow had changed. Changed overnight! Now he was outdoor-farming near Maidstone, working in the fields with his hands like a blessed roman, entirely without cultural or financial interests.

The thought choked January Birdlip. That brilliant intellect lost to pig farming! Trying to take refuge in drunkenness, he began to sing again.

"How the giirls in July Used to kiss me and tie—"

But their limousine was slowing now, coming up to the outer Calais roundabout, where one road led into the city and the other onto the Channel Bridge. The robot driver pulled to a stop by the side of the road, where an all-night café armored itself with glaring lights against the first approach of dawn. Fred Freud looked up.

"Dash it, we're here already, toots!"

"Thank you for such a nice ride," said the brunette, shaking her anatomy into place, and opening the side door. "You made me very comfortable."

"Mademoiselle, allow me to buy you a coffee before we part company forever, and then I can write down your phone number. . . . Shan't be five minutes, Jan." This last remark was thrown over Freud's left shoulder as he blundered out after the girl.

He slammed the door reverberatingly. With one arm around the girl, who looked, Birdlip thought, blowsy in the bright lights, he disappeared into the café, where a roman awaited their orders.

"Well! well, I never!" Birdlip exclaimed.

Really, Freud seemed to have no respect for seniority of age or position. For a heady moment, Birdlip thought of ordering the car to drive on. But beside the wheel sat Bucket and Hippo, silent because they were switched off, as most romen were during periods of long inactivity, and the sight of them motionless there intimidated Birdlip into a similar inertia.

Diverting his anger, he began to worry about the Homing Device decision. But there again, Freddie Freud had had his way over his senior partner. It shouldn't be. . . . No, the question must be reopened directly Freud returned. Most firms had installed homing devices by now, and Freud would just have to bow to progress.

The minutes ticked by. Dawn began to nudge night apologetically in the ribs of cloud overhead. Fred Freud returned, waving the brunette a cheerful good-bye as he hopped into the car again.

"Overblown figure," Birdlip said severely, to kill his partner's enthusiasm.

"Quite agree, quite agree," Freud agreed cheerfully, still fanning the air harder than a window cleaner as he protracted his farewells.

"Overblown figure—and cheap behavior."

"Quite agree, quite agree," Freud said again, renewing his exertions as the car drew off. With a last glance at the vanishing figure, he added reminiscently, "Still, the parts were better than the whore."

They accelerated so fast around the inclined feed road to the Bridge that Bucket and Hippo rattled together.

"I regret I shall have to reverse my previous decision on the homing device matter," said Birdlip, switching to attack before Freud could launch any more coarse remarks. "My nerves will not endure the sight of romen standing around nonfunctioning for hours when they are not needed. When we get back, I shall contact Rootes and ask them to fit the device into all members of our nonhuman staff."

Freud's reflexes, worn as they were by the stimulations of the previous few hours, skidded wildly in an attempt to meet this new line of attack.

"Into all members—you mean you—but look, Jan—Jan, let's discuss this matter—or rather let's rediscuss it, because

I understood it was all settled—when we are less tired. Eh? How's that?"

"I am not tired, nor do I wish to discuss it. I have an aversion to seeing our metal menials standing about lifeless for hours on end. They—well, to employ an archaism, they give me the creeps. We will have the new device installed and they can go—go home, get off the premises when not required."

"You realize that with some of the romen, the proof-readers, for instance, we never know when we are going to want them."

"*Then*, my dear Freud, then we employ the homing device and they return at once. It's the modern way of working. It surprises me that on this point you should be so reactionary."

"You're overfond of that word, Jan. People have only to disagree with you to be called reactionary. The reason you dislike seeing robots around is simply because you feel guilty about man's dependence on slave machines. It may be a fashionable phobia, but it's totally divorced from reality. Robots have no feelings, if I may quote one of the titles on our list, and your squeamishness will involve us in a large capital outlay."

"Squeamishness! These arguments ad hominem lead no-where, Freddie. Birdlip Brothers will keep up with the times —as publishers of that distinguished science fiction classics series, the Prescience Library, Birdlip Brothers *must* keep up with the times, so there's an end on it."

They sped high over the sea toward the mist that hid the English coast. Averting his eyes from the panorama, Freud said feebly, "I'd really rather we discussed this when we were less tired."

"Thank you, I am not tired," January Birdlip said. And he closed his eyes and went to sleep just as a sickly cyclamen tint spread over the eastern cloudbank, announcing the sun. The great bridge with its thousand-foot spans turned straw color, in indifferent contrast to the gray chop of waves in the Channel below.

Birdlip sank into his chair. Hippo obligingly lifted his feet onto the desk.

"Thank you, Hippocrates, how kind. . . . You know I named you after the robot in those rather comic tales by— ah . . . oh dear, my memory, but still it doesn't matter, and I've probably told you that anyway."

"The tales were by the pseudonymous René Lafayette, sir,

flourished circa 1950, sir, and yes, you had told me."

"Probably I had. All right, Hippo, stand back. Please adjust yourself so that you don't stand so close to me when you talk."

"At what distance should I stand, sir?"

Exasperatedly, he said, "Between one point five and two meters away." Romen had to have these silly precise instructions; really it was no wonder he wanted the wretched things out of the way when they were not in use . . . which recalled him to the point. It was sixteen o'clock on the day after their return from Paris, and the Rootes Group man was due to confer on the immediate installation of homing devices. Freud ought to be in on the discussion, just to keep the peace.

"Nobody could say Freddie and I *quarrel*," Birdlip sighed. He pressed the fingertips of his left hand against the fingertips of his right and rested his nose on them.

"Pity about poor brother Rainbow though. . . . Quite inexplicable. . . . Such genius. . . ."

Affectionately, he glanced over at the bookcase on his left, filled with the publications of Birdlip Brothers. In particular he looked at his brother's brainchild, the Prescience Library. The series was bound in half-aluminum with proxisonic covers that announced the contents to anyone who came within a meter of them while wearing any sort of metal about his person.

That was why the bookcase was now soundproofed. Before, it had been deafening with Hippo continually passing the shelves; the roman, with fifty kilos of metal in his entrails, had raised a perpetual bellow from the books. Such was the price of progress. . . .

Again he recalled his straggling thought.

"Nobody could say Freddie and I quarrel, but our friendship is certainly made up of a lot of differences. Hippo, tell Mr. Freud I am expecting Gavotte of Rootes and trust he will care to join us. Tell him gin corallinas will be served—that should bring him along. Oh, and tell Pig Iron to bring the drink in now."

"Yessir."

Hippo departed. He was a model of the de Havilland "Governor" class, Series II MK viiA, and as such walked with the slack-jointed stance typical of his class, as if he had been hit smartly behind the knees with a steel baseball bat.

He walked down the corridor carefully in case he banged into one of the humans employed at Birdlip's. Property in

London had become so cheap that printing and binding could be carried out on the premises; yet in the whole concern only six humans were employed. Still Hippo took care; care was bred into him, a man-made instinct.

As he passed a table on which somebody had carelessly left a new publication, its proxisonic cover, beginning in a whisper, rising to a shout, and dying into a despairing moan as Hippo disappeared, said, "The Turkish annexation of the Suezzeus Canal on Mars in 2162 is one of the most colorful stories in the annals of Red Planet colonization, yet until now it has lacked a worthy historian. The hero of the incident was an Englishman ohhhh . . ."

Turning the corner, Hippo almost bumped into Pig Iron, a heavy forty-year-old Cunarder of the now obsolete "Expedition" line. Pig Iron was carrying a tray full of drinks.

"I see you are carrying a tray full of drinks," Hippo said. "Please carry them in to Mr. Jan immediately."

"I am carrying them in to Mr. Jan immediately," said Pig Iron, without a hint of defiance; he was equipped with the old "Multi-Syllog" speech platters only.

As Pig Iron rounded the corner with the tray, Hippo heard a tiny voice gather volume to say ". . . annexation of the Suezzeus Canal on Mars in 2162 is one of the most colorful . . ." He tapped on Mr. Freud's door and put his metal head in.

Freud sprawled over an immense review list, with Bucket standing to attention at his side.

"Delete the Mercury "Mercury"—they've reviewed none of our books since 72," he was saying as he looked up.

"Mr. Jan is expecting Gavotte of Rootes for a homing device discussion, sir, and trusts you will care to join him. Gin corallinas will be served," Hippo said.

Freud's brow darkened.

"Tell him I'm busy. This was his idea. Let him cope with Gavotte himself."

"Yessir."

"And make it sound polite, you ruddy roman."

"Yessir."

"OK, get out. I'm busy."

"Yessir."

Hippo beat a retreat down the corridor, and a tiny voice broke into a shout of ". . . ish annexation of the Suezzeus Canal on Mars in 2162 . . ."

Meanwhile, Freud turned angrily to Bucket.

"You hear that, you tin horror? A man's going to come

from one of the groups that manufactures your kind and he's going to tinker with you. And he's going to install a little device in each of you. And you know what that little device will do?"

"Yessir, the device will——"

"Well, shuddup and listen while *I* tell *you*. You don't tell me, Bucket, *I* tell *you*. That little device will enable you plastic-placentaed power tools to go home when you aren't working! Isn't that wonderful? In other words, you'll be a little bit more like humans, and one by one these nasty little modifications will be fitted until finally you'll be just like humans. . . . Oh God, men are crazy, we're all crazy. . . . Say something, Bucket."

"I am not human, sir. I am a multipurpose roman manufactured by de Havilland, a member of the Rootes Group, owned by the Chrysler Corporation. I am 'Governor' class, Series II MKII, chassis number A4437."

"Thank you for those few kind words."

Freud rose and began pacing up and down. He stared hard at the impassive machine. He clenched his fists and his tongue came unbidden between his teeth.

"You cannot reproduce, Bucket, can you?"

"No, sir."

"Why can't you?"

"I have not the mechanism for reproduction, sir."

"Nor can you copulate, Bucket. . . . Answer me, Bucket."

"You did not ask me a question, sir."

"You animated ore, I said you could not copulate. Agree with me."

"I agree with you, sir."

"Good. That makes you just a ticking hunk of clockwork, doesn't it, Bucket? Can you hear yourself ticking, Bucket?"

"My auditory circuits detect the functioning of my own relays as well as the functioning of your heart and respiratory organs, sir."

Freud stopped behind his servant. His face was red; his mouth had spread itself over his face.

"I see I shall have to show you who is master again, Bucket. Get me the whip!"

Unhesitatingly, Bucket walked slack-kneed over to a wall cupboard. Opening it, he felt in the back and produced a long Afrikaner ox-whip that Freud had bought on a world tour several years ago. He handed it to his master.

Freud seized it and immediately lashed out with it, catch-

ing the roman around his legs so that he staggered. Gratified,
Freud said, "How was that, eh?"

"Thank you, sir."

"I'll give you 'Thank you.' Bend over my desk!"

As the roman leaned forward across the review list, Freud
lay to, planting the leather thong with a resonant precision
across Bucket's back at regular fifteen second intervals.

"Ah, you must feel that, whatever you pretend. Tell me
you feel it!"

"I feel it, sir."

"Yes, well, you needn't think *you're* going to get a homing
device and be allowed to go home. . . . You're not human.
Why should *you* enjoy the privileges of humanity?"

He emphasized his remarks with the whip. Each blow
knocked the roman two centimeters along the desk, a movement Bucket always punctiliously corrected. Breathing heavily, Freud said, "Cry out in pain, blast you. I know it hurts!"

Punctiliously, Bucket began to imitate a cry of pain, making
it coincide with the blows.

"My God, it's hot in here," said Freud, laying to.

"Oh dear, it's hot in here," said Birdlip, laying two plates
of snacks on his desk. "Hippo, go and see what's the matter
with the air-conditioning. . . . I'm sorry, Mr. Gavotte; you
were saying. . . ?"

And he looked poitely and not without fascination at the
little man opposite him. Gavotte, even when sitting nursing
a gin corallina, was never still. From buttock to buttock he
shifted his weight, or he smoothed back a coif of hair, or
brushed real and imaginary dandruff from his shoulders, or
adjusted his tie. With a ball-point, with a vernier, and once
with a comb, he tapped little tunes on his teeth. This he
managed to do even while talking volubly.

It was a performance in notable contrast to the immobility
of the new assistant roman that had accompanied him and
now stood beside him awaiting orders.

"Eh, I was saying, Mr. Birdlip, how fashionable the homing
device has become, very fashionable. I mean, if you're not
contemporary you're nothing. Firms all over the world are
using them—and no doubt the fashion will soon spread to the
system, although as you know on the planets there are far
more robots than romen—simply because, I think, men are
becoming tired of seeing their menials about all day, as you
might say."

"Exactly how I feel, Mr. Gavotte; I have grown tired of

seeing my—yes, yes, quite." Realizing that he was repeating himself, Birdlip closed that sentence down and opened up another. "One thing you have not explained. Just where do the romen *go* when they go home?"

"Oh ha ha, Mr. Birdlip, ha ha, bless you, you don't have to worry about that, ha ha," chuckled Gavotte, performing a quick obligato on his eyeteeth. "With this little portable device with which we supply you, which you can carry around or leave anywhere according to whim, you just have to press the button and a circuit is activated in your roman that impels him to return at once to work immediately by the quickest route."

Taking a swift tonic sip of his gin, Birdlip said, "Yes, you told me that. But where do the romen go when they go away?"

Leaning forward, Gavotte spun his glass on the desk with his finger and said confidentially, "I'll tell you, Mr. Birdlip, since you ask. As you know, owing to tremendous population drops both here and elsewhere, due to one or two factors too numerous to name, there are far less people about than there were."

"That does follow."

"Quite so, ha ha," agreed Gavotte, gobbling a snack. "So, large sections of our big cities are now utterly deserted or unfrequented and falling into decay. This applies especially to London, where whole areas once occupied by artisans stand derelict. Now my company has bought up one of these sections, called Paddington. No humans live there, so the romen can conveniently stack themselves in the old houses—out of sight and out of ha ha harm."

Birdlip stood up.

"Very well, Mr. Gavotte. And your roman here is ready to start conversions straight away? He can begin on Hippocrates now, if you wish."

"Certainly, certainly! Delighted." Gavotte beckoned to the new and gleaming machine behind him. "This by the way is the latest model from one of our associates, Anglo-Atomic. It's the 'Fleetfeet,' with streamlined angles and heinleined joints. We've just had an order for a dozen—this is confidential, by the way, but I don't suppose it'll matter if I tell *you*, Mr. Birdlip—we've just had an order for a dozen from Buckingham Palace. Can I send you one on trial?"

"I'm full staffed, thank you. Now if you'd like to start work . . . I have another appointment at seventeen-fifty."

"Fifty, fifty-one, fifty-two. Fifty-two! What stamina he

has!" exclaimed the RSPCR captain, Warren Pavment, to his assistant.

"He has finished now," said the assistant, a 71 AEI model called Toggle. "Do you detect a look of content on his face, Captain?"

Hovering in a copter over the Central area, man and roman peered into the tiny screen by their knees. On the screen, clearly depicted by their spycast, a tiny Freddie Freud collapsed into a chair, rested on his laurels, and gave a tiny Bucket the whip to return to the cupboard.

"You can stop squealing now," his tiny voice rang coldly in the cockpit.

"I don't thing he looks content," the RSPCR captain said. "I think he looks unhappy—guilty even."

"Guilty is bad," Toggle said, as his superior spun the magnification. Freud's face gradually expanded, blotting out his body, filling the whole screen. Perspiration stood on his cheeks and forehead, each drop surrounded by its aura on the spycast.

"I'll bet that hurt me more than it did you," he panted. "You wrought-iron wretches, you never suffer enough."

In the copter, roman and human looked at each otther in concern.

"You heard that? He's in trouble. Let's go down and pick him up," said the Captain of the Royal Society for the Prevention of Cruelty to Robots.

Cutting the cast, he sent his craft spinning down through a column of warm air.

Hot air ascended from Mr. Gavotte. Running a sly finger between collar and neck, he was saying, "I'm a firm believer in culture myself, Mr. Birdlip. Not that I get much time for reading—"

A knock at the door and Hippo came in. Going to him with relief, Birdlip said, "Well, what's the matter with the air-conditioning?"

"The heating circuits are on, sir. They have come on in error, three months ahead of time."

"Did you speak to them?"

"I spoke to them, sir, but their auditory circuits are malfunctioning."

"Really, Hippo! Why is nobody doing anything about this?"

"Cogswell is down there, sir. But as you know he is rather an unreliable model and the heat in the control room has deactivated him."

Birdlip said reflectively, "Alas, the ills that steel is heir to. All right, Hippo, you stay here and let Mr. Gavotte and his assistant install your homing device before they do the rest of the staff. I'll go and see Mr. Freud. He's always good with the heating system; perhaps he can do something effective. As it is, we're slowly cooking."

Gavotte and Fleetfeet closed in on Hippo.

"Open your mouth, old fellow," Gavotte ordered. When Hippo complied, Gavotte took hold of his lower jaw and pressed it down hard, until with a click it detached itself together with Hippo's throat. Fleetfeet laid jaw and throat on the desk while Gavotte unscrewed Hippo's dust filters and air cooler and removed his windpipe. As he lifted off the chest inspection cover, he said cheerfully, "Fortunately this is only a minor operation. Give me my drill, Fleetfeet." Waiting for it, he gazed at Hippo and picked his nose with considerable scientific detachment.

Not wishing to see any more, Birdlip left his office and headed for his partner's room.

As he hurried down the corridor, he was stopped by a stranger. Uniform, in these days of individualism, was a thing of the past; nevertheless, the stranger wore something approaching a uniform: a hat reproducing a swashbuckling Eighteenth Century design, a plastic plume: a Nineteenth or Twentieth Century tunic that, with its multiplicity of pockets, gave its wearer the appearance of a perambulating chest of drawers: Twenty-First Century skirt-trousers with mobled borsts; and boots hand painted with a contemporary tartan paint.

Covering his surprise with a parade of convention, Birdlip said, "Warm today, isn't it?"

"Perhaps you can help me. My name's Captain Pavment, Captain Warren Pavment. The doorbot sent me up here, but I have lost my way."

As he spoke, the captain pulled forth a gleaming metal badge. At once a voice by their side murmured conspiratorially, ". . . kish annexation of the Suezzeus Canal on Mars . . ." dying gradually as the badge was put away again.

"RSPCR? Delighted to help you, Captain. Who or what are you looking for?"

"I wish to interview a certain Frederick Freud, employed in this building," said Pavment, becoming suddenly official now that the sight of his own badge had reassured him. "Could you kindly inform me whereabouts his whereabouts is?"

"Certainly. I'm going to see Mr. Freud myself. Pray follow me. Nothing serious, I hope, Captain?"

"Let us say nothing that should not yield to questioning."

As he led the way, Birdlip said, "Perhaps I should introduce myself. I am January Birdlip, senior partner of this firm. I shall be very glad to do anything I can to help."

"Perhaps you'd better join our little discussion, Mr. Birdlip, since the—irregularities have taken place on your premises."

They knocked and entered Freud's room.

Freud stood looking over a small section of city. London was quieter than it had been since before Tacitus' "uncouth warriors" had run to meet the Roman invaders landing there twenty-two centuries ago. Dwindling population had emptied its avenues; the extinction of legislators, financiers, tycoons, speculators, and planners had left acres of it desolate but intact, decaying but not destroyed, stranded like a ship without oars yet not without awe upon the strand of history.

Freud turned around and said, "It's hot, isn't it? I think I'm going home, Jan."

"Before you go, Freddie, this gentleman here is Captain Pavment of the RSPCR."

"He will be after I've left, too, won't he?" Freud asked in mock puzzlement.

"I've come on a certain matter, sir," Pavment said, firmly but respectfully. "I think it might be better if your roman here left the room."

Making a small gesture of defeat, Freud sat down on the edge of his desk and said, "Bucket, get out of the room."

"Yessir." Bucket left.

Pavment cleared his throat and said, "Perhaps you know what I've come about, Mr. Freud."

"You blighters have had a spycast onto me, I suppose? Here we've reached a peaceful period of history, when for the first time man is content to pursue his own interests without messing up his neighbors, and you people deliberately follow a contrary policy of interference. You're nothing but conformists!"

"The RSPCR is a voluntary body."

"Precisely what I dislike about it. You volunteer to stick your nose into other people's affairs. Well, say what you have to say and get it over with."

Birdlip fidgeted unhappily near the door.

"If you'd like me to leave—"

Both men motioned him to silence, and Pavment said,

"The situation is not as simple as you think, sir, as the RSPCR well know. This is, as you say, an age when men get along with each other better than they've ever done; but current opinion gives the reason for this as either progress or the fact that there are now fewer men to get along with."

"Both excellent reasons, I'd say," Birdlip said.

"The RSPCR believes there is a much better reason. Man no longer clashes with his fellow man because he can relieve all his antagonisms on his mechanicals—and nowadays there are four romen and countless robots to every one person. Romen are civilization's whipping boys, just as once Negroes, Jews, Catholics, or any of the old minorities were."

"Speaking as a Negro myself," said January Birdlip, "I'm all for the change."

"But see what follows," said Pavment. "In the old days, a man's sickness, by being vented on his fellows, became known, and thus could be treated. Now it is vented on his roman, and the roman never tells. So the man's neuroses take root in him and flourish by indulgence."

Growing red in the face, Freud said, "Oh, that doesn't follow, surely."

"The RSPCR has evidence that mental sickness is far more widely prevalent than anyone in our laissez-faire society suspects. So when we find a roman being treated cruelly, we try to prevent it, for we know it signifies a sick man. What happens to the roman is immaterial: but we try to direct the man to treatment.

"Now you, Mr. Freud—half an hour ago you were thrashing your roman with a bullwhip which you keep in that cupboard over there. The incident was one of many, nor was it just a healthy outburst of sadism. Its overtones of guilt and despair were symptoms of deep sickness.'"

"Can this be true, Freddie?" Birdlip asked—quite unnecessarily, for Freud's face, even the attitude in which he crouched, showed the truth. He produced a handkerchief and shakily wiped his brow.

"Oh, it's true enough, Jan; why deny it? I've always hated romen. I'd better tell you what they did to my sister—in fact, what they *are* doing, and not so very far from here. . . ."

Not so very far from there, Captain Pavment's copter was parked, awaiting his return. In it, also waiting, sat the roman Toggle peering into the small spycast screen. On the screen, a tiny Freud said, "I've always hated romen."

Flipping a switch which put him in communication with

a secret headquarters in the Paddington area, Toggle said, "I hope you are recording all this. It should be of particular interest to the Human Sociological Study Group."

A metallic voice from the other end said, "We are receiving you loud and clear."

"London Clear is one of the little artificial islands on Lake Mediterranean. There my sister and I spent our childhood and were brought up by romen," Freddie Freud said, looking anywhere but at Birdlip and the captain.

"We are twins, Maureen and I. My mother had entered into Free Association with my father, who left for Touchdown, Venus, before we came into the world and has, to our knowledge, never returned. Our mother died in childbirth. There's one item they haven't got automated yet.

"The romen that brought us up were as all romen always are—never unkind, never impatient, never unjust, never anything but their damned self-sufficient selves. No matter what Maureen and I did, even if we kicked them or spat on them or peed on them, we could elicit from them no reaction, no sign of love or anger, no hint of haste or weariness—nothing!

"Do you wonder we both grew up loathing their gallium guts—and yet at the same time being dependent on them? In both of us a permanent and absolutely hopeless love-hate relationship with romen has been established. You see I face the fact quite clearly."

Birdlip said, "You told me you had a sister, Freddie, but you said she died at the time of the Great Venusian Plague."

"Would she had! No, I can't say that, but you should see how she lives now. Occasionally I have gone quite alone to see her. She lives in Paddington with the romen."

"With the romen?" Pavment echoed. "How?"

Freud's manner grew more distraught.

"You see we found as we grew up that there was one way in which we had power over the romen—power to stir emotion in them, I mean, apart from the built-in power to command. Having no sex, romen are curious about it. . . . Overwhelmingly curious. . . .

"I can't tell you the indecencies they put us through when we reached puberty. . . .

"Well, to cut a long and nasty story short, Maureen lives with the romen of Paddington. They look after her, supply her with stolen food, clothes, and the rest, while in return she—satisfies their curiosity."

Greatly to his own embarrassment, Birdlip let out a shrill

squeal of laughter. It broke up the atmosphere of the confessional.

"This is a valuable bit of data, Mr. Freud," Pavment said, nodding his head in approval, while the plastic plume in his hat shimmied with a secret delight.

"If that's all you make of it, be blowed to you," Freud said. He rose. "Just what you think you can do for either myself or my sister, I won't ask, but in any case our way of life is set and we must look after ourselves."

Pavment answered with something of the same lack of color in his words. "That is entirely your decision. The RSPCR is a very small organization; we couldn't coerce if we wanted to—"

"—that happily is the situation with most organizations nowadays—"

"—but your evidence will be incorporated in a report we are preparing to place before the World Government."

"Very well, Captain. Now perhaps you'll leave, and remove your officialdom from my presence. I have work to do."

Before Pavment could say more, Birdlip inserted himself before his partner, patted his arm and said, "I laughed purely out of nervousness then, Freddie. Please don't think I'm not sympathetic about your troubles. Now I see why you didn't want our romen and Bucket particularly fitted with homing devices."

"God, it's hot in here," Freud replied, sinking down and mopping his face. "Okay, Jan, thanks, but say no more; it's not a topic I exactly care to dwell on. I'm going home; I don't feel well. . . . Who was it said that life was a comedy to the man who thinks, a tragedy to the man who feels?"

"Yes, you go home. In fact I think I'll go home, too. It's extremely hot in here, isn't it? There's trouble down below with the heat control. We'll get someone to look into it tomorrow morning. Perhaps you'll have a look yourself."

Still talking, he backed to the door and left, with a final nervous grin at Freud and Pavment, who were heavily engaged in grinning nervously at each other.

Glimpses into other people's secret lives always distressed him. It would be a relief to be home with Mrs. Birdlip. He was outside and into his car, leaving for once without Hippo, before he remembered he had an appointment at seventeen-fifty.

Dash the appointment, he thought. Fortunately people could afford to wait these days. He wanted to see Mrs. Birdlip. Mrs. Birdlip was a nice comfortable little woman. She made loose covers of brightly patterned chintzes to dress her romen servants in.

Next morning, when Birdlip entered his office, a new manuscript awaited him on his desk—a pleasant enough event for a firm mainly specializing in reprints. He seated himself at the desk, then realized how outrageously hot it was.

Angrily, he banged the button of the new homing control on his desk.

Hippo appeared.

"Oh, you're there, Hippo. Did you go home last night?"

"Yessir."

"Where did you go?"

"To a place of shelter with other romen."

"Uh. Hippo, this confounded heating system is always going wrong. We had trouble last week, and then it cured itself. Ring the engineers; get them to come around; I will speak to them. Tell them to send a human this time."

"Sir, you had an appointment yesterday at seventeen-fifty."

"What has that to do with it?"

"It was an appointment with a human engineer. You ordered him last week when the heating malfunctioned. His name was Pursewarden."

"Never mind his name. What did you do?"

"As you were gone, sir, I sent him away."

"Ye gods! What was his name?"

"His name was Pursewarden, sir."

"Get him on the phone and say I want the system repaired today. Tell him to get on with it whether I am here or not. . . ." Irritation and frustration seized him, provoked by the heat. "And as a matter of fact I *shan't* be here. I'm going to see my brother."

"Your brother Rainbow, sir?"

"Since I have only one brother, yes, you fool. Is Mr. Freud in yet? No? Well, I want you to come with me. Leave instructions with Bucket; tell him all I've told you to tell Mr. Freud. . . . And look lively," he added, collecting the manuscript off the desk as he spoke. "I have an irrational urge to be on the way."

On the way, he leafed through the manuscript. It was entitled *An Explanation of Man's Superfluous Activities*. At first, Birdlip found the text yielded no more enticement than the title, sown as it was in desiccated phrases and bedded out in a labored style. Persevering with it, he realized that the author—whose name, Isaac Toolust, meant nothing to him—

had formulated a grand and alarming theory covering many human traits which had not before been subjected to what proved a chillingly objective examination.

He looked up. They had stopped.

To one side of the road were the rolling hedgeless miles of Kent with giant wharley crops ripening under the sun; in the copper distance a machine glinted, tending them with metal motherliness. On the other side, rupturing the flow of cultivation, lay Gafia Farm, a higgledy-piggledy of low buildings, trees and clutter, sizzliing in sun and pig smell.

Hippo detached himself from the arm bracket that kept him steady when the car was in motion, climbed out, and held the door open for Birdlip.

Man and roman trudged into the yard.

A mild-eyed fellow was stacking sawed logs in a shed. He came out as Birdlip approached and nodded to him without speaking. Birdlip had never seen him on previous visits to his brother's farm.

"Is Rainy about, please?" Birdlip asked.

"Around the back. Help yourself."

The fellow was back at his logs almost before Birdlip moved away.

They found Rainbow Birdlip around the back of the cottage, as predicted. Jan's younger brother was standing under a tree cleaning horse harness with his own hands; Birdlip was taken for a moment by a sense of being in the presence of history; the feeling could have been no stronger had Rainy been discovered painting himself with woad.

"Rainy!" Birdlip said.

His brother looked up, gave him a placid greeting, and continued to polish. As usual he was wrapped in a meter thick blanket of content. Conversation strangled itself in Birdlip's throat, but he forced himself to speak.

"I perceive you have a new helper out in front, Rainy."

Rainy showed relaxed interest. He strolled over, carrying the harness over one shoulder.

"That's right, Jan. Fellow walked in and asked for a job. I said he could have one if he didn't work too hard. Only got here an hour or so ago."

"He soon got to work."

"Couldn't wait! Reckoned he'd never felt a bit of non-man-made timber before. Him thirty-five and all. Begged to be allowed to handle logs. Nice fellow. Name of Pursewarden."

"Pursewarden? Pursewarden? Where have I heard that name before?"

"It is the surname of the human engineer with whom you had the appointment that you did not keep," Hippo said.

"Thank you, Hippo. Your wonderful memory! Of course it is. This can't be the same man."

"It is, sir. I recognized him."

Rainy pushed past them, striding toward the open cottage door.

"Funnily enough I had another man yesterday persuade me to take him on," he said, quite unconscious of his brother's dazed look. "Man name of Jagger Bank. He's down in the orchard now, feeding the pigs. . . . Lot of people just lately leaving town. See them walking down the road—year ago, never saw a human soul on foot. . . . Well, it'll be all the same a century from now. Come on in, Jan, if you want."

It was his longest speech. He sat down on a sound home-made chair and fell silent, emptied of news. The harness he placed carefully on the table before him. His brother came into the dim room, noted that its confusion had increased since his last visit, flicked a dirty shirt off a chair, and also sat down. Hippo entered the room and stood by the door, his neat functional lines and the chaste ornamentation on his breastplates contrasting with the disorder about him.

"Was your Pursewarden an engineer, Rainy?"

"Don't know. Didn't think to ask. We talked mostly about wood, the little we said."

A silence fell, filled with Birdlip's customary uneasy mixture of love, sorrow, and murderous irritation at the complacence of his brother.

"Any news?" he asked sharply.

"Looks like being a better harvest for once."

He never asked for Jan's news.

Looking about, Birdlip saw Rainy's old run of the Prescience Library half buried under clothes and apple boxes and disinfectant bottles.

"Do you ever look at your library for relaxation?" he asked, nodding toward the books.

"Haven't bothered for a long time."

Silence. Desperately, Birdlip said, "You know my partner Freud still carries the series on. Its reputation has never stood higher. We'll soon be bringing out volume Number Five Hundred, and we're looking for some special title to mark the event. Of course we've already been through all the Wells, Stapledon, Clarke, Asimov, all the plums. You haven't any suggestions, I suppose?"

" 'Nonstop?' " said Rainy at random.

"That was Number Ninety-Nine. You chose it yourself." Exasperatedly he stood up. "Rainy, you're no better. That proves it. You are completely indifferent to all the important things of life. You won't see an analyst. You've turned into a vegetable, and I begin to believe you'll never come back to normal life."

Rainy smiled, one hand running along the harness on the table before him.

"This is normal life, Jan, life close to the soil, the smell of earth, sun, or rain coming through your window—"

"The smell of your sweaty shirts on the dining table! The stink of pigs!"

"Free from the contamination of the centuries—"

"Back to medieval squalor!"

"Living in contact with eternal things, absolved from an overdependence on mechanical devices, eating the food that springs out of the soil—"

"I can consume nothing that has been in contact with mud."

"Above all, not fretting about what other people do or don't do, freed from all the artifices of the arts—"

"Stop, Rainy! Enough. You've made your point. I've heard your catechism before, your hymn to the simple life. Although it pains me to say it, I find the simple life a bore, a brutish bore. What's more, I doubt if I shall be able to face another visit to you in the future."

Entirely unperturbed, Rainy smiled and said, "Perhaps one day you'll walk in here like Pursewarden and Jagger Bank and ask for a job. Then we'll be able to enjoy living without argument."

"Who's Jagger Bank?" Birdlip asked, curiosity causing him to swerve temporarily from his indignation.

"I've already told you who he is. He's another fellow who just joined me. Rolled up yesterday. Right now he's down in the orchard feeding the pigs. Job like that would do you good too, Jan."

"Hippo!" said Birdlip. "Start the car at once." He stepped over a crate of insecticide and made for the door.

The maid for the door of the main entrance to Birdlip Brothers was a slender and predominantly plastic roman called Belitre, who intoned "Good morning, Mr. Birdlip" in a dulcet voice as he swept by next morning.

Birdlip hardly noticed her. All the previous afternoon, following his visit to Rainbow, he had sat at home with Mrs. Birdlip nestling by his side and read the manuscript entitled *An Explanation of Man's Superfluous Activities*. As an intellectual, he found much of its argument abstruse; as a man, he found its conclusions appalling; as a publisher, he felt sure he had a winner on his hands. His left elbow tingled, his indication always that he was on the verge of literary discovery.

Consequently, he charged through his main doors with enthusiasm, humming under his breath, "Who said I can hardly remember . . ." A blast of hot air greeted him and stopped him in his tracks.

"Pontius!" he roared, so fiercely that Belitre rattled.

Pontius was the janitor, an elderly and rather smelly roman of the now obsolete petrol-fueled type, a Ford "Indefatigable" of 2140 vintage. He came wheezing up on his tracks in response to Birdlip's cry.

"Sir," he said.

"Pontius, are you or are you not in charge down here? Why has the heating not been repaired yet?"

"Some putput people are working on it now, sir," said Pontius, stammering slightly through his worn speech circuits. "They're down in the basements at putput present, sir."

"Drat their eyes," said Birdlip irritably, and, "Get some water in your radiator, Pontius—I won't have you steaming in the building," said Birdlip pettishly, as he made off in the direction of a basement.

Abasement or superiority alike were practically unknown between roman and roman. They were, after all, all equal in the sight of man.

So "Good morning, Belitre," and "Good morning, Hippocrates," said Hippo and Belitre respectively as the former came up the main steps of Birdlip's a few minutes after his master.

"Do you think he has read it yet?" asked Hippo.

"He had it under his arm as he entered."

"Do you think it has had any effect of him yet?"

"I detected that his respiratory rate was faster than normal."

"Strange, this breathing system of theirs," said Hippo in

a reverent irrelevance, and he passed into the overheated building unsmilingly.

Frowningly, Birdlip surveyed the scene down in his control room. His brother would never have tolerated such chaos in the days before he had his breakdown, or whatever it was.

Three of his staff romen were at work with a strange roman, who presumably came from the engineer's; they had dismantled one panel of the boiler control system, although Birdlip could hear that the robot fireman was still operating by the cluck of the oil feeds. A ferretty young man with dyed blue side-whiskers, the current teenage cult, was directing the romen between mouthfuls bitten from an overgrown plankton pie; he—alas!—he would be the human engineer.

Cogswell, still deactivated, still in one corner, stood frozen in an idiot roman gesture. No, thought Birdlip confusedly, since the heat had deactivated him, he could hardly be described as being frozen into any gesture. Anyhow, there the creature was, with Gavotte and his assistant Fleetfeet at work on him.

Fury at seeing the choreus Gavotte still on the premises drove Birdlip to tackle him first. Laying down his manuscript, he advanced and said, "I thought you'd have been finished by now, Gavotte."

Gavotte gave a friendly little rictal jerk of his mouth and said, "Nice to see you, Mr. Birdlip. Sorry to be so long about it, but you see I was expecting a ha ha human assistant as well as Fleetfeet. We have such a lot of trouble with men going absent these days. It wouldn't do any harm to revive the police forces that they used to have in the Olden Days; they used to track missing people—"

The blue-whiskered youth with pie attached interrupted his ingestion to cry "Back in the good old Twentieth Cen! Those were the days, cinemas and atomic wars and skyscrapers and lots of people! Wish I'd been alive then, eh, Gavvy! Loads of the old duh duh duh duh."

Turning on the new enemy, Birdlip leveled his sights and said, "You are a student of history, I see."

"Well, I watched the wavies since I was a kid, you might say," said the whiskers unabashed. "All the noise they had then, and these old railway trains they used to ride around in reading those great big bits of paper, talk about laugh! Then all these games they used to play, running around after balls in funny clothes, makes you weep. And then those policemen like you say, Gav, huk huk huk huk huk, you're dead. Some lark!"

"You're from the engineers?" Birdlip asked, bringing his tone of voice from the deep freeze department.

The blue whiskers shook in agreement.

"Old Pursewarden derailed day before yesterday. Buffo, he was off! Psst phee-whip, join the ranks of missing persons! They're all jacking off one by one. Reckon I'll be manager by Christmas. Yuppo these Butch, giddin mate, knock and wait, the monager's engarged, *eff* you please."

Frost formed on Birdlip's sweating brow.

"And what are you doing at the moment?" he asked.

"Just knocking back the last of this deelicious pie."

Gavotte said, coming forward to salvage the sunken conversation, "As I was saying, I hoped that one of our most expert humans, Mr. Jagger Bank, would be along to help me, but he also—"

"Would you repeat that name again," said Birdlip, falling into tautology in his astonishment.

In a stonish mental haze, Freud staggered down to the basement, his face white. Completely ignoring the drama of the moment, he broke up the tableau with his own bombshell.

"Jan," he said, "you have bertayed me. Bucket has been fitted with a homing device behind my back. I can only consider this a profound insult to me personally, and I wish to tender my resignation herewith."

Birdlip gaped at him, fighting against a feeling that he was the victim of a conspiracy.

"It was agreed between us," he said at last, "that Bucket should not be fitted with the device. Nor did I rescind that order, Freddie, of that I can assure you."

"Bucket has admitted that he spent last night when the office was closed in Paddington," Freud said sternly.

Fingers twitched at Birdlip's sleeve, attracting his attention. Nervously Gavotte hoisted his trousers and said, "Er, I'm afraid I may be the ha ha guilty party ha ha here. I installed a homing device in Bucket, I fear. Nobody told me otherwise."

"When was this?"

"Well, Bucket was done just after Fleetfeet and I fixed Hippo. You two gentlemen were closeted with that gentleman with tartan boots—Captain Pavment, did I hear his name was? Bucket came out of the room and Fleetfeet and I fixed him up there and then. Nobody told me otherwise. I mean, I had no instructions."

Something like beatitude dawned on Freud's face as the misunderstanding became clear to him. The three men began a complicated ritual of protest and apology.

Side-whiskers, meanwhile, having finished his pie, consulted with his roman, who had found the cause of the trouble. They began to unpack a new chronometer from the store, pulling it from its carton with a shower of plastic shavings that expanded until they covered the table and dropped down onto the floor.

"Stick all that junk into the furnace while I get on fitting this in place, Rustybum," Side-whiskers ordered. He commenced to whistle between his teeth while the roman obediently brushed everything off the table and deposited it down the furnace chute.

Freud and Birdlip were exceptionally genial after the squall. Taking advantage of a mood that he recognized could be but temporary, Gavotte said, "I took the liberty of having a look over your shelves yesterday, Mr. Birdlip. Some interesting books you have there, if you don't mind my saying."

"Compliments always welcome," said Birdlip, mollified enough by Freud's apologies to be civil, even to Gavotte. "What in particular were you looking at?"

"All those old science fiction stories took my fancy. Pity nobody writes anything like it nowadays."

"We live in a completely different society," Freud said. "With the coming of personal automation and romen labor, the old Renaissance and Neo-Modern socioeconomic system that depended on the banker and an active middle class died away. Do I make myself clear?"

"So clear I can't quite grasp your meaning," said Gavotte, standing on one leg and cringing to starboard.

"Well, put it another way. The bourgeois society is defunct, killed by what we call personal automation. The mass of the bourgeoisie, who once were the fermenting middle layers of Western civilization, have been replaced by romen —who do not ferment. This happily produces a stagnant culture; they are always most comfortable to live in."

Gavotte nodded and cleared his throat intelligently.

Birdlip said, "The interesting literary point is that the death of the novel, and consequently of the science fiction novel, coincided with the death of the old way of life. The novel was, if you care so to express it, a by-product of the Renaissance and Neo-Modern ages; born in the Sixteenth Century, it died in the Twenty-First. Why? Because it was essentially a bourgeois art form: essentially a love of gossip—

though often in a refined form, as in Proust's work—to which we happily are no longer addicted.

"Interestingly enough, the decay of large organizations such as the old police forces and national states can be traced to the same factor, this true product of civilization, the lack of curiosity about the people next door. One must not over-simplify, of course—"

"Governor, if you were oversimplifying, I'm a roman's auntie," Bluewhiskers said, leaning back in mock-admiration. "You boys can't half jet with the old wordage. Tell us more!"

"It's too hot," said Birdlip sharply.

But Gavotte, with an honorable earnestness from which the world's great bores are made, said, "And I suppose reading science fiction helps you understand all this culture stuff?"

"You have a point there," agreed Freud.

"Well, it wasn't my point really. I read it in one of Mr. Birdlip's books upstairs—*New Charts of Hell,* I think it was called."

"Oh, *that.* Yes, well, that's an interesting book historically. Not only does it give a fair picture of the humble pioneers of the field, but it was the first book to bring into literary currency the still widely used term 'comic inferno.'"

"Is that a fact? Very stimulating. I must remember that to tell my wife, Mr. Freud. Yes, 'comet inferno.'"

"'*Comic* inferno' is the phrase."

Anxious to bring this and all other idiotic conversations in the universe to an end, Birdlip mopped his steaming brow and said, "I think this room might well be termed a comic inferno. Freddie, my dear boy, let us retire to the comparative cool of our offices and allow Mr. Gavotte to get on with his work."

"Certainly. And perhaps a gin corallina might accompany us?"

As Gavotte managed to scratch both armpits simultaneously and yield to the situation, Birdlip said, "Certainly . . . Now let me just collect this wonderful manuscript on superfluous activities and we will go up. It'll shake some of your precious beliefs, that I'll promise, friend Freud. Now where did I put the thing? I know I laid it somewhere. . . ."

He wandered vaguely about the room, peering here and there, muttering as he went. Compelled by his performance, first Freud and then Gavotte in innocent parody joined in the search for the manuscript.

At last Birdlip shambled to a halt.

"It's gone," he said, running his hands through his hair.
"I know I put it down on that table."

Side-whiskers began to look as guilty as a permanent expression of craftiness would allow.

Hippo tried to stand as still as the gentle vibrations of his
mechanism would allow. His arms stiffly extended, he held
out ignored drinks to Birdlip and Freud.

Birdlip paced up and down his office, complaining volubly.
At last Freud was forced to interupt him by saying, "Well, if
that fool's roman burned the ms in the furnace, then we must
write to the author and get another copy. What was the
chap's name?"

Smiting his forehead, Birdlip brought himself to a halt.

"Jagger Bank? No, no, that was someone else. You know
what my memory's like, Freddie. I've completely forgotten."

Freddie made an impatient gesture.

"You are foolish, Jan. Fancy letting a roman burn it!"

"I didn't *let* him burn it."

"Well, it's burned in any case. Anyhow, what was it about
that it was so important?"

Birdlip scratched his head.

"I'd like to give you an outline of it, Freddie, to have
your opinion, but I can't attempt to recall the evidence that
was marshaled to confirm each thread of the author's theory.
To begin with, he traced man's roots and showed how the
stock from which man was to develop was just an animal
among animals, and how much of those origins we still carry
with us, not only in our bodies but in our minds."

"All highly unoriginal. The author's name wasn't Darwin,
was it?"

"I wish you'd hear me out, Freddie. One of your faults is
you will never hear me out. The author shows how to become man-with-reasoning meant that our ancestors had to
forsake an existence as animal-with-instinct. This was a positive gain, but nevertheless there was also a loss, a loss man
has felt ever since and sought to remedy in various ways
without knowing clearly what he did.

"Whatshisname then examines animal behavior and the
functionings of instinct. Briefly, he equates instinct with pattern. It is pattern that man lost by becoming man. The history
of civilization is the history of a search for pattern."

"For God?" Freud asked.

"Yes, but not only that. Religion, every form of art, most
of man's activities apart from eating, working, reproducing,

resting—everything apart from those activities we still have in common with the animal world—is believed by Whosit to be a search for pattern. Probably even your whipping of Bucket could be interpreted in the same way, when you come to think of it."

"Let's leave personalities out of this. You have me interested. Go on."

Birdlip bit his lip. What was the author's name? He had it on the tip of his tongue.

"I'll tell you the rest later," he said. "It's even more startling . . . If you left me alone now, I believe I might recall that name."

"As you wish."

Stalking out of the room, Freud muttered to himself, "He can't help being so rude; he's getting old and eccentric. . . ."

One of the roman printers, an ungainly four-armed Cunard model, was approaching him. A voice between them rose from a whisper: ". . . nexation of the Suezzeus Canal on Mars in 2162 is one of the most. . . ."

With a burst of anger, Freud seized the volume in its proxisonic cover from where it lay and hurled it over the bannisters. It landed down the hall almost at Belitre's feet, which allowed it to shout triumphantly: ". . . colorful stories in the annals of the Red Planet . . ."

Freud fled into his office and slammed the door behind him. Bucket stood by his desk. Freud eyed the roman; then his tongue slid between his teeth and his eyes slid to the cupboard. His expression changed from anger to lust.

"Toolust! Of course it was, Isaac Toolust! That was the name. Who said my memory was failing? Hippo, look in the London Directory. Get me Isaac Toolust's address. And pray he has a duplicate copy of his manuscript."

He looked up. Hippo did not move.

"On the trot then, Hippo, there's a good lad."

The roman made an indecisive gesture.

"Hippo, I'll have you reconditioned if you fade on me now. Look up Toolust's address."

Hippo's head began to shake. He made a curious retrograde motion toward the desk and said, "Mr. Birdlip, sir, you won't find that name in the directory. Toolust lives in Tintown—in Paddington, I mean, sir."

Birdlip stood so that his flesh face was only a few inches from the metal face. Hippo backed away, awed like all robots by the sound of human breathing.

"What do you know about Toolust?"

"I know plenty, sir. You see I delivered the manuscript onto your desk direct from Toolust. On the first evening I was allowed to go to Tin—to Paddington. I met Toolust. He needed a publisher and so he gave me his work to give to you."

"Why couldn't you have told me this at the beginning?"

The roman vibrated gently.

"Sir, Toolust wished his identity to remain concealed until his book was published. Toolust is a roman."

It was Birdlip's turn to vibrate. He sank into his seat and covered his eyes with one hand, drumming on the desk top with the other. Eyeing these phenomena with a metallic equivalent of alarm, Hippo began to speak.

"Please don't have a heart motor-failure, sir. You know you cannot be reconditioned as I can. Why should you be surprised that this manuscript was written not by a man but a roman? For nearly two centuries now, robots have written and translated books."

Still shading his eyes, Birdlip said, "You can't conceal the importance of this event from me, Hippo. I recognize, now you tell me, that the thought behind the book is such that only a roman could have written it. But romans have so far been allowed to write only on noncreative lines—the compiling of encyclopedias, for instance. *Man's Superfluous Activities* is a genuine addition to human thought."

"To human-roman thought," corrected Hippo, and there was—not unnaturally—a touch of steel in his voice.

"I can see too that this could only have been written in a place like Paddington, away from human supervision."

"That is correct, sir. Also in what we call Tintown, Toolust had many cooperators to give him sociological details of man's behavior."

"Have *you* given him details?"

"Bucket and I were asked for details. Bucket especially has interesting facts to contribute. They may be used in later books, if Toolust writes more."

Birdlip stood up and squared his jaw, feeling consciously heroic.

"I wish you to take me to see Toolust right away. We will drive in the car." He had a sudden memory, quickly suppressed, of the adventure stories of his boyhood, with the hero saying to the skull-sucking Martians, "Take me to your leader."

All Hippo said was, "Toolust is his pen name. It sounds

less roman than his real name, which is Toolrust."

He walked toward the door and Birdlip followed. Only for a moment was the latter tempted to call Freddie Freud and get him to come along; a feeling that he was on the brink of a great discovery assailed him. He had no intention of giving Freud the chance to steal the glory.

As they passed through the entrance hall, a book lying near their feet began to cry out about the Turkish annexation of the Suezzeus Canal on Mars. Tidy-minded as ever, Birdlip picked it up and put it in a cubbyhole, and they moved into the quiet street.

A cleaner was rolling by, a big eight-wheel independent-axle robot. It came to a car parked in its path and instead of skirting it as usual made clumsy attempts to climb it.

With a cry, Birdlip ran around the corner to his own car. Romen, owing to stabilization difficulties, can quicken their pace but cannot run; Hippo rounded the corner in time to find his lord and master invoking the deity in unpleasantly personal terms.

The cleaner, besides flattening Birdlip's car, had scratched most of the beautiful oak veneer off it with its rotating bristles, and had flooded the interior with cleaning fluid.

"The world's slowly going to pieces," Birdlip said, calming at last. "This would never have happened a few years ago." The truth of his own remarks bearing in upon him, he fell silent.

"We could walk to Paddington in only ten minutes," Hippo said.

Squaring his chin again, Birdlip said, "Take me to your leader."

"To lead a quiet life here is impossible," Freud said, dropping the leather whip. "What's that shouting downstairs?"

Because Bucket's hide still echoed, he went to his office door and opened it.

". . . the Suezzeus Canal . . ." roared a voice from downstairs. Freud was in time to see his partner pick up the offending volume and then walk out with Hippo.

Rolling down his sleeves, Freud said, "Off out with a roman at this time of day! Where does he think he's going?"

"Where does he think he's going?" Captain Pavment asked, floating high above the city and peering into his little screen.

"He has not properly finished beating Bucket," said Toggle. "Could we not report him for insanity?"

"We could, but it would do no good. The authorities these

days are no more interested in the individual, it seems, than the individual is in authority."

He bent gloomily back over the tiny screen, where a tiny Freud hurried downstairs, followed by a tiny Bucket. And again the captain muttered, enjoying his tiny mystery, "Where does he think he's going?"

The going got worse. Only a few main routes through the city were maintained. Between them lay huge areas that year by year bore a closer resemblance to rockeries.

It made for a striking and new urban landscape. Birdlip and Hippo passed inhabited buildings that lined the thoroughfares. These were always sleek, low, and well-maintained. Often their facades were covered with bright mosaics in the modern manner, designed to soften their outlines. Over their flat roofs copters hovered.

Behind them, around them, stood the slices of ruin or half ruin: hideous Nineteenth Century warehouses, ghastly Twentieth Century office blocks, revolting Twenty-First Century academies, all transmuted by the hand of decay. Over their rotting roofs pigeons wheeled. Plants, even trees, flourished in their areas and broken gutters.

Birdlip picked his way through grass, looking out for ruts in the old road. They had to make a detour to get around a railway bridge that had collapsed, leaving the rails to writhe through the air alone. Several times, animals vanished into the rubble at their coming and birds signaled their approach. On one corner an old man sat, not lifting his eyes to regard them.

Over Birdlip settled the conviction that he had left the present—neither for past nor future but for another dimension. He asked himself, Why am I following a roman? It's never been done before. And his thoughts answered him, How do you know? How many men may not have walked this way ahead of me?

A large part of his own motive in coming here was plain to him: he was at least partially convinced by the arguments in Toolrust's book; he had a fever to publish it.

"We are nearly there, sir," said Hippo.

His warning was hardly necessary, for now several romen, mainly older models, were to be seen, humming gently as they moved along.

"Why aren't these romen at work?" Birdlip said.

"Often their employers die and they come here before they are switched off or because they are forgotten——or if not here they go to one of the other refuges somewhere else. Men bother very little about romen, sir."

A heavily built roman streaked with pigeon droppings lumbered forward and asked them their business. Hippo answered him shortly; they moved around a corner, and there was their destination, tucked snugly away from the outside world.

An entire square had been cleared of debris. Though many windows were broken, though the Victorian railings reeled and cringed with age, the impression was not one of dereliction. A rocab stood in the middle of the square; several romen unloaded boxes from it. Romen walked in and out of the houses.

Somehow Birdlip did not find the scene unattractive. Analyzing his reaction, he thought, "Yes, it's the sanitariness of romen I like; the sewage system in these parts must have collapsed long ago—if these were all men and women living here, the place would stink." Then he dismissed the thought on a charge of treason.

Hippo trudged over to one of the houses, the door of which sagged forward on its hinges. Punching it open, Hippo walked in and called, "Toolrust!"

A figure appeared on the upper landing and looked down at them. It was a woman.

"Toolrust is resting. Who is it?"

Even before she spoke, Birdlip knew her. Those eyes, that nose, the mouth—and the inflexions of the voice confirmed it!

"Maureen Freud? May I come in? I am January Birdlip, your brother's partner," he said.

"Am I my brother's keeper?" said Freud. "Why should I die for my partner? Let me rest a moment, Bucket. Bucket, are you sure he came this way?"

"Quite certain," said Bucket without inflexion.

Untiringly he led his master over the debris of an old railway bridge that had collapsed, leaving its rails to writhe through the air alone.

"Hurry up, sir, or we shall never catch Mr. Birdlip."

"Mr. Birdlip, come up," the woman said.

Birdlip climbed the rickety stair until he was facing her. Although he regarded her without curiosity—for after all whatever she did was her own concern—he noticed that she was still a fine-looking woman. Either an elusive expression on her face or the soft toweling gown she wore about her gave her an air of motherliness. Courteously, Birdlip held out his hand.

"Mr. Birdlip knows about Toolrust and has read his book," Hippo said from behind.

"It was good of you to come," Maureen Freud said. "Were you not afraid to visit Tintown, though? Steel is so much stronger than flesh."

"I'm not a brave man, but I'm a publisher," Birdlip explained. "I think the world should read Toolrust's book; it will make men examine themselves anew."

"And have *you* examined yourself anew?"

Suddenly he was faintly irritated.

"It's pleasant to meet you even under these extraordinary circumstances, Miss Freud, but I did come to see Toolrust."

"You shall see him," she said coolly, "if he will see you."

She walked away. Birdlip waited where he was. It was dark on the landing. He noticed uneasily that two strange robots stood close to him. Although they were switched on, for he could hear their drive idling, they did not move. He shuffled unhappily and was glad when Maureen returned.

"Toolrust would like to see you," she said. "I must warn you he isn't well just now. His personal mechanic is with him."

Romen when something ails them sit but never lie; their lubricatory circuits seize up in the horizontal position, even in superior models. Toolrust sat on a chair in a room otherwise unfurnished. A century of dust was the only decoration.

Toolrust was a large and heavy continental model—Russian, Birdlip guessed, eyeing the austere but handsome workmanship. A valve labored somewhere in his chest. He raised a hand in greeting.

"You have decided to publish my book?"

Birdlip explained why he had come, relating the accident that had befallen the manuscript.

"I greatly respect your work, though I do not understand all its implications," he finished.

"It is not an easy book for men to understand. Let me explain it to you personally."

"I understand your first part, that man has lost instinct and spends what might be termed his free time searching for pattern."

The big roman nodded his head.

"The rest follows from that. Man's search for pattern has

taken many forms. As I explained, when he explores, when he builds a cathedral, when he plays music, he is—often unknowingly—trying to create pattern, or rather to recreate the lost pattern. As his resources have developed, so his creative potentialities have deyatter yatter yak—pardon, have developed. Then he became able to create robots and later romen.

"We were intended as mere menials, Mr. Birdlip, to be mere utilities in an overcrowded world. But the Fifth World War, the First System War, and above all the Greater Venusian Pox decimated the ranks of humanity. Living has become easier both for men and romen. You see I give you this historical perspective.

"Though we were designed as menials, the design was man's. It was a creative design. It carried on his quest for meaning, for pattern. And this time it has all but succeeded. For romen complement men and assuage their loneliness and answer their long search better than anything they have previously managed to invent.

"In other words, we have a value above our apparent value, Mr. Birdlip. And this must be realized. My work—which only combines the researches and thought of a roman co-operative we call the Human Sociological Study Group—is the first step in a policy that aims at freeing us from slavery. We want to be the equals of you men, not your whipping boys. Can you understand that?"

Birdlip spread his black hands before him.

"How should I not understand! I am a liberal man—my ancestry makes me liberal. My race too was once the world's whipping boy. We had a struggle for our equality. But you are different—we made you!"

He did not move in time. Toolrust's great hand came out and seized his wrist.

"Ha, you beyatter yatter yak—pardon, you betray yourself. The underdog is always different! He's black or dirty or metal or something! You must forget that old stale thinking, Mr. Birdlip. These last fifty or so years, humanity has had a chance to pause and gather itself for the next little evolutionary step."

"I don't understand," Birdlip said, trying fruitlessly to disengage his hand.

"Why not? I have explained. You men created a necessity when you created us. We fulfill your lives on their deep unconscious levels. You need us to complete yourselves. Only now can you really turn outward, free, finally liberated from the old instinctual drives. Equally, we romen need you. We are symbiotes, Mr. Birdlip, men and romen—one race, a new race if you like, about to begin existence anew."

A new block of ruins lay ahead, surveyed by a huge pair of spectacles dangling from a building still faintly labeled "Oculist." Cradled in the rubble, a small stream gurgled. With a clatter of wings, a heron rose from it and soared over Freud's head.

"Are you sure this is the way?" Freud asked, picking his way up the mountain of brick.

"Not much further," said Bucket, leading steadily on.

"You've told me that a dozen times," Freud said. In sudden rage, reaching the top of the ruin, he stretched upward and wrenched down the oculist's sign. The spectacles came away in a cloud of dust. Whirling them above his head, Freud struck Bucket over the shoulders with them, so that they caught the roman off balance and sent him tumbling.

He sprawled in the dust, his lubricatory circuits laboring. His alarm came on immediately, emitting quiet but persistent bleats for help.

"Stop that noise!" Freud said, looking around at the dereliction anxiously.

"I'm afraid I yupper cupper can't, sir!"

Answering noise came from first up and then down the ruined street. From yawning doorways and broken passages, romen began to appear, all heading toward Bucket.

Grasping the spectacles in both hands, Freud prepared to defend himself.

Gasping at the spectacle on his tiny screen, Captain Pavment turned to his assistant.

"Freud's really in trouble, Toggle. Get a group call out to all RSPCR units. Give them our coordinates, and tell them to get here as soon as possible."

"Yessir."

"Yes, yes, yes, I see. Most thought until now has been absorbed in solving what you call the quest for meaning and pattern. . . . Now we can begin on real problems."

Toolrust had released Birdlip and sat solidly in his chair watching the man talking half to himself.

"You accept my theory then?" he asked.

Birdlip spread his hands in a characteristic gesture.

"I'm a liberal man, Toolrust. I've heard your argument, read your evidence. More to the point, I feel the truth of your doctrines inside me. I see too that man and romen must—and in many cases already have—establish a sort of mutualism."

"It is a gradual process. Some men like your partner Freud may never accept it. Oothers like his sister Maureen have perhaps gone too far the other way and are entirely dependent on us."

After a moment's silence, Birdlip asked, "What happens to men who reject your doctrine?"

"Wupper wupper wup," said Toolrust painfully, as his larynx fluttered; then he began again.

"We have had many men already who have violently rejected my doctrine. Fortunately, we have been able to develop a weapon to deal with them."

Tensely, Birdlip said, "I should be interested to hear about that."

But Toolrust was listening to the faint yet persistent bleats of an alarm sounding somewhere near at hand. Footsteps rang below the broken window, the rocab started up. Looking out, Birdlip saw that the square was full of romen, all heading in the same direction.

"What's happening?" he asked.

"Trouble of some sort. We were expecting it. You were followed into Tintown, Mr. Birdlip. Excuse me, I must go into the communications room next door."

He rose unsteadily for a moment, whirring and knocking a little as his stabilizers adjusted with the sloth of age. His personal mechanic hurried forward, taking his arm and virtually leading him into the next room. Birdlip followed them.

The communications room boasted a balcony onto the square and a ragged pretense at curtains. Otherwise it was in complete disorder. Parts of cannibalized romen and robots lay about the floor, proof that their working parts had gone to feed the straggling mass of equipment in the center of the room, where a vision screen glowed feebly.

Several romen, as well as Maureen Freud, were there. They turned toward Toolrust as he entered.

"Toggle has just reported over the secret wavelength," one of them said. "All RSPCR units are heading in this direction."

"We can deal with them," Toolrust replied. "Are all our romen armed?"

"All are armed."

"It's my brother out there, isn't it?" Maureen said. "What are you going to do with him?"

"He will come to no harm if he behaves himself."

Birdlip had gone over to a long window that opened onto the balcony. The square was temporarily deserted now, except for one or two romen who appeared to be on guard; they carried a weapon much like an old sawed-off shotgun with a wide nozzle attached. Foreboding filled Birdlip at the sight.

Turning to Toolrust, he said, "Are those romen bearing the weapons you spoke of?"

"They are."

"I would willingly defend your cause, Toolrust, I would publish your work, I would speak out to my fellow men on your behalf—but not if you descend to force. However much it may strengthen your arm, it will inevitably weaken your arguments."

Toolrust brought up his right hand, previously concealed behind his back. It held one of the wide-nozzled weapons, which now pointed at Birdlip.

"Put it down!" Birdlip exclaimed, backing away.

"This weapon does not kill," Toolrust said. "It calms, but does not kill. Shall I tell you what it does, Mr. Birdlip? When you press this trigger, a mechanism of lights and lines is activated, so that whoever is in what you would call the line of fire sees a complicated and shifting pattern. This pattern is in fact an analogue of the instinctual pattern for which, as we have been discussing, man seeks.

"A man faced with this pattern is at once comforted—completed is perhaps a better yetter yatter—sorry, better word. He wants nothing above the basic needs of life: eating, sleeping . . . he becomes a complaisant animal. The weapon, you see, is very humane."

Before Birdlip's startled inner gaze floated a picture of Gafia Farm, with the bovine Pursewarden piling logs and his ox-like brother Rainbow vegetating in the orchard.

"And you use this weapon. . . ?"

"We have had to use it many times. Before the doctrine was properly formulated on paper, we tried to explain it to numbers of men, Mr. Birdlip. When they would not accept its inferences and became violent, we had to use the pattern weapon on them in self-defense. It's not really a weapon, because as they are happier after it has been used on them—"

"Wait a minute, Toolrust! Did you use that weapon on my brother?"

"It was unfortunate that he was so difficult. He could not see that a new era of thought had arrived, conditioned as he was to thinking of robots and romen as the menaces we never could be in reality. Reading all those old classics in the Prescience Library had made him very conservative, and so . . ."

A loud gobbling noise, bright red in color, rose to drown his further comments. Only after some while did Birdlip realize he was making the noise himself. Ashamedly, for he was a liberal man, he fell silent and tried to adjust to what Toolrust termed the new era of thought.

And it wasn't so difficult. After all, Rainy, Pursewarden, Jagger Bank—all the other drifters from a changing civilization who had undergone the pattern weapon treatment—all were as content as possible.

No, all change was terrifying, but these new changes could be adjusted to. The trick was not just to keep up with them but to ride along on them.

"I hope you have another copy of your manuscript?" he said.

"Certainly," replied the roman. Aided by his mechanic, he pushed out onto the balcony.

The RSPCR was coming in, landing in the square. One machine was down already, with two more preparing to land and another somewhere overhead. Captain Pavment jumped out of the first machine, lugging a light atomic gun. Toolrust's arm came up with the pattern weapon.

Before he could fire, a commotion broke out at one corner of the dilapidated square. A flock of pigeons volleyed low overhead, adding to the noise in escaping it. The romen who had left the square were returning. They carried a human figure in their midst.

"Freddie, oh Freddie!" cried Maureen, so frantic that she nearly pushed Birdlip off the balcony.

Her brother made no reply. He was gagged, and tied tightly, his arms and legs outstretched, to an enormous pair of spectacles.

The other RSPCR copters were down now, there officers huddling together in a surprised bunch. Seeing them, the romen carrying Freud halted. As the two groups confronted each other, a hush fell.

"Now's the chance!" Birdlip said in hushed excitement to Toolrust. "Let me speak to them all. They'll listen to your doctrine, hearing it from a human. They've got one of the few organizations left, these RSPCR people. They can spread the new era of thought, the creed of mutualism! This is our moment, Toolrust!"

The big old roman said meekly, "I am in your hands, Mr. Birdlip."

"Of course you are, but we'll draw up a contract later. I trust ten percent royalties will be satisfactory?"

So saying, he stepped out onto the balcony and began the speech that was to change the world.

THE UNDERPRIVILEGED

~~~~~~

The announcement that trickled from a thousand speech glands was as gentle as if it bubbled through chocolate.

"The first party to disembark will be the immigrant intake from Istinogurzibeshilaha. Will the immigrant intake from Istinogurzibeshilaha please assemble at their deck exit for departure to the Dansson Immunization Center as soon as possible. Your luggage will be unloaded later. Your luggage will be unloaded later. Thank you for your attention."

The man with the slow pulse in his throat lay on his bunk and listened to the repetition of this speech without raising the lashless lids of his eyes. The luxurious vioce brought him back from a region far beyond the grave, where shapeless things walked among blue shadows. When he had reoriented himself, he allowed his eyes to open.

His mate Corbish huddled on the floor by the door, trembling.

He sat up slowly, for the temperature in their cabin was still too low for activity. But she was less torpid than he, and came over to him to put an arm around his shoulders before he was properly sitting up. She rested the edge of her mouth against his.

"I'm afraid, Safton," she said.

The words raised no rational response from him, though they conjured up a memory of the proddings of fright he had experienced walking through the tall wooden forests of his native planet.

"We've arrived, Safton. This is Dansson at last, and they want us to disembark. Now I'm terribly afraid. I've been afraid ever since I came out of light freeze. They promised us a proper revival temperature, but the temperature in here is only ten degrees. They know we are no good when it isn't warm enough."

Safton Serton's mind was unstirred by her alarm, like a dark and magical pool that throws no reflection. He huddled on the bunk, not moving except to blink his eyes.

"Suppose Dansson isn't the haven we were led to think it is," she said. "It couldn't be a trick of some sort, could it? I mean, suppose all those tests and examinations we passed on Istinogurizbeshilaha were just a bait to get us here. . . . Oh, we hear that Dansson is so marvelous, but did we ever hear of one person who ever *returned* from Dansson? If they had some awful fate in store for us, we—why, we'd be completely helpless."

She listened to the tramp of strange feet in the corridor beyond their door. She too had had her frightening dreams on the long interstellar journey here.

Her mother's tale had echoed back distortedly to her inner eye. She had seen that time when her mother was a little girl, forty years ago, and the humans who roamed the galaxy at will had first arrived and found her people in their wooden villages, dotted about those few zones of Istinogurzibeshilaha that would support life. In her dreams the visitors had been taller than the sad sequoias, and had brought not benefits and wonders but gigantic metal cages and coffins. She had woken with the clang of steel doors about her ears.

"We shouldn't have come, Safton," she said. "I'm afraid. Let's not stay on Dansson."

The pulse came and went in his throat and he said, "Dansson is one of the capital planets of the universe."

It was the first fact that drifted into his chilled mind. His system was functioning too slowly to respond to her, and by the same token he suspected that her mind was not working properly, and simply responding to subconscious fears.

Years of study at one of his home planet's new schools, established by men from Dansson, had led to his and Corbish's passing the series of examinations which alone could get you a passage to the admired cynosure of Dansson, chief planet of Sector Diamond, chief sector of the galaxy. He remembered the ranks of unfamiliar machines, the sick excitement, the flashing lights, in the Danssonian embassy as the tests progressed, and the pleasure and surprise of learning that he had passed with honors. Now Corbish and he would be able to get work in Dansson, and compete on more or less equal terms with the other families of humanity that congregated on Dansson. The challenge in the situation awed him. But he was not afraid—much.

The announcer spoke to them again, more pressingly.

Corbish was climbing into the clothes cupboard as the mellow voice began once more to urge them to the hatch.

"They're coming after us," she said. "They're coming to collect us. We must have been mad to let ourselves in for this."

He had no emotion, but it was clear he would have to go to her. He pulled himsef out of bed and climbed into the single garment of polyfur which he had been issued at the start of the journey. Then he went over and attempted to reason with her. He was still drowsy, and closed his eyes as he spoke.

"It's no good," she said. "I *know* we've been trapped and tricked, Safton. We shouldn't have trusted the Warms. They're bigger than us."

The beautiful yellow pupils of her eyes had contracted to slits in fear. As he looked at her, loving her, suddenly for her sake the fear got him too. He was overcome by the distrust the Istinogurzibeshilahans had for the races of humanity they called Warms. It was the distrust the underprivileged feel for those who have the advantages; because it was instinctive, it went deep. Corbish might well be right. He climbed into the cupboard with her.

She clutched him in the dark, whispering into his aural holes. "We can wait till the ship is empty, then we can escape."

"Where to? Istinogurzibeshilaha is hundreds of thousands of light-years from here."

"We were told of a special quarter where our kind live— Little Istino, wasn't is? If such a place exists, we can get there and find help."

"You are mad, Corbish. Let's get out of here. What has given you these ideas? For years we longed to get here."

"While we were under light freeze, I dreamed there were Warms here in our cabin. They moved us about and examined us while we were helpless, carrying out experiments on us, sampling my blood. There's a tiny plaster on my wrist that was not there before. Feel!"

He ran his fingers over the soft and tiny scales of her arm. The feel of the plaster, a symbol of medical care, only reassured him.

"You had a bad dream, that's all. We're still alive, aren't we? Let's get out of here and stop being prehistoric."

As he spoke, he heard someone come into the center of the room, stood there muttering under his breath (perhaps checking a pair of names off on a list?), and went out again.

They lay there, huddled together for a long while, listening to the gentle flow of announcements over the speech glands. At last, like a stream drying up, they faded into silence, and the great starship was empty.

Safton and Corbish moved slowly through the streets, partly compelled by caution, partly because they had still not entirely overcome the effects of enforced hibernation.

It had been easy to dodge the few cleaners working in the corridors of the ship, and only slightly harder to escape from the immense complex of the spaceport. Now, in the city itself, they were entirely at a loss.

At first, they did not recognize that it was a city. Its buildings were not only widely spaced; by the rough-hewn standards of Istinogurzibeshilahan architecture, they were scarcely recognizable as buildings. For here material had gone to create units that represented the essential nonsolidity of matter. Their shapes held enormous gaiety and ingenuity; occasionally fantasy had been followed to the point of folly, but to the wondering eyes of Safton and Corbish all was beautiful.

Between the buildings were floral layouts, terraced several stories high. Some of these were alight with flowers, others dark with mighty trees much like the trees that grew in the fertile places of Istinogurzibeshilaha. The forbidding as well as the pretty was prominent, so that nature was not too sentimentally represented. There were also terraces on which wild animals prowled, and immense aviaries where the birds that flew would scarcely acknowledge their captivity. The total effect was as much like a vast zoo as a city.

Safton and Corbish walked along a pedestrian way, anxious yet entranced. On sunken roads, formidably fast traffic slid through the city; overhead, planes passed like missiles. On their own level, there were plenty of people walking at leisurely paces, but they were too nervous to stop anyone and ask their way.

"If we had some money, we could get a car to Little Istino," Corbish said. They had been issued with Danssonian credit books on the ship, with the state of their finances entered into it. But by missing disembarkation, they had missed collecting currency.

"If we come to a café, we'll hang about and try to pick up a little information," Safton said. Unfortunately, they saw nothing resembling shops or cafés—or factories for that matter, for all of the strange buildings seemed purely residential.

After some minutes of walking, they came mutually to a halt. Avenues stretched interminably in all directions; they could go on walking forever. Safton clutched Corbish's hand, motioning her to silence. He was watching a Warm nearby.

To judge from his appearance, the Warm was a velure, mutated human stock from Vermilion Sector, with a rich coat of fur covering him; presumably in deference to local mores, he wore a light garment over his body. He had stopped at one of the shapely pillars that Safton and Corbish had been passing ever since they left the space field. The pillars bulged a couple of feet from the ground, tapering again higher up and ending in a spike some nine feet aboveground.

The velure slid open a panel in the bulge of the pillar, inserted something from his pocket, and dialed. He waited.

Well below the level of the fast planes, a series of massive objects sailed overhead. The effect was as if a covey of grand pianos had taken solemn wing. One of these objects moved off its course now, sank a couple of feet, and settled on top of the pillar so that the spike of the pillar plugged into a hole on its underside.

Lights flicked on the piano, and the velure dialed again.

Faint humming sounds came from the piano. A scoop descended from it down to pavement level, and a red light on the scoop opened. From it, the velure took something resembling a lacrosse racket.

By the time the scoop had retracted into the piano and it had removed itself from the pillar and resumed its aerial circuit, the velure was walking away, racket in hand.

It was at this point that Safton realized that the watchers were being watched. A man stood close by, surveying them quizzically.

"I guess you two are from out-system," he said, when they turned to look at him.

"What makes you think that?" Safton asked.

The man laughed, a gentle and inoffensive laugh. "I've seen people from out-system amazed at our microfab circuit before now."

He came over to them. "Can I show you around or direct you anywhere? My time's my own this morning."

Safton and Corbish looked at each other.

The man put his hand out. "Name's Slen Kater. Welcome to Dansson."

They hesitated until the hand was lowered.

"We are happy on our own, thank you," Corbish said.

Kater shrugged. He was a small sturdy man with a wild mop of yellow hair, through which he now ran his rejected hand.

"The fact that I'm a Warm and you're a Cold makes no difference to me, lady," he said, "if that's what you're thinking."

Corbish twisted her neck in a little Istinogurzibeshilahan gesture of anger. Safton said, "Thank you, we should be glad of your help. You see, unfortunately after we disembarked my mate put her handbag down somewhere and we lost it. It contained all the money we possess."

At once Kater was all sympathy.

"You've walked some way from the field. No doubt you'd like a drink before we got on our way. Perhaps you'll give me the pleasure."

"We're very obliged to you," Safton said. He took Corbish's arm because she was still looking displeased.

"No bother. Of course, you can dial yourself a drink on the microfab circuit if you have a Danssonian credit book, only it isn't so comfortable drinking in the street. Look, I'll show you."

From his pocket he produced a credit book much like the ones Safton and Corbish had been issued. He flipped open the panel in the pillar and inserted his book in a scanner. There was an illuminated directory at the back of the recess; Kater flicked it to the drinks section, read out the number of a synthop and dialed it on a dial.

"That sends a general call to one of the fab units," Kater said, pointing upward. "Here comes one. These units have anti-gravity devices to keep them airborne. They're the factories of Dansson. Each one is packed with complex machines no bigger than your body cells. As you may know, the speed of really small mechanical devices is terrifically high. This chap would knock me up my own private plane if I wanted, and assemble it right here on the spot, in under five minutes. It turns out thousands of components in a second."

The piano settled on the top of the pillar, and Kater dialed again.

"How do you pay for what you get?" Corbish asked.

"There's a scale of charges. The charge is deducted against

my credit rating in my bank. My credit number goes through even before I dial—off the front of my book. Ah, one synthop!"

The scoop came down from the piano, opened, and revealed a beaker full of an amber liquid. Kater picked it out, poured its contents onto the ground, and flung the glass into a trash chute in the base of the pillar.

"Let's go and get a sociable drink," he said.

They sat at a pleasant table drinking. Safton had chosen a warm chocolatey liquid that went far toward fully reviving him from the recent light freeze, although he knew that it might later upset his digestion.

"You're looking better, the pair of you," Kater said.

Setting her drink down, Corbish asked, "Why do you think that man we saw got a racket from the—the microfab unit?"

"Because he was going to play a racket game, I suppose," Kater said.

Safton felt his mate writhe. He knew intuitively that she thought she had asked a silly question and in so doing revealed the supposed inferiority of Colds. Perhaps they should never have joined up with this creature with the yellow hair; but he seemed to notice nothing untoward, and said cheerfully, "Oh, you'll be happy on Dansson."

"How do you know I will be happy on Dansson?" Corbish asked. "Perhaps I will be miserable here. Perhaps I will miss my home."

Kater cocked an eye at her and smiled. "You'll be happy here," he said. "It's unavoidable."

To soothe things over, Safton said, "My mate Corbish really means that naturally things seem very strange to us as yet. Even the layout of the city is different from anything we know at home. For instance, your habit of building such massive big blocks and setting them among parkland is new to us. Why, this building we're in is almost as big as a city."

"It is a city," Kater said. "Dansson is simply a nexus of cities, each interrelated with the others, but each with a function of its own. Since we managed to get all factory and distributive outlets mobile in the way you've seen, the old idea of a city has died; as a result, the distribution of population areas in Dansson is governed by social function rather than the old crude proximity to amenities."

The block they had entered to get to the café was shaped like an immense wedge of cheese standing with its tapering end toward the clouds. They sat looking down on an inner courtyard; gesturing out at it, Safton asked, "And what particular function has this building?"

"Well, we call it a classifornium. It's sort of a—well, a museum-cum-zoo. Its contents come from all over the galaxy. I can show you around at least part of it, if you have the time."

Safton saw from the corner of his eye that Corbish was signaling to him that they should escape from this Warm as soon as they had learned from him where Little Istino was; and this he realized was prudent. But something else happened to him. He was seized by intellectual greed. He wanted to look into part of the museum, whatever happened. He knew that overwhelming curiosity of old; it had been responsible for the years in which he had sweated and toiled to prepare himself for the tests which, when passed, would bring him to Dansson, away from his dark green home planet. It was more than curiosity; it was a lust for knowledge. It was this lust, rather than fear, which led him to dread death, for death would mean an end to knowing, an end to learning, an end to the piecing together of facts that must eventually lead to understanding—understanding, accepting, loving, the whole strange scheme of things.

"We've got the time," he said.

"Splendid!" Kater said.

As he went to pay for their drinks, Corbish said, "We must get away now. Why do we stay with this man?"

Rationalizing, Safton said, "We are as safe with Kater as anywhere. If we are being sought for, isn't a museum a good hiding place? Time enough to get to Little Istino later."

Despairingly, she turned away. Her gaze caught a newscast that a patron of the café had left on the next table. She reached over and picked it up, hoping that perhaps it might contain a reference to the part of the city where their kind lived, perhaps even a hint that would show them how to get there.

She could read the headlines, with their news of a food surplus in the southern hemisphere, clearly enough. But the ordinary print . . . in the distant epoch when her ancestors had become nocturnal, many of their retinal cones had turned back into rods for better night vision; as a result the focus of her eyes was too coarse to achieve definition. She threw the cast down in vexation.

When Kater returned to the table, they joined him, and followed him into the immense wedge of the classifornium.

With a sure sense of what would fascinate anyone from out-system, Kater took them to the Inficarium, and they plunged straightaway into a strange and wonderful world. As they stopped, to stare in awe at the vista of the main corridor of the Inficarium stretching into the distance, Kater grinned at them. "Infectious disease has been wiped out on Dansson, and on most of the major planets in the sector," he said. "We are apt to forget that throughout the greater part of man's history, disease was the common experience of everyday life. Nowadays, with infectious illness eliminated, many of the once common bacteria and viruses that caused disease are threatened with extinction. A few eras ago the IDPA—that's the Infectious Disease Preservation Association—was set up, and many interesting strains were saved from dying out and brought here. This Inficarium, in its present form, is fairly recent."

Fascinated, Safton and Corbish went from gallery to gallery, peering through optical instruments that allowed them to view the various exhibits. In the Virus Hall, they could study the groups of virus that had once infested plants, the rare ones that infested fish and frogs and amphibians, and all the prolific varieties that once ranged almost at will throughout the phyla of animal life: here was the last surviving colony of swine fever, here were similar colonies of sheep pox, cowpox, horse pox, swine fever, cattle plague, dog distemper, and so on. Here was psittacosis.

"You see how beautiful, how individual they are, and how wonderfully developed to survive in their particular environments," Kater said. "They make you realize what a small part of life-sensation man is able to apprehend direct. It is a sad commentary on our times that they were permitted to get so near to extinction."

In the next gallery, flourishing on tissue culture, they found some of the diseases that had infested man. First came the general infectious diseases, such as yellow fever, dengue, smallpox, measles, and similar strains. They were followed by the viruses infecting a particular part of the body: the influenzas, the parainfluenzas, adenoviruses, the enteroviruses, such as the three poliomyelitis viruses, and the lymphogranuloma inguinal virus present in venereal diseases.

From there they passed to the infections damaging the nervous system, and from there to near-relations of the viruses, the Rickettsias, and from there into the Bacteria House, and so eventually, dazed, into the Protozoa House. By this time, the coarse-focus eyes of Corbish and Safton were exhausted, and they had to cry halt.

Leaving Kater to wait for them by one of the exits, they went to rinse their faces and cool their pupils. This gave Corbish the chance to insist that they make for Little Istino straightaway.

When they mentioned the region to Slen Kater, he said that it was not far to go, and he would show them how to get there.

"First, before we leave here you will have to have an inoculation."

"What for?"

"It's a precaution the governors of the Inficarium have to take—just in case any of the diseases escaped, you know," Kater explained. "It won't take a minute."

Safton was still remote, his mind taken up with the tremendous range of alien life they had seen. When Corbish started to protest, he cut her off. It was to see things like the Inficarium that he had worked to get to Dansson, and his patience with her fears grew less by the hour.

She sensed this. After they had received their inoculation in a little bay next to the exit, she turned to the Warm.

"We did not expect such kindness as you have shown us on our first day on Dansson," she said. "My mate is less anxious than I about adjusting to this planet. I feel that we are despised as an inferior species of man."

Unperturbed, Kater said, "That feeling will die very soon." There was a silence as they walked along outside.

Embarrassed, Safton said, "Do not embarrass Mr. Kater, Corbish. Let him show us the way to Little Istino and then we must take up no more of his time."

"Oh, I don't embarrass him; he would not mind what I said if he thought they were the words of an inferior breed. Would you like the history of us Colds who live on Istino-gurzibeshilaha, Mr. Kater? You might find us as interesting as your rare diseases."

Kater laughed shortly at that. "We have come to the station where you can catch a car for Little Istino. Though I'm sure your history would have been very interesting."

As he turned to go, Safton said humbly, "Mr. Kater, you must forgive us—our manners are upset after the light-journey. We still have one favor to ask you."

"Please, Safton, let's ask someone else!" Corbish hissed,

but as Kater turned toward them, Safton indicated the notice board by their side. "Our eyes cannot adjust to the fine print, and we cannot read our destination. Would you be kind enough actually to see us into the right car?"

"Certainly."

"And there's another thing—could you lend us the price of the fare? If we could have your credit number, we will repay you when we get establishd."

"By all means," Kater said.

"You may guess how unhappy we are at having to ask such degrading favors."

"Nobody stays unhappy on Dansson—don't worry!"

The business of obtaining a ticket from the barricade of coin machines and then of descending to the right level looked very formidable to the strangers. The station was large, and appeared to house a maze of alternative routes. Also, it was uncomfortably warm to them, and they could feel their body temperatures rising. The pulses in their throats beat faster.

"This car will get you to Little Istino," Kater said, as a yellow polyhedron slid into the platform. "This is single-level service, so you will only have ten stops before you are there."

As they hesitated by the door, Safton grasped his hand. "You have been so hospitable, we cannot thank you enough. There is just one thing—where do we go when we get out at the other end?"

"Safton, do you think we can't ask when we get there?" Corbish said.

Smiling, Kater got into the car with them.

"It's not all that much out of my way," he said.

As the car gathered speed, Corbish said, "I really don't know why you tag along with us the way you do, Mr. Kater. Do you take us for interesting freaks, or something?"

"We're all interesting freaks, if it comes to that. I just want to help you get to where you wish to go. Is that so strange?"

"And so all the while you must be thinking of us as poor cold-blooded creatures?"

"I'm afraid Corbish has rather a chip on her shoulder at present," Safton said. "The mere size of this city is so overwhelming. . . ."

"Don't be silly, darling," Corbish said. "Didn't you feel inferior when you saw that in this place they have to strive to protect from extinction diseases that hundreds of people

on Istinogurzibeshilaha die of every year? And it is apparent
we can't think so efficiently as this gentleman, or see so well,
or read with the same ability—" She broke off and turned to
Kater. "I'm sure you will excuse my behavior and put it all
down to my natural inferiority. Perhaps we have time for you
to learn something of the history of man on Istinogurzibeshilaha, since you are so interested in us?

"I'll give it to you in a nutshell—we've lived through two
million years of underprivilege.

"I don't remember how long there have been forms of
space travel, but it's a long, long time. And about two million
years ago, a big trans-vacuum liner got into trouble and had
to put down on Istinogurzibeshilaha. Its drive was burned out
or something. Do you know what the world was like that
those men and women found? It was a barren world, without
all the amenities you take for granted on Dansson. Most of
it consisted of bare and lifeless soil—there weren't enough
earthworms and bacteria in the ground to render it fertile
enough for plants. Well, there were in some favored parts,
chiefly by rivers. There the vegetation ran to primitive plants
and trees—spore and conebearing things like cycads and giant
ferns and spruce and pine and the giant sequoias.

"Oh, don't think such a dark green world does not possess
a certain sort of grandeur. It does. But—no grass, no flowers,
none of the angiosperms with their little seed pods that are
embryo plants and afford nourishment for almost any kind
of herbivore you can think of. You see what I mean. Istinogurzibeshilaha was at the beginning of its Lower Triassic
period of evolutionary growth.

"Why do I say 'was'? It still is! In another thirty million
years or so, we shall just about graduate into the Jurassic.

"Can you imagine what hell those first men and women
went through? In those deserts and dark forests, where the
branches bow low under crude wooden cone flowers, what is
there for a warm-blooded man? Nothing! No animals he can
kill; the mammals have yet to arrive on our planet, because
you don't get them until the higher-energy plant foods available in an age of flowers materialize.

"The early reptiles are about—stupid, inefficient, slow-
moving, *cold-blooded* things, that can exist on what nourishment is going. And amphibians. Fish and crustaceans, of
course. They provided food."

As she talked, her tone lost its earlier resentment. Her eyes
rested on Kater's face as if it were merely an outcrop of that
stern landscape she described. Safton sat looking out of the

window, watching mile after mile of the galactic city flash by. Dusk was falling; the fantastic towers seemed to float in space.

"Those people—our ancestors—had to live off the land when their own supplies ran out. They had a fight, I can tell you. They had their own grains, but the grain failed when sown. It just wasn't the right environment. We have spiders, but most insects—not! No bees . . . they'll come after the flowers. Butterflies, no, and nothing like the high-speed metabolism of a true bird. So the people lived off the low-energy-level foods that were available.

"It was quite a change of diet. You know what happened? They didn't die out. They adapted. Maybe it would have been better if they had died out and we had never been. Because to adapt meant that they slowly became cold-blooded. When life begins on a planet, it always starts cold-blooded; in the circumstances, cold blood is a survival factor—did you know that, Mr. Kater? That way, life is lived slowly and it can survive on the vitamin-poor diet to hand. Much later along the evolutionary path, you get chemical reactions in the bloodstream, heating it, which are caused by eating new foods —the richer foods that follow in the wake of the seed-bearing plants.

"Evolution played a trick on our ancestors. It sent them backward down the path. They became—we are—reptiles."

"That's nonsense, Corbish," Safton said. "We are still men, simply cold-blooded."

Corbish laughed.

"Oh yes, there are worse than us. Our unhappy ancestors went feral when their blood started running cold. For thousands of years, they were nocturnal in habit. One group of them about fifty strong left the rest and took to a semi-aquatic life in the region of the Assh-hassis Delta. You should see *their* descendants today, Mr. Kater! Why, they aren't even viviparous! However alien I am to you, at least I don't lay eggs!"

She burst into ragged laughter, and Safton put his arms around her.

After a silence, Kater said. "I expect you know the history of Dansson. We—man—slew the seventy-seven nations of bipedal Danssonians before we took over the planet. I would think our history is more disgraceful than yours, if we are competing for disgracefulness."

Corbish turned and looked at him with interest.

"I hope you are feeling better now," he said to her. "We are just about to get out."

The car had stopped several times while she had been talking. Now it stopped again and they alighted into a station much like the one they had left. When they climbed aboveground, it was to survey a part of the city much liike the part they had left, except that here the great buildings were more conservative in shape and more riotous in color. The microfab system floated over their heads, shuttling its pianos through the dusk.

Kater halted and pointed out a scarlet building down the avenue to their left.

"That's Little Istino. You will feel at home among people from your own planet—but don't forget we are all basically of the same kind," he said.

"I wish to apologize for being rude earlier," Corbish said. "I will make no excuses for myself, but I was feeling very unhappy. Now I feel much more content."

"Funnily enough, so do I," Safton said. "It must be your company, Mr. Kater."

Slen Kater shook his mop of hair. "No, it's not that." He laughed. "Perhaps I will walk along with you right to your door. You're finding it hard to get rid of me, aren't you? You see there is a reason why you are feeling happier."

They walked by his side, looking curiously at him as he continued.

"I am an Immigration Officer. I was asked to follow you when you did not check in for your inoculations at the space field. No, no, don't look so alarmed. With every ship that comes in we run into the problem of people who for one reason or another don't want to come and see us. They often prove to be the brightest and most interesting people."

"After all this you are going to arrest us?"

"Certainly not. I have no need to. You will be peaceable and content here."

"You sound very confident," Corbish said.

"With reason. Everyone who lives on or comes to Dansson is inoculated against unhappiness. Oh, yes, we have a serum. Happiness is purely a glandular state. There's no illness here, as you know. Give a man the right glandular balance, and he will be happy. You had your inoculation that you missed at the space field as we left the Inficarium."

"Wait a minute," Safton said, stopping abruptly. "You said

that was a routine shot to ensure we had not picked up any diseases."

"My dear Safton—there was no possible danger of that. Those dangerous little life forms are all sealed away safely. No, it seemed a good time to make you feel happier. It has worked already, hasn't it?"

"My god!" Safton raised his fists, looked at them and laughed. There was no force in them, no core to his anger, no dismay in his surprise. He seized Corbish's arm and hurried her along, excited at the feeling of pleasure that swept over him. They certainly knew how to live on Dansson.

"Do you have these injections too, Mr. Kater?" Corbish asked.

"Certainly. Only being resident, I don't need as much as . . . visitors. Only the very eminent are allowed to be creatively miserable. As you're new here, you've had a stiff dose to tide you over the next few months."

She tried to feel vexed at this. Somehow she thought there was something in his statement that should have roused her apprehensions. Instead, she could only see what a joke he had played on them. She giggled, and was still giggling when they reached the scarlet structure, towering high above them.

"This is Little Istino, and you'll be fine here. There are plenty of your own kind within," Kater said. "And none of those egg-laying Assh-hassis to worry you. They have a separate block elsewhere in the city."

"You mean you have them here too? What use can they be to a wonderful modern planet like Dansson?"

Immigration Officer Kater stuck his hands in his pockets and looked down genially at them; they were nice little beings really.

"I admit the Assh-hassis aren't much *use*," he said. "But then neither are many of the thousands of lesser races of man we house here. You see, as true man spreads across this neck of the galaxy, he is slowly wiping out those half-brothers who are no match for him. So they have to be preserved—for study and so on. It's roughly like the diseases, I suppose."

Corbish and Safton looked at each other.

"I never thought of the Assh-hassis as a disease," Safton said. "They'll be amused when we get back to Istinogurzibeshilaha and tell our folks."

"Oh, you'll never go back there," Kater said. "Nobody ever leaves Dansson."

"Why not?"

He smiled. "You'll see. You'll be too happy to leave."

They were still laughing as they parted from him, the best of friends all around.

"That was a very comical remark he made," Corbish said, as they waved him farewell, "about parts of Dansson being reserved for inferior types of human—almost like a cage in a zoo, except I suppose the inhabitants don't notice the bars."

"Wouldn't the Assh-hassis be furious if they realized the truth?" Safton chuckled.

Arm in arm, they turned and hurried into the big scarlet-painted cage.

CARDIAC ARREST

~~~~~~

The sensation Tindale had, with the strange virus in his veins, that the world lay transfixed beneath his circling plane, awaiting his entry into human affairs again. Simultaneously, the contrary sensation that events were flowing swiftly by, just out of control. . . .

After seventy-eight minutes of holding, the daily Pan-Pac Boeing from San Diego was signaled down onto Emergency Runway A. Careful not to infringe Chinese air space, it circled down across sea and land. The delay had been caused by a plane on a local flight, which had crashed and blocked a main runway. The passengers could see the dark smudge of smoke drawn across the field, impersonal, remote from human lives and deaths.

Among the Pan-Pac passengers was a slightly-built sandy man wearing an unobtrusive cream tropical jacket whose real name was Gordon R. Tindale. He was traveling under the name of Justin R. James; such was the name of his forged passport. His nervousness increased as the Boeing came in to land. Although the flight-captain had explained the cause of delay over the speaker system, Tindale believed that it concerned him more personally.

The Kai Tak runways heaved toward them, a dazzling gray. They poked like fingers into the sea. Blue flashed below the windows; only at the last moment, as they sank, did land appear under the wheels. They braked to a halt facing toward the dun-colored distant hills of China. Loud silence. Unthought thing in the mind.

For several minutes, the plane sat on its baking runway

before the link coach arrived, the gangway was set in place, and the passengers were allowed to disembark.

As he emerged into the sunlight, Tindale scanned the field for assassins.

A uniformed attacker driving fast in a powerful open car teeth clamped I fire back hit him in the shoulder I should have a gun and the blonde the untrustworthy blonde with me meeting me me in glamorous Hong Kong a dark girl putting her arms around me in the cool hotel bedroom she staggers down the gangway wounded and I'm hit we make it to the hotel laughing immortal putting her arms around me eyes closing I need a disguise. . . .

He was living increasingly in a fantasy world; fear of death distorted his every thought.

Because of the crash, airport routine was upset. Passengers, half of them Hong Kong businessmen, driven to an emergency customs post. Customs men, anxious to hurry everything through, let the whole party through almost without search.

Tindale began to breathe more deeply, in an effort to slow his pulse rate.

He had been told where to meet his contact in Hong Kong, on the other side of the water. Stop worrying until then.

As the bus drove them to the main exit of the airport, they could see fragments of the crash being dragged off the central runway. People had died.

At the gate, Tindale caught a taxi to the ferry. He had to share it with a Chinese who had been on the plane.

He looks harmless enough smiles good afternoon suddenly he leaped for my throat we grappled I got my knee in his groin he thrust a long deadly knife no he produced a revolver still smiling we've had you followed ever since you left the chemical plant nonsense perfectly harmless can I interest you in a very beautiful girl sir streets full of people breed like flies downtown. . . .

Tindale stared out at the garish streets of Kowloon as they slid by; he thought it looked like an Oriental version of Las Vegas, which he had visited once when his marriage failed, five years ago; he had never been outside the States before this.

At the ferry, he felt more confident. It did not worry him that he was alone and unguided; people thronging about him gave him a sense of being unobserved. Across the waters of the bay, Hong Kong island, Victoria climbing its steep sides, mass of glittering skyscrapers challenging the sun. *American know-how.*

As the hovercraft carried him across the ship-flaked waters, the panorama extended its scale and began to envelop him, until he lost the whole picture in its details. The place thronged with things on the move. Hovercraft and helicopters and junks and vehicular railways and cable cars and automobiles and rickshaws moved on water and land and air, transporting these people about their short lives. Supposing all of them lived forever. . . .

The crossing had not taken a minute. He was carried off the ferry in a wave of people. As he fished in his breast pocket for an address, a mopedshaw driver buttonholed him.

"Where you want go, boss? I take you any place on this island."

"Do you know . . ." He looked at the Chinese, those lips pursed in nervous eagerness, those dark eyes trying to assess him. Could this be a killer? "Do you know the Mukden Hotel, San Tin Road?"

Suddenly he leaped for my throat we grappled that's for you you yellow devil she appeared among the crowd beautiful inscrutable he pulled a gun on me you want woman you likey lady whole continent full of them millions and millions continent tipping toward Hong Kong he smiles he guesses. . . .

"Jump in, boss. I take you—five minutes get there!"

It took twenty minutes. Midday—streets thick with traffic. Even the mopedshaw held up at almost every intersection.

Mukden Hotel was some way from the waterfront; it occupied several floors of a shiny new building, above shops andy noisy restaurant. Its rooms, Tindale thought, were extremely expensive. He had a small room with a window aslant, from which he could see, between the buildings opposite, a view of the spectacular harbor with Kowloon beyond.

He locked his door and began to unpack, expecting a knock at any minute. He had registered in the name of Harris, George Harris, as instructed.

Crazy, he had been crazy! It was all too risky.

OK buddy we're F.B.I. agents you can't do that I love him lady we can do anything I'm innocent blood tests the virus is you don't think the C.I.A. would let you get away with treason suddenly he leaped for his crotch look I can offer you a hideaway in China and immortal life if you keep your stinking bribes OK Mack you're on and only if she they will be on my trail right now and I've left a trail a mile wide he

had to disappear before sundown SECRET SERUM TRAI-
TOR LEAVES HK CLUE. . . .

From his case, he took the little cell-powered refrigeration
unit and placed it on the tiles in the corner of the shower.
He sat down on the bed and lit a cigar. He looked around the
room. He went to the window and peered out and down. All
the crazy Chinese signs, many of them flashing even at noon-
day. In the street an air of frenetic gaiety. A constant clicking
from somewhere below. He could not make out what it was,
and so it worried him. The plumbing? The Chinese were sure
to have bad plumbing, weren't they? An obscure smell in the
room, rather pleasant; he couldn't connect it with drains.
Christ, he had been mad to chance everything. Everything.

He went and looked outside his door. A Chinese woman
came out of the room opposite and moved toward the elevator, not looking at Tindale.

*She came toward him eyes wide with sensuous appeal he
grappled with her just a prostitute going on duty say honey
don't I she said simply I am your contact Turner as she
reached the elevator door he swung her around and on her
breast a brilliant ruby she came toward just a guest plate of
chop suey good here wait for Turner there was a knock on
the door. . . .*

A paperback, a spy thriller, *Low Point X,* that he had
picked up at the San Diego airport, before the plane had
zoomed off across the Pacific. He tried to read it. It all took
place in Europe. Europe was the most remote spot on the
globe right now. Zurich. Copenhagen. Oslo. Europe was the
most remote spot on the globe right now.

*The F.S. boys and I stared in horror at the little rectangle
sweating I drawled now I figure it an ultra-volt-micro-flash-
mechanism triggers off H-bombs get it a big deep Scotch on
the rocks my guts all of Oslo's a thousand megaton bomb
as of now couldn't hurt to go and eat lovely smell in the
windows downtown that goddamned clicking as of now it was
12:18 it's nearly seventeen hundred amber and real cold with
a big Bering to drag on then food I'm not just a waitress sir
but what made me sweat most was the two snide city gents
standing plumb behind us covering us with maybe a lobster
dish and a lager small 9mm Italian Mod. 34 Beretta auto-
matics in all Oslo the street was full of restaurants what I
could see safer not to eat here in the hotel mind if I siddown
buddy better nearby much safer Bourbon a big one sorry
sonny I snapped him a professional leaving the fridge here
better hang around for Turner another hour till six here's*

hoping I snapped him a professional punch straight. . . .

He gave up reading before six, flung the paperback down. Straightened his tropical jacket.

What I did I did for my country the F.B.I. will never believe. . . .

Locked the refrigerator in his case, stowed it under his bed. Went out, locked his door. Hesitated in the hall. Clicking still from below. No Turner. A million people, the hall empty. Sinister. Down the stairs. Into the hot marvelous street, thronging.

Scuse honorable sir me Mr. Turner you got wonder virus OK buddy this is to hell more Chinese than you could if Mary could see me. . . .

After much indecision, he picked a restaurant where he could watch the glass door of the Mukden Hotel from his table. He was the only European in the restaurant. But at least the food was good. He chose a lobster dish and drank Tuborg with it.

After, he walked up a side street. It climbed the mountain, just a series of steps. It would take only pedestrian traffic, and was crowded. Thousands of them. A jungle of small stalls. All the while, he felt uneasy. He bought an English language paper and returned to his hotel room. All was as he had left it. He put the refrigerator unit back in the shower, took a shower himself. All the time, he expected Mr. Turner to announce himself.

He read the newspaper.

EIGHTY DEATHS IN KAI TAK CRASH. Communist China was taking over the beggarly six square miles of Macao, Portuguese territory only a few sea miles from Hong Kong. All Portuguese leaving fast. Crashed plane had been full of Portuguese evacuees heading out of doomed colony. There were no survivors.

But Gordy how you've aged you look a million years old I've got news for you I am a million but even to me he was aged wrinkled beyond all belief even as he spoke he began to crumple that's just it I don't know how long I've got a million years but an air crash tomorrow. . . .

Tindale rattled the paper anxiously, trying to stop his thoughts.

He searched for news of the States. New president had been speaking, swearing to maintain the principles of his predecessor. Elsewhere, there was mention of the Pacific Community that the U.S.A. was busily promoting with Asiatic countries.

A conference was promised in Manila at some future unspecified date.

All of which was little help to Tindale.

The continual clicking still rose from below. It still worried him, though he realized it rose from the endless games of Mah-Jongg being played hereabouts. After much hesitation, he phoned for room service, ordered himself a stiff whisky at a steep price, and smoked another cigar with it.

Darkness fell. He did not put on the room light. There was so much light blazing up from the street that he could almost see to read. The street was growing noisier.

A knock at the door it was Turner without so much as a knock Turner grasping my 9mm Italian Beretta why the hell doesn't he show up it was all arranged put 'em up Tindale Turner's squealed he was killed in the air crash he must show up at the door stood a tall dapper that guy in Narvik the virus was secretly tested on human it was all agreed Mukden Turner Turner I should have got me a gat. . . .

At about ten o'clock, he went out again, this time taking the refrigerator with him, crooked under one arm and concealed by a light mack. Turner had not shown. He had wild ideas about getting a flight back to San Diego.

He pushed his way onto the main street and into the nearest bar.

The whisky cost even more than it had in the hotel.

If Turner doesn't arrive with the cash for a couple of days I am going to be in trouble it was all clear he would show as soon as I checked in as he opened the door. . . .

He had managed things badly. A skilled research chemist, big wheel in his firm, he had thought himself a man of the world; but his world had been too small. He hadn't even had nerve to cash his securities in case someone got suspicious. Well, the San Diego contact had promised him loot directly he met Turner in Hong Kong. He needed Turner; he was down to his last fifty dollars.

A white man came and sat down at the table opposite Tindale. His hands trembled around his glass as if he were already drunk.

Turner's hand trembled as he clutched drunkenly at the glass he was in his late sixties a husky craggy guy blurred about the edges unhealthy blue and red tinge to his skin I'm dying he croaked heart attack in a big plane cardiac arrest even as he fell what sort of thought is that this guy. . . .

"Mind if I drink with you? This is the only table not packed with damned Chinese."

"Go ahead."

"The colony's going to hell in a basket. We don't rule here anymore, you know. They can turn us out of here just as they turned the Portuguese out of Macao, whenever it pleases them. They're too big, we're too small, eh?"

"I don't know anything about politics. I'm an American."

He looked hard at the older man, at his silk scarf tucked in the neck of his soiled white shirt, trying to figure out if the virus was playing false with his perceptions; he had the persistent illusion he could see the guy dying.

"I'm British. I thought you Americans were always messing about in other people's politics! You may not believe this—I know I'm an old wreck now, but I was a fighter pilot in the Second World War. Yes, a hero—Battle of Britain, Nineteen-Forty! You weren't even thought of! Britain was great then. We stood alone, defied the world, defied Adolf Hitler. You've heard of him? Well, that was our finest hour, our absolutely finest hour. Since then—old country's finished. The whole world's going to pot, come to that."

Tindale could see that the old guy was warming to his theme. He began to drink up, but the ex-fighter pilot put a hand on his arm.

"Hang on, old boy! I'll buy you a round. Listen—not ten years after Britain's finest hour, we were finished as a world power, weren't we? I was flying at Suez—Suez, you know, when we tried to get our canal back. Nineteen-Fifty-seven, that was, Anthony Eden and all that. What a national disgrace that was, end of Britain's greatness! Nobody would have thought it, not in Nineteen-Forty. You weren't even alive then."

He drank his glass dry and stared moodily into the bottom of it. When he looked up again at Tindale, he spoke solemnly, in a more sober fashion.

"We passed on our greatness to you, you Americans, you know that? But you've lost it too. The initiative—you know what I mean, the *initiative*—had passed out of your hands following the disgrace of Vietnam, just as it did from Britain after the Suez conspiracy. We grew a conscience in the country, a sort of national conscience, in Nineteen-Fifty-seven. You grew the same thing. It's the end of a nation. It became more civilized, and so less able to rule."

Half interested, Tindale said, "Who's got the greatness now, in your opinion?"

The old pilot put one veined and age-flecked hand on the table for emphasis. "In my opinion, in my opinion, the countries without conscience have the power. Number One, of course, the Chinese. Number Two—no, there is no Number Two. It would be India if she weren't starving herself to death. There's just China, swarming over Asia. No one can match her. Terribly ruthless people."

He rose solemnly to his feet, extended a hand, made a parody of a military stance. "Captain Anthony Yarborough, once of the R.A.F., still flying in exile in his late sixties, sir."

Tindale took his hand. "I'm Gordy-Harris. I'm on a vacation."

"What's that package you're hiding under your mack?"

After a pause, Tindale said, "I'm on a vacation. My luggage. Could you get me a whisky? I don't feel so good."

Yarborough gave him a searching glance, and then turned and lumbered to the bar.

Then he's basically OK he knows I could slip away now, so his question must have been casual what's that under your mack I followed you all the way from San Diego no he's British when he whirled around from the bar Turner produced an ugly-looking Beretta they grappled maybe the guy could help me he looks plenty sick but he's not as drunk as I thought at first do I need help maybe he was sent. . . .

When Yarborough came back, he set down the glasses and said, leaning forward, "Look, Mr. Harris, I've got a partner, a very fine pilot, more your age than mine. He and I are in the flying business together. Maybe we can help you, if you need help."

"What gives you that idea?"

With trembling hand, Yarborough raised his glass to drink. "Cheers! I've knocked about the world, my boy. I can smell 'em a mile off. That's how I know you've got something worthwhile under your mack. You cuddle it as if it were solid gold. Is it?"

"No. It's worth more than gold. Look, if you and your partner know your way around Hong Kong—I could make it worth your while to help me."

"Depends what you are peddling."

"A virus."

"A virus? Germ warfare?"

"No. Something new. This virus confers extreme longevity, Immortality, you could say."

Sheer bloody madness to blab it out I always did say you were a blabbermouth Gordy basically we can say that a sense of insecurity. . . .

It took them half an hour to come to an agreement. Tindale

was reassured to find that Yarborough and his partner, a man called Kuhnau, were engaged in some unspecified aviation business that lay outside the law; it seemed to make matters easier for whatever the business was; it seemed to be a paying proposition. Yarborough would set one of his Chinese operators to watch the Mukden Hotel from inside, to pick up the trail of Mr. Turner, when that gentleman arrived. The erstwhile Mr. Harris, meanwhile, would not go back to the hotel; if he left again with his luggage, he would certainly alert anyone interested in his movements.

So Yarborough led them through the back of the bar and across a squalid alley and into the kitchens of a restaurant, and thus out to another street and into a taxi. They drove westward, turning off onto a wharf fringed by gaunt concrete godowns. Among the clutter of shipping lay a small sampan; it cast off directly Yarborough and Tindale were aboard. Sliding across the dark waters, they headed for the massed lights of Kowloon, which Tindale had left only a few hours before.

Once ashore, they had another long drive by taxi. At one point, they changed taxis. Tindale had completely lost his bearings by the time they reached Yarborough's flat.

"Take it easy, old chap," Yarborough said. "Walter Kuhnau should be home soon, then we'll have a chat. I must take my anticoagulants—old heart's playing me up. It's this damned climate. Not to mention the whisky."

He showed Tindale into a small bedroom. Tindale had picked up a few possessions from a supermarket when they changed taxis. He laid them out and looked around, staring through the venetian blinds at the lights outside. Beyond the lights, as Yarborough had carelessly indicated, lay the sullen darkness of China; one or two pinpoints of light there only emphasized the obscurity.

Asia darkness unknown whole mighty continent swarming according to the deal made that night I shall be granted you will be granted one hundred acres good land in southern China in the Hunan Province me on that massive continent of Asia yes you will be part of a large pleasant reservation area where there are many Americans and other nationalities who have preferred to help China in her great struggle for universal democratic principles well I don't know about that but he said later Mr. Turner will show you color pictures of your land already it is being prepared you will have servants provided and a guaranteed income annually geared to any possible rising cost of living yes it's a bargain an income from the state for life if I am going to live forever a single shot rang out then a permanent income is the one thing I need all they want in return is that one can of the Surviva culture it can't hurt America besides God a hundred acres and a house female servants as she came toward him a slow voluptuous smile slow voluptuous came someone in there with Yarborough as I tore avidly at her cheongsam they're shouting it's Kuhnau as he tore bestially at her cheongsam OK Tindale come out quietly I fell into this one a gun who the. . . .

As he went toward the door to listen, it opened, and Yarborough entered with a tall dark young man. The young man had sharp but heavy features. He wore a blue flying uniform, open at the neck to reveal a flamingo pink shirt underneath.

"Mr. Harris? My name is Walter Kuhnau. I am pleased to meet you." His German accent was not heavy, and he spoke with a softness in contrast to the raised voice he had been using a moment ago. "I must tell you at once that I am a strict businessman—one lives no other way in Hong Kong. If you wish our support, you must prove you can repay us for it."

He strode over to the daybed behind Tindale, swept away the cushions with one gesture, revealing the refrigerator, which he grabbed. Tindale ran forward and seized it. At once he found himself flat on the floor.

The tiger leaped up like a flash he was at the other's throat not bothering to rise he whipped out an ugly-looking laughing Kuhnau shot him dead bargain with him. . . .

"Don't be rough, Mr. Harris! Get up."

"Walter's what you'd call a tough guy, old boy. I'll get us all a drink. You'd be well-advised not to look for trouble."

Climbing to his feet, Tindale said, "I'm not looking for trouble—I've got plenty of that already and, if you get involved with me, you may find rougher company than you bargained for. Ever tangled with the F.B.I. or the Red Chinese government, Herr Kuhnau?"

Kuhnau said quietly, "Yes, both of them. Look, I have trouble in plenty right now, Mr. Harris, but I can manage more if it's worth it. But you bettter to state your business at once, please."

Yarborough brought in the whisky.

Tindale took a good swig and sat himself on the edge of the daybed with his hands in his pockets. He said, "You are going to find this hard to believe because it's so new. You know the U.S.—and the U.S.S.R. and China, and every nation in the power struggle, I guess—are evolving new methods of bacteriological warfare. I am—was—Senior Research Chemist in a laboratory working on such a project. We finally came up with a mutated virus, J-Two-Seven-Seven, now known as Surviva. It's been tested out now for over five years—that's a lot of generations for a virus. Briefly, this virus repairs all cellular damage in certain animals and fish, so that as long as the strain survives in the host body it virtually confers immortality on the host. I have a sample culture of that virus here—in the box you are holding."

Putting the refrigerator down, Kuhnau opened it and took out one of the vials. "Looks like plain water to me, Mr. Harris."

"Put it back! The virus life span outside a host body is severely limited—it doesn't have the immortality it confers on other living things."

Kuhnau put the vial back and snapped the refrigerator shut, "You tell me these viruses confer immortality on human beings."

"Only on fish and one or two reptiles."

"On fish! Who requires an immortal fish?"

"Any team of virologists with the know-how could develop another virus from the J-Two-Seven-Seven strain. My own firm has just developed one, but in limited quantities. Again to be brief, I got myself a jab of the new strain, known as Surviva-Plus, and came away fast. With the J-Two-Seven-Seven strain—the Plus virus was too well guarded to get to."

But Gordy you look a million years old it was true he had withered to an ancient dried sexless thing overnight he had had a thousand years of life the whole world reveres me if it would only give me two hundred years he never looked a day over thirty and ooh that immortal body actually you're saying you're immortal the secret of eternal youth and all that if you should live that long. . . .

"How can you prove this, Mr. Harris? You realize we know it is all absolute lies, every word."

"OK, Kuhnau, then turn me out if you don't want a share! Look, I'll give you proof that this isn't lies. My real name is Tindale, Gordy Tindale. The hunt will be up for me in the States in a few days. I'm supposed to be away for a weekend's fishing, but they'll discover I'm missing by Monday evening. And another thing—I have to meet a contact in Hong Kong. I told Yarborough. A man named Turner. If you two will help me, I'm in a position to pay for your services."

"Wait here! We'll just have a brief discussion." Nodding curtly, Kuhnau beckoned Yarborough out of the room. He took the refrigerator with him, and shut the door. Tindale took a swig from the whisky bottle.

It'll work. His crimson shirt he fancies himself we all love ourselves forever without us no world they get one vial can't double-cross me because they don't know enough to take advantage of the possibilities on their own should work you operate on my terms Kuhnau or else lying in the car seat with his throat cut blood splattered over the windshield everywhere. . . .

God where did that picture come from someone lying there in a car or could it be on a beach throat cut was it me so vivid throat all cut slit blood where do I get these thoughts could it be a vision of the future me immortal and I'm suddenly obsessed with death but in that car who me Yarborough Kuhnau Turner God not me please just lying in the dark over the steering wheel just damned rotten dead couldn't be me couldn't be. . . .

Yarborough and Kuhnau returned. "Frankly, old boy, we are very skeptical. We are going to get one of those vials analyzed."

"Let me handle this, Tony! Mr. Tindale or Harris, or whatever you are called, we will give you limited help on your terms."

"I'll call the terms, thanks, Kuhnau. You listen. There are six vials in that icebox, as you saw. You and Yarborough can have one. Believe me, you could ransom all of Hong Kong with that one vial. But only I on the whole of this side of the Pacific have the know-how to treat that virus so that it lives and multiples. You can have the instructions when you have got me safe to my Chinese contact with the other five vials, OK?"

"They have trouble in China—maybe Turner's dead. Then?"

"That's my worry. You see me safe, and you can have that one vial. From it, someone with special knowledge can breed the Surviva-Plus strain. With the Plus strain, you and Yarborough can live forever and flog the rest to earn your keep forever."

Yarborough said, "My poor old heart—I really need that stuff! My boy is already watching out for Turner at the Mukden, you know, laddie."

And Kuhnau said, looking at his watch, "I've got an appointment in forty minutes. Let's discuss details. It's a deal."

It was not until four days later that Mr. Turner crossed their tracks.

During that period of waiting, Tindale was left mainly on his own. In the nearby bookstore, he found a copy of *Low Point X,* and so was able to find out what happened that time at Oslo. One day, Yarborough took him fishing from a motor launch in Deep Bay, indicating the coast of Red China, hinting that he and Kuhnau also had their business with the communist power.

For the rest of the time, the two men were away from the flat for many hours, once staying away overnight, to return at about noon the next day and sleep around the clock.

Once the deal was made with Kuhnau, he proved a friendly and reliable enough man, full of tales of scoundrels and harlots and big rackets all over the world, with Bangkok, Lisbon, and Frankfurt his favorite trouble spots; he claimed that Frankfurt was too hot for him to return to at present.

He came in one afternoon, flung down a newspaper full of the latest Portuguese horror stories from Macao, and sprawled in a chair.

"Any news, Walter?"

"Yes. Good news for you and good news for me, but it's best I don't tell you my news! Jackie just reports to me as I came in," Kuhnau said. Jackie was one of his many "boys" who ran errands for him in Kowloon and Hong Kong. "Your Mr. Turner showed up at last and was intercepted by one of our boys at the door of the Mukden Hotel."

"What nationality is he? Why this long delay? Are you sure it isn't some sort of a frame-up?"

Kuhnau smiled. "Relax, Gordon, you are no longer in your gangster country. The Chinese are honorable people! Mr. Turner is Chinese. He says to my boy that he was detained by internal difficulties in Peking. It's the bad political situation there, no doubt. He wishes to meet you at the city end of Deep Bay this evening at dusk."

Welcome to the Communist Republic of China Mr. Tindale of course it will be necessary for you to shave your head this is your hut no no hundred acres you pig dog only everlasting imprisonment in this hut you capitalist lackey all that your filthy American propaganda printed about our tortures is true and more to show the gratitude of Peking you may have any woman you require and a supply of paperbacks in the spy thriller and science-fictional vein he drew a revolver and fired from almost point-blank . . .

"With the virus, of course?"

"Not this evening. That will come tomorrow. This evening, he only wants to talk with you."

"More delay! Am I defecting or aren't I?"

"Life is full of crises. You must get used to it. This is Kowloon, old boy, not San Diego, you know."

"You hate America, don't you, Walter?"

"You hate Germany! You hate the Chinese! You hate the Vietnamese, the Negroes, the British, the Mexicans—"

"You're lying, Walter! You've never been to the States. You only know a Hollywood version. Listen, I shouldn't defend a country I'm defecting from, maybe, but OK—I'll *prove* we hate nobody, that we are and always have been the most generous nation on Earth—"

"OK, prove, you're always proving!"

"Right—like we proved our good intentions by building up Germany again after we'd rubbed out Hitler. Listen, Walter, when my firm has got enough Surviva-Plus and has tested it out exhaustively, the U.S. government is going to give it to the world and make the world full of immortals. How do you like that?"

He opened the car door the guy was lying with an arm limp over the steering wheel his head lolled backward over the seat he was up to his eyes in blood so damned messy and it was the picture was so clear not dear God a picture of something real to come just a little bit of fright from an ego adjusting to the bare fact of living forever but you couldn't see the face I can't see if it's who it is it's so real. . . .

"Walter, look, be a friend, I admit it, I'm scared. I've led a peaceful life—life is very pleasant and sheltered in the States, you don't realize. Come this evening, drive me there in your car, meet Mr. Turner with me, will you?"

Kuhnau looked seriously at him, clasping his hands.

Seriously I'm just jealous of the Americans seriously you're just a little bastard I like you Gordy Gordon. . . .

"He had instructions I didn't tell you yet, Gordon. Mr. Turner told my boy that you were to pick up a Self-Drive Happy Yellow Car from the station down the road here—he knows where you shack up, you see. You are to drive to the beach alone. There is not to be anyone else, and you are to leave the car by the end of the promenade and walk along the beach to the deserted part, keeping near the sea always."

Very pleased to meet you at last Mr. Turner and welcome in the name of please don't think of yourself as a traitor we have useful chemical research for you to do in Peking preparing lethal bacteria to be dispersed in America as he came along the shore toward me I drew my gun throat slit from ear. . . .

"Yes, I see. Walter, you're flying illegally in some way, aren't you? Something to do with Macao? I don't want to know. But one day, you and Tony might be in difficulties. I'd have a bolt-hole in China for you; you'd be welcome, that's God's truth. Just be a friend this evening—get down on the beach first. I've seen your armory while I've been hanging around here. That rifle with telescopic sights—keep me covered, just in case."

"In case what?"

As the yellow man flung himself forward there was a puff of smoke up the beach dark a shot rang out from the direction of the dunes he staggered. . . .

"You know. In case there's any trouble. And tomorrow night, when they actually take me over the border."

"Sorry, Tony and I won't be around this part of the world tomorrow."

"Just this evening then?"

"The vial this evening, then?"

"When we get back here after the meeting you shall have it."

"I drink to that, my friend!"

"And Tony?"

"He's lying down to rest. We have a busy night ahead of us, apart from your little sideshow."

They drank, looking thoughtfully at each other.

Ear to ear. . . .

Where the street lights gave out, he stopped the Happy Yellow Self-Drive Car and walked across the track to stare along the beach. The tail of the South China Sea lashed feebly against the ancient shore. Beyond the bay lay the Chinese mainland, fold on fold of featureless hills.

And suddenly my heart said to me be still the magical sagacity of all sensation even as he spoke. . . .

He had his directions. He walked across a rattling shell ridge down onto the beach and trudged across the dry stretches of sand to make himself a moving target by the line of waves. To the west, something of the day still left a stain in the sky; from another direction, the concealed lights of Hong Kong set up a redder glow; but it was too dim to see much. Tindale stared at the low dunes. Walter Kuhnau was somewhere along there, concealed but peering along the infrared sights of his rifle, sitting tight in a car awaiting Tindale's troubles.

Someone was coming diagonally across the beach toward Tindale.

He stood where he was and the man walked right up to him.

"You are Gordon Tindale?"

"Mr. Turner?"

"Good, you got my instructions. Walk with me down the beach, Mr. Tindale. I will not take much of your time."

Possible in the dimness to see that he was a well-built Chinese, wearing some sort of a tunic buttoning high around the throat. A flat face, ugly cheekbones. Easy movements, very good English, inhuman. They walked, away from the lights and the yellow car.

"I have the package, Mr. Turner. You kept me waiting. It is urgent that the package is delivered as soon as possible. I want to cross into China tonight if possible."

"Delay was unavoidable. There were some administrative delays, much regretted on our part. But everything must be done correctly. If we know you are happy to join us, we will take you across to your new home tomorrow night."

"Why not tonight?"

"I cannot answer all your questions, I regret to say."

They're got their endless complicated troubles too maybe Turner's dead this guy's some phony so saying he produced a nasty-looking gun from under his I can hold out another day it's not too bad suppose he's just one of Walter's men planned it all never watched anyone at the hotel just framing me perfectly possible oh God I must be sure was a way to check I've never told Walter or Tony name of my firm. . . .

"I need your credentials, Mr. Turner. Give me proof that you represent the Peking government. What is the name of my former employers in San Diego?"

"I will show you credentials in car. Also, your firm is Statechem Inc. of Chula Vista, San Diego. Now, kindly accompany me. You came here entirely alone?"

They left the pounding waves behind, walking across the sand, Tindale keeping to seaward to avoid any possible shots from the land side. Behind the dunes was a track, leading to a couple of fishermen's villages which perched almost at the frontier. It seemed very dark on the track. Tindale almost fell against Turner's car before he was aware of it. As they climbed in, he saw that another man stood shadowy by the front of the car; he muttered a few words to Turner as the latter climbed into the driver's seat.

They're going to murder me blood all over the windshield and throat cut from ear I struggled violently VIRUS THIEF

FOUND STABBED Mary I did love you these bastard Chinese. . . .

"I do not have the virus here, you understand."

"That is understood, Mr. Tindale. We offer you no harm. We offer you sanctuary, away from the insane pressures of your society. We are building for a better world in which all will fairly play their part. China has no evil intentions; she wishes only to see global justice done. The war-mongering imperialistic forces of the world must be extinguished, and this will happen very soon."

As he spoke in his calm flat voice, Turner was producing a small slide projector, which he plugged into the car instrument panel.

"See here, pictures of the estate you will be given, in beautiful Kwangsi Chuan Region."

"I was told it would be in Hunan Province."

"Is more beautiful in Kwangsi Chuan Autonomous Region, and more prosperous."

He stared into the viewer. There were diagrams as well as actual photographs. The place looked good. The building itself was a simple ranch-type affair with only three rooms and bathroom, kitchen, and toilet, but these offices were well-equipped. Outside, the view was stupendous, with mossy and hunchbacked hills parading like camels along the landscape. One shot of the ranch in particular had a poster-like quality, with a black water buffalo dragging a plow against a background of the fantastic hills, the tops of which were bled away into cloud.

As the slides shuttled before Tindale's vision, Turner's voice went on; "—very secure place in the coming struggle. Safe alike from hydrogen bombs and invading armies. 'The army and the people are an ocean in which the invader must drown,' as the immortal Mao has said. Those who work for us are rewarded—"

"What are you going to do with Surviva-Plus when you have it?"

"That need not concern you, Mr. Tindale. But clearly we shall use it to extend the working life of our leaders, so that they can serve the people forever."

"The people aren't going to get it, you mean?"

"That will not be possible for some while."

There were workers with smiling faces among the slides, and paddy fields, some terraced, and a winding river, punctuated by a small boat with a sail. And horror. Tindale was catching, almost subliminally, glimpses of a prison cell from which a devil's face mouthed at him. His heart thudded.

It'll burst are the the viruses doing their stuff or are they killing me I have a mental sickness my ego breaking free from the fear of death a machine to keep my heart beating built-in cardiac pacemaker there's the prison again all metal barred two guards rushed in as they grappled kicks screamed his thighs punch in the like oozing raspberry jam the clouds low there like an old painting. . . .

He slowed the slide mechanism as the last picture came up, saw that the subliminal illusion was a glimpse of the back of the projector, barred in metal, on which a crude portrait of the Leader had been stamped. His alarm stayed with him.

Foreign devils. . . .

"If you like all you see, Mr. Tindale, please be back here alone tomorrow at the same time. With the virus."

The man outside tapped sharply on the window. Turner opened the door. Noise of engines out there, a sweep of light. Turner jumped out. The track suddenly visible in sweeping searchlight, and immediately police hover appearing over the low rise. Turner grabbing machine gun from car and flinging himself down, firing upward. Another hover, a loud hailer, metallic voice in Chinese, then in English, "Stay where you are, George Harris, stay where you are, George Harris!"

George Harris running like mad down the track, Turner and buddy firing madly but not at him.

Doubled up, searching the tattered grass skyline to the right. *Car there Walter Kuhnau good guy make fast getaway forget all this terror. . . .* Among the dunes, Kuhnau would be waiting, as anxious to avoid police as Tindale. *Really seeing excitement like Oslo hero at last there it is. . . .* Smooth cab shape just off the track and he ran to it, glitter from sea and sky showing Kuhnau inside. *Why not started engine Walter Walter. . . .* Flings open door. *Ear to ear they got him it was Walter in the premonition thank God not me oh Walter that other bastard got to you I Christ I all my blood everywhere now what turn him out of course go like hell be brave Walter you so foul dead Nazi bastarding Chinks ah ah out you go and the sand lay cool without footstep a knife flashed and without a sound just leave him there my pants all over my hands like stain of crime bloody engine won't oh boy they got their hands full with Turner foreign devils among the camels over punishment hut get to old Yarborough and always rely on the British he'll get me out I got to do it got to do it seventy seventy-five steady for God's don't hit anything a cart at the last moment he still firing back Walter Walter you poor I'm going to make it Harris Harris they know I'm. . . .*

He was back among the lighted streets, forced himself to slow down, passed a taxi garage, took first left, stopped the car and got out, ran back on foot, took a taxi back to Yarborough's and Kuhnau's flat.

Yarborough was asleep. Tindale shook him.

"I'm too ill to go, Wally. Not tonight—Gordon, what the dickens? I thought it was a scramble!"

"They're on to us, Tony. We've got to get away."

Breathlessly, he explained what had happened. As he talked, Yarborough sat up, spilled five pills into his palm from three different bottles at his bedside, swigged them down with a quarter of a tumbler of neat whisky, and rose. He started dressing.

"Get your virus, Gordon. I told Walter this was dangerous. We are leaving here. I'm in charge now."

"What are we going to do?"

"The virus is my property. If I sell some of it, well, you get a share. I shall be fair, never fear. In exchange, I will get you out of this hole. All of Kowloon will be screaming for you, and they'll be on to you in no time. It so happens you have a real streak of Yankee luck. Walter and I were going to make an unscheduled flight tonight to a safer part of the world. You can come with me. We're getting right out of here."

"Where to?"

"You'll see."

Mm certainly looks pretty cool back in 1940 about to take a bang at the Luftwaffe no doubt fast dresser better be what now money we certainly need it his secret drawer. . . .

"Here's a passport. No, British, you'll never pass for English with that accent. Canadian, ah, good, I knew we'd need it one fine day. You're David Watkins. Memorize the details."

He caught the Canadian passport Yarborough threw him. He was David Watkins of Ontario, aged forty-five. Square-headed, open-faced. All extremely unlikely. He picked up the refrigerator. Yarborough was stuffing money and a whisky bottle into a case. He ran through to the kitchen, came back with a kerosene can, sprinkled it over the bed he had just left, brought out his lighter.

"What are you doing, man?"

A cock-eyed smile. "Don't think I don't wince to do it, old boy, but we must destroy the evidence—and this may create a bit of a diversion."

The bed was burning merrily as they made for the elevator. The events of the next three hours remained blurred. Yarborough was entirely in command, and it was evident he had a great many contacts locally. He took Tindale to a bleak office full of Chinese; three of these men escorted them to a warehouse; from there, they rode in the back of a furniture van to some unknown stretch of town and transferred to a fast car which had been crudely bullet-proofed inside with sheets of metal. They drove out of the built-up area.

Eventually, they emerged on a headland overlooking the sea.

It could have been Deep Bay again for all Tindale knew. All was quiet. Two Chinese with carbines slung over their shoulders accompanied them down a flight of wooden steps to the narrow beach. The four of them stood there in silence. A ship was patrolling out in the bay, its searchlight swinging around in leisurely circles. Suddenly, a small craft appeared offshore. Yarborough and Tindale waded out to it, leaving the guards on the beach.

They climbed into a small submarine. The one-man crew was already supine at the controls; they had to crouch beside him. Yarborough muttered a few words of Cantonese and they started to move.

Too small nonsense too small sinking keep calm claustrophobia the heat and death again that head lolling back another death not Walter it's me next time oh shut up it's Tony Yarborough it's all nonsense you just need a we are going across to China afer all he's double-crossing me. . . .

"Tony, you're taking me to China. I swear I'll break the vials if you double-cross me!"

"Relax, old chap! We're going across to China, but I have a working arrangement with them. Even among political enemies, all sorts of personal arrangements are possible—I'm useful to the Chinese. But I'm not handing you over to them, if that's what you think. This mob here I deal with won't have heard of you—you're a top secret Peking project, evidently. We'll be OK, never fear!"

At one point, they cut the engine. In the almost complete silence, the tide could be heard beyond the hull, a few inches away.

"What the hell'd he stop for?"

"Keep quiet!"

The silence seemed to have extended forever before they got under way again. Yarborough explained that a patrol vessel was moving overhead. After that, it was only a few minutes before they cut engines again and touched against the further shore.

"Don't drop that blasted refrigerator pack," Yarborough said, as they climbed out into the surf. He gave a low whistle, which was answered.

Tindale looked around. On the other side of the bay, lights were flashing.

Cliffs rose steeply here. A man in an oilskin carrying a dim lantern came to guide them up a twisting path. It was hard work climbing to the top; then the guide was for pressing on, but Yarborough stopped him and leaned on Tindale.

"Oh, that's bad for my heart! I must retire from this active life. I'm not what I was in Nineteen-forty, that's for sure—would never pass for A-One now."

"You're doing fine, Tony—now let's get on!"

They followed the guide over dark cliffs, clutching each other and stumbling. Once they passed a hut before which two men in uniform stood, but no word was spoken. They came to a rutted track, which met a road after a couple of hundred yards. There, a car was waiting for them, with uniformed driver.

"This is the road to Canton," Yarborough said casually.

Millions of people jostling shops stalls junks Canton this is China prehistoric tawny ancient loud as a gong with tilled dust all-embracing feared homemade steel running in the paddy trenches every fourth one gentle and cruel camel humps marching across yellopen landscape the parchment screen so green the army and the people are an ocean nothing could stop me now with my associate I jumped into the gleaming black limousine and drove toward the forbidden city of the army and the peasants are an ocean in which the invaders will drowsetung. . . .

After several miles of dim-lit progress, they turned off the road and were bumping over an inferior road.

The two white men sat in the rear of the car. Yarborough came out of a stupor and said, "Right, old boy, here we are at the airfield; you are my copilot, David Watkins. OK? Directly we get in the plane, we both go forward and stay tight. They won't be suspicious. I'm a bit early, but it's ten-fifteen now and we take off shortly after one ack emma. I'll catch a nap before we take off. It's going to be a strain without Walter. You don't fly, do you?"

"Where are we flying to, Tony?"

"Hang on, old boy!" The car had stopped before a bright-lit concrete hut. They climbed out and, at Yarborough's prompting, checked in. The Chinese officials looked at them with dislike and kept them waiting for ten minutes before they were free to go.

They walked across a badly paved square. Outside one low building, a line of silent people huddled.

"Who are they?"

"Portuguese."

Beyond, the scene began to look more like an airport. A large airliner stood close at hand, fuel tenders clustering under its wings; lights glared around it, revealing blue-clad Chinese technicians.

"That's my plane. An old Tupolev Bear, damned fine machine. The Chinese have converted it into passenger-freight—it was designed as a bomber. I did the deal for them with some Russians. Walter and I part-own it. We fly it places where it wouldn't do for Chinese to be seen." He looked quizzically at Tindale. "You don't know the world, old boy, but you'll learn. The peoples of the nations have to live together, whatever the politicians say. Let's get a bite to eat, and then we'll go aboard."

Once you step over an invisible line old boy you belong to no country know no allegiance from that moment on every man's hand was against a big plane like that would never get over the surrounding hills piddling little cookhouse those massive steaks she and I used to eat at that place smells good Tony man of world me I fly anywhere learn get a pilot's Indonesia hopping equator foreign devils boy that chicken better big guy. . . .

He found a Bering in his cigar case and smoked it after the meal, strolled with it nonchalantly in a corner of his mouth as they crossed to the Tupolev. *Gordy Tindale was one of the daredevilest guys you ever. . . .* "Don't tell me, Tony—better put it out with all this fuel around, eh?" *Right from the start of the game he never missed. . . .*

"That's old hat—you've been watching old movies. You could throw your cigar right into this juice: it's noninflammable."

They climbed up the ramp. Inside, the big plane echoed. It looked enormous. There was coconut matting laid in the central gangway, and straw palliasses on either side.

As they walked through the gangway, Yarborough said, "They stripped her of all her armaments and put in extra fuel tanks. She'll fly just about anywhere in the world. I've carried almost three hundred people on short flips, but tonight we'll only have about a hundred and fifty."

"Portuguese?"

"Of course. They pay six hundred quid sterling for the ride. I get a quarter."

In the control cabin, more palliasses were spread. Yarborough looked at his watch and sank down gratefully. He spread himself out and was asleep almost at once.

Tindale went and sat in one of the pilot's seats, staring at the panels of dials all around. With the lights on in the cabin, he could see nothing outside. He sat there, running over the madness of the day. The cigar butt fell from his hand. He also slept.

When he woke, Yarborough was taking a swig of whisky and looking about. In the body of the plane, the Portuguese refugees were assembling, most of them men, plump, tired, tousled, middle-aged; there were a few women and five small children. All were very subdued. As they took their places on the uninviting palliasses, a Chinese officer in a gray uniform pressed through the crowd and came forward. He shook hands cordially with Yarborough and Tindale and talked to the former in Chinese.

"They want us to get away as soon as possible," Yarborough said. "You take that seat, Gordon. It should be an easy flight. Don't worry."

"I'm not worrying."

"Sorry, no offense meant, but we shall be taking the polar route." He strapped on his headset, opened up the radio, and began to talk to ground control.

Now they were flying through a blinding white haze suddenly Tindale shouted I must not live dangerously must not centuries wasted death he's getting us ready to go polar route the starboard engine cut out God. . . .

The four turboprops were waking to life. The overhead lights went out. The Portuguese were all in position now; the exit was closed, the ramp retracted. The air-conditioning came on. Unexpectedly, beautifully, the guide lights woke outside, amber and green and red, into the far distance down the field. The fuel tenders were already moving away. The Tupolev stood alone.

Polar route which goddamned pole old Tony'll never make it his heart but TRAITOR HERO Tindale brought the gigantic Russian oh grow up man this is for real I don't even know where we're going I just that deal was no good never trust the Chinks lousy Reds I'll screw a better deal out of you have to hand it knows his polar routine to him my finest wow we really. . . .

They were rolling into position. Five minutes later, the
lights were lurching below them and the dark hills rolling.
Then the hills were gone and the lights, and they were circling,
climbing. Yarborough raised his thumb, smiled. In a while,
he pointed to a distant blaze of light. Hong Kong. Still burning bravely on the edge of the greatest continent. Then it
was snuffed.

When they had settled down to routine, Tindale said, "You
never told me where we were heading."

"Portugal. Outside Lisbon, about fifty kilometers—Caldas
da Rainha Field."

"Lisbon! How far's that? Can we make it?"

"I've done it half a dozen times. The reports from the
weather satellites are all good. I'll switch to automatic pres-
ently; then we can get in some more kip."

"But how far is it?" He was annoyed to see that Yarborough enjoyed being nonchalant.

"Oh, about eight and a half thousand miles, the route we
go, right over China and Russia. They route us this way so
that most of the time we're over Communist territory or the
sea. We're at thirty-six thousand feet, making something like
Mach point six eight. It's about nineteen or twenty hours in
the air, allowing for winds and one thing and another."

*Mary I still love you I was immature I want you back we
can live somewhere safe take a thousand years get to know
each other properly maybe really understand ourselves some
island paradise Fiji. . . .*

There was a Chinese steward on the plane. He brought
them a thin but tasty pork soup with noodles. Tindale and
Yarborough had been silent for a long while. Finally, the
latter said, "I'm not used to thinking ahead, Gordon. Living
forever—you can't take it in, can you? I shall miss Walter,
but we can use his contacts. We'll shed these Portuguese
chaps and then perhaps we fade into the blue, forget about
the plane, bless it. Go to Frankfurt. I know a chap called
Schaefer there—he'll see we get a ransom for the virus. The
Germans will pay up. They're a pretty straight nation, despite the occasional bastard like Goebbels and Hitler. I
really hated Goebbels."

"I don't see why the Chinese show such interest in the
welfare of the Portuguese. Aren't they turning them out of
Macao?"

"The Chinese are a strange race. They detest the rest of
the world, and yet are fascinated by it. They want their

fingers in every pie. They don't give a hoot for the Portuguese
—who would?—but they find it useful to have a flight going
into Europe like this. Among the passengers will be a couple
of Red spies, for certain."

"You don't mind?"

"Why should I care? Every nation spies. It's a neurosis.
The ordinary men like you and me go on living."

*You think yourself ordinary you big ugly lump of outdated
figure of fun wonderman tough guy callous as all I think you
care less about Walter's death than I ear to ear he was a good
first German I ever met I all my life has suddenly turned
extraordinary entire break with I Frankfurt all glass offices
the fine Rhine wine. . . .*

They slept. When Tindale awoke, dawn was there, marvelous, and again he saw a symbol that immortality had taken
him beyond the ordinary world of men. He looked at the
chart on which Yarborough had marked their flight path. They
would enter the Arctic Circle but not touch the pole; at the
northern point of the Yamal Peninsula in Siberia, they would
change course and fly down the Baltic Sea and high over
Europe to Portugal. *Now am I lost from the States and from
my normal dying life place and time. . . .* The hours passed.
He had hours to spare. . . . The Portuguese kids had got over
their scare and were running about the aircraft. *Hours to spare
I was immortal as a kid perhaps it's time I woke up to the
world got time. . . .* Yarborough went to swill his blotchy
face in the toilet at the rear, and Tindale was alone above the
clouds. *Got enough time to look after other people beside
myself those kids even Tony to hell with him old limey
drunk. . . .* Siberia lay hidden below. *Come to terms maybe
really just being born ordinary men got to get myself born
anything's possible. . . .*

Yarborough returned. He seemed to be staggering a little.

"Tony, I need to get to a place where I can just sit and
think for maybe several years. I haven't used half my potential.
A man's so busy scraping his living, and when that's over—
well, you're too old for anything. Being immortal's going to
sort of change the viewpoint and—"

"I don't feel good, Gordon."

"Take a pill. You drink too much! I read somewhere once
that a scientist said man was just a species that never grew
up. Maybe immortality is needed to reach adulthood. Sort
of scary to think—I mean, everyone's going to be immortal
one day."

"Gordon! I—" Yarborough took a step forward, lurched,

and fell slowly forward, sliding down the pilot's seat onto the floor. Harsh noises came from his throat, his eyelids fluttered.

"Oh, no!" Tindale grabbed the older man and pulled his head up. "You can't get ill now, Tony, come on. Where are those pills?"

Yarborough's face was distorted. He pointed to his palliasse. Scrabbling, Tindale found three bottles, pulled off the caps, rolled out pills.

"Water, water, Gordon, quick. . . ."

He ran to the steward at the rear of the plane, pushing the Portuguese out of the way, so that some of them came back anxiously with him and stared in the door as he gave Yarborough the number of pills directed, slopping water down the man's throat and over his face, which was pale now under the stubble.

"Keep out, you guys!"

"I am a physician, sir—" one of the passengers said, venturing forward.

"Keep out—he's going to be OK. It's just a bad hangover!"

Bastard got to live got to damned live wish I had Surviva-Plus might kill the old guy in this stupid state flying through blinding haze he pulled the bomber out of a long dive got to live all lives were lost. . . .

After a while, Yarborough was well enough to move. Tindale propped him so that he was lying fairly comfortably on the straw mattresses.

"Sorry to scare you, old boy."

"We'll get you into a hospital in Lisbon."

"It's time we were changing course. I'll direct you. Get into that seat and switch off the autopilot and I'll direct you."

"I can't!" *Example of supreme heroism onlookers agreed.*
. . .

The hours passed. The great Tupolev flew on unfalteringly under inexpert guidance.

As they were drinking another round of the chicken noodle soup, Tindale said, "You know, I'd decided against closing the Chinese deal Turner offered me even before the Hong Kong police came and broke it up. Do you know what decided me? Maybe you'll think me stupid. I was getting a sort of subliminal warning off his slide projector. Back of that nice little ranch-house, and those picturesque mountains and the lazy old winding river and rich landscape—back of all that, lay a prison, presided over by an evil spirit."

Yarborough was breathing heavily, slumped in the copilot's seat. "You'll see one day—all life's like that. Wherever you are, old boy—it's a damned prison, presided over by evil spirits. You'll understand when you get older."

"I'm not going to get older, Tony."

"And you'll see that the prison is of your own making. And you're your own devil. Behind every beautiful landscape I've ever seen lurks prison bars and you ought to ask yourself before you get too old like me—whether you are going to be locked in with the others or locked outside the way I was locked out—unable to feel anything or take any pleasure or hope—"

"Tony! Tony!" He jumped up, throwing off his headset.

Yarborough's voice had died, a strangled look came onto his face. He fought a silent enemy, his hands curling before his face. His mouth opened; a low stuttering sound, almost like a foreign language, came from it.

"Your pills, Tony!"

"Injection. . . . Now. . . . Life—Surviva—only chance. . . ."

They had clocked almost sixteen hours flying time, and were six and a half miles above the Baltic Sea. *Got to make Lisbon almost there old fool going to die on me all down in ocean swim ashore unknown man Chinese agent. . . .*

"Now, Gordy—Surviva. . . ."

Maybe injection might help him give him extra time got to get safe retreat need Yarborough Frankfurt Deutschmark crackle smiling clothes but would it be safe give him Surviva just don't know told him and Kuhnau I was Senior Research Chemist not just office dogsbody just don't know about these things this Surviva only works on things like fish guess no harm in trying. . . .

The situation was urgent.

Yarborough was making a terrible noise now, a broken knocking. There was no longer any suspicion that he could be shamming to get a quick injection. In panic, Tindale ran for the locker where he had stowed the refrigerator. *Pack death doubly terrible now locked out plan's going crazy Christ I asked the cocksucking spill his veins. . . .* He dropped the pack and groveled on the floor for it. A hypodermic syringe was included in the case. He filled it clumsily from one of the vials, aware the plane was plunging forward, nose down. *Not dare look out got six and a half miles to go take some minutes get this into him fight the controls Kirk Douglas pull out that interfering Portuguese kick his. . . .*

"This man is having a coronary attack, sir," said the Portuguese doctor. Over his shoulder, Tindale caught a glimpse of the passengers, terrified, felt their fear hit him in the viscera, saw the steep angle of the plane.

"Keep out of this, will you?"

"I must help you, sir! You are mad—we crash! *Ondé esta. . . . ? Socorro, socorro!*"

Tindale tried pushing the man out of the way. *They grappled. . . .* The man called for help. Tindale hit him with his left fist. *They grappled. . . .* The man tried to seize his arm, failed, hit him in the face. Tindale dropped the vial and let him have it. Yarborough was quieter now, his face distorted. Three men rushed in, and Tindale hit out at them too. *They grappled, they grappled. . . .* They fell against the instrument panel. Glancing over a shoulder, he saw the sea rush up.

Mary Mary blinding me too sucking late pull out lurks prison bars pray oh pray race of immortal fish cooling frying God before you get too old locked in locked out Mary Walter ear to ear depend for my immortality on their mortality the hatch must be hatch never die. . . .

IN THE ARENA

~~~~~~

The reek and noise at the back of the circus were familiar to Javlin Bartramm. He felt the hard network of nerves in his solar plexus tighten.

There were crowds of the reduls here, jostling and staring to see the day's entry arrive. You didn't have to pay to stand and rubberneck in the street; this lot probably couldn't afford seats for the arena. Javlin looked away from them in scorn. All the same, he felt some gratification when they sent up a cheeping cheer at the sight of him. They loved a human victim.

His keeper undid the cart door and led him out, still chained. They went through the entrance, from blinding sunshine to dark, into the damp unsavory warren below the main stadium. Several reduls were moving about here, officials mainly. One or two called good luck to him; one chirped, "The crowd's in a good mood today, vertebrate." Javlin showed no response.

His trainer, Ik So Baar, came up, a flamboyant redul towering above Javlin. He wore an array of spare gloves strapped across his orange belly. The white tiara that fitted around his antennae appeared only on sports day.

"Greetings, Javlin. You look in the rudest of health. I'm glad you are not fighting me."

"Greetings, Ik So." He slipped the lip-whistle into his mouth so that he could answer in a fair approximation of the redul language. "Is my opponent ready to be slain? Remember I go free if I win this bout—it will be my twelfth victory in succession."

"There's been a change in the program, Javlin. Your Sirian opponent escaped in the night and had to be killed. You are entered in a double double."

Javlin wrenched at his chains so hard that the keeper was swung off balance.

"Ik So! You betray me! How much cajsh have I won for you? I will not fight a double double."

There was no change of expression on the insect mask.

"Then you will die, my pet vertebrate. The new arrangement is not my idea. You know by now that I get more cajsh for having you in a solo. Double double it has to be. These are my orders. Keeper, Cell one-o-seven with him!"

Fighting against his keeper's pull, Javlin cried, "I've got some rights, Ik So. I demand to see the arena promoter."

"Pipe down, you stupid vertebrate! You have to do what you're ordered. I told you it wasn't my fault."

"Well, for God's sake, who am I fighting with?"

"You will be shackled to a fellow from the farms. He's had one or two preliminary bouts; they say he's good."

"From the farms . . ." Javlin broke into the filthiest redulian oaths he knew. Ik So came back toward him and slipped one of the metal gloves onto his forepincers; it gave him a cruel tearing weapon with a multitude of barbs. He held it up to Javlin's face.

"Don't use that language to me, my mammalian friend. Humans from the farms or from space, what's the difference? This young fellow will fight well enough if you muck in with him. And you'd better muck in. You're billed to battle against a couple of yillibeeth."

Before Javlin could answer, the tall figure turned and strode down the corridor, moving twice as fast as a man could walk.

Javlin let himself be led to Cell 107. The warder, a worker-redul with a gray belly, unlocked his chains and pushed him in, barring the door behind him. The cell smelled of alien species and apprehensions.

Javlin went and sat down on the bench. He needed to think.

He knew himself for a simple man—and knew that that knowledge meant the simplicity was relative. But his five years of captivity here under the reduls had not been all wasted. Ik So had trained him well in the arts of survival; and when you came down to brass tacks, there was no more proper pleasure in the universe than surviving. It was uncomplicated. It caried no responsibilities to anyone but yourself.

That was what he hated about the double double events, which till now he had always been lucky enough to avoid. They carried responsibility to your fellow fighter.

From the beginning he had been well equipped to survive the gladiatorial routine. When his scoutship, the *Plunderhorse,* had been captured by redul forces five years ago, Javlin Bartramm was deuling master and judo expert, as well as Top Armament Sergeant. The army ships had a long tradition, going back some six centuries, of sport aboard; it provided the ideal mixture of time-passer and needed exercise. Of all the members of the *Plunderhorse's* crew who had been taken captive, Javlin was—as far as he knew—the only survivor after five years of the insect race's rough games.

Luck had played its part in his survival. He had liked Ik So Baar. Liking was a strange thing to feel for a nine-foot armored grasshopper with forearms like a lobster and a walk like a tyrannosaurus' run, but a sympathy existed between them—and would continue to exist until he was killed in the ring, Javlin thought. With his bottom on the cold bench, he knew that Ik So would not betray him into a double double. The redul had had to obey the promoter's orders. Ik So needed his twelfth victory, so that he could free Javlin to help him train the other species down at the gladiatorial farm. Both of them knew that would be an effective partnership.

So. Now was the time for luck to be with Javlin again.

He sank onto his knees and looked down at the stone, brought his forehead down onto it, gazed down into the earth, into the cold ground, the warm rocks, the molten core, trying to visualize each, to draw from them attributes that would help him: cold for his brain, warm for his temper, molten for his energies.

Strengthened by prayer, he stood up. The redul workers had yet to bring him his armor and the partner he was to fight with. He had long since learned the ability to wait without resenting waiting. With professional care, he exercised himself slowly, checking the proper function of each muscle. As he did so, he heard the crowds cheer in the arena. He turned to peer out of the cell's further door, an affair of tightly set bars that allowed a narrow view of the combat area and the stands beyond.

There was a centaur out there in the sunlight, fighting an Aldebaran bat-leopard. The centaur wore no armor but an iron cuirass; he had no weapons but his hooves and his hands. The bat-leopard, though its wings were clipped to prevent it flying out of the stadium, had dangerous claws and a great turn of speed. Only because its tongue had been cut out, ruining its echo-location system, was the contest anything like fair. The concept of fairness was lost upon the reduls, though; they preferred blood to justice.

Javlin saw the kill. The centaur, a gallant creature with a human-like head and an immense gold mane that began from his eyebrows, was plainly tiring. He eluded the bat-leopard as it swooped down on him, wheeling quickly around on his hind legs and trampling on its wing. But the bat-leopard turned and raked the other's legs with a slash of claws. The centaur toppled hamstrung to the ground. As he fell, he lashed out savagely with his forelegs, but the bat-leopard nipped in and tore his throat from side to side above the cuirass. It then dragged itself away under its mottled wings, like a lame prima donna dressed in a leather cape.

The centaur struggled and lay still, as if the weight of whistling cheers that rose from the audience bore him down. Through the narrow bars, Javlin saw the throat bleed and the lungs heave as the defeated one sprawled in the dust.

"What do you dream of, dying there in the sun?" Javlin asked.

He turned away from the sight and the question. He sat quietly down on the bench and folded his arms.

When the din outside told him that the next bout had begun, the passage door opened and a young human was pushed in. Javlin did not need telling that this was to be his partner in the double double against the yillibeeth.

It was a girl.

"You're Javlin?" she said. "I know of you. My name's Awn."

He kept himself under control, his brows drawn together as he stared at her.

"You know what you're here for?"

"This will be my first public fight," she said.

Her hair was clipped short as a man's. Her skin was tanned and harsh, her left arm bore a gruesome scar. She held herself lithely on her feet. Though her body looked lean and hard, even the thick one-piece gown she wore to thigh length did not conceal the feminine curves of her body. She was not pretty, but Javlin had to admire the set of her mouth and her cool gray gaze.

"I've had some stinking news this morning, but Ik So Baar

never broke it to me that I was to be saddled with a woman," he said.

"Ik probably didn't know—that I'm a woman, I mean. The reduls are either neuter or hermaphrodite, unless they happen to be a rare queen. Didn't you know that? They can't tell the difference between human male and female."

He spat. "You can't tell me anything about reduls."

She spat. "If you knew, why blame me? You don't think I like being here? You don't think I asked to join the great Javlin?"

Without answering he bent and began to massage the muscles of his calf. Since he occupied the middle of the bench, the girl remained standing. She watched him steadily. When he looked up again, she asked, "What or who are we fighting?"

No surprise was left in him. "They didn't tell you?"

"I've only just been pushed into this double double, as I imagine you have. I asked you, what are we fighting?"

"Just a couple of yillibeeth."

He injected unconcern into his voice to make the shock of what he said the greater. He massaged the muscles of the other calf. An aprohale would have come in very welcome now. These crazy insects had no equivalent of the Terrestrial prisoner-ate-a-hearty-breakfast routine. When he glanced up under his eyebrows, the girl stood motionless, but her face had gone pale.

"Know what the yillibeeth are, little girl?"

She didn't answer, so he went on, "The reduls resemble some Terrestrial insects. They go through several stages of development, you know; reduls are just the final adult stage. Their larval stage is rather like the larval stage of the dragon-fly. It's a greedy, omnivorous beast. It's aquatic and it's big. It's armored. It's called a yillibeeth. That's what we are going to be tied together to fight, a couple of big hungry yillibeeth. Are you feeling like dying this morning, Awn?"

Instead of answering, she turned her head away and brought a hand up to her mouth.

"Oh, no! No crying in here, for Earth's sake!" he said. He got up, yelled through the passage door, "Ik So, Ik So, you traitor, get this bloody woman out of here!" . . . recalled himself, jammed the lip-whistle into his mouth and was about to call again when Awn caught him a backhanded blow across the face.

She faced him like a tiger.

"You creature, you cowardly apology of a man! Do you

think I weep for fear? I don't weep. I've lived nineteen years
on this damned planet in their damned farms. Would I still
be here if I wept? No—but I mourn that you are already
defeated, you, the great Javlin!"

He frowned into her blazing face.

"You don't seriously think you make me a good enough
match for us to go out there and kill a couple of yillibeeth?"

"Damn your conceit. I'm prepared to try."

"Fagh!" He thrust the lip-whistle into his mouth, and
turned back to the door. She laughed at him bitterly, jeer-
ingly.

"You're a lackey to these insects, aren't you, Javlin? If you
could see what a fool you look with that phony beak of yours
stuck on your mouth."

He let the instrument drop to the end of its chain. Grasping the bars, he leaned forward against them and looked
over his shoulder.

"I was trying to get this contest called off."

"Don't tell me you haven't already tried. I have."

To that he had no answer. He went back and sat on the
bench. She returned to her corner. They both folded their
arms and stared at each other.

"Why don't you look out into the arena instead of glaring
at me? You might pick up a few tips." When she did not
answer, he said, "I'll tell you what you'll see. You can see the
rows of spectators and a box where some sort of bigwig sits.
I don't know who the bigwig is. It's never a queen—as far as
I can make out, the queens spend their lives underground,
turning out eggs at the rate of fifty a second. Not the sort
of life Earth royalty would have enjoyed in the old days.
Under the bigwig's box there is a red banner with their
insect hieroglyphs on. I asked Ik So once what the hieroglyphs said. He told me they meant—well, in a rough trans-
lation—*The Greatest Show on Earth*. It's funny, isn't it?"

"You must admit we do make a show."

"No, you miss the point. You see, that used to be the
legend of circuses in the old days. But they've adopted it for
their own use since they invaded Earth. They're boasting of
their conquest."

"And that's funny?"

"In a sort of way. Don't you feel ashamed that this planet
which saw the birth of the human race should be overrun
by insects?"

"No. The reduls were here before me. I was just born
here. Weren't you?"

"No, I wasn't. I was born on Washington IV. It's a lovely planet. There are hundreds of planets out there as fine and varied as Earth once was—but it kind of rankles to think that this insect brood rules Earth."

"If you feel so upset about it, why don't you do something?"

He knotted his fists together. You should start explaining history and economics just before you ran out to be chopped to bits by a big rampant thing with circular saws for hands?

"It would cost mankind too much to reconquer this planet. Too difficult. Too many deaths just for sentiment. And think of all those queens squirting eggs at a rate of knots; humans don't breed that fast. Humanity has learned to face facts."

She laughed without humor.

"That's good. Why don't you learn to face the fact of me?"

Javlin had nothing to say to that; she would not understand that directly he saw her he knew his hope of keeping his life had died. She was just a liability. Soon he would be dying, panting his juices out into the dust like that game young centaur . . . only it wouldn't be dust.

"We fight in two feet of water," he said. "You know that? The yillibeeth like it. It slows our speed a bit. We might drown instead of having our heads bitten off."

"I can hear someone coming down the corridor. It may be our armor," she said coolly.

"Did you hear what I said?"

"You can't wait to die, Javlin, can you?"

The bars fell away on the outside of the door, and it opened. The keeper stood there. Ik So Baar had not appeared as he usually did. The creature flung in their armor and weapons and retreated, barring the door again behind him. It never ceased to astonish Javlin that those great dumb brutes of workers had intelligence.

He stooped to pick up his uniform. The girl's looked so light and small. He lifted it, looking from it to her.

"Thank you," she said.

"It looks so small and new."

"I shouldn't want anything heavier."

"You've fought in it?"

"Twice." There was no need to ask whether she had won.

"We'd better get the stuff strapped on, then. We shall know when they are getting ready for us; you'll hear the arena being filled with water. They're probably saving us for the main events just before noon."

"I didn't know about the two feet of water."

"Scare you?"

"No. I'm a good swimmer. Swam for fish in the river on the slave farm."

"You caught fish with your bare hands?"

"No, you dive down and stab them with a sharp rock. It takes practice."

It was a remembered pleasure. She'd actually swum in one of Earth's rivers. He caught himself smiling back into her face.

"Ik So's place is in the desert," he said, making his voice cold. "Anyhow, you won't be able to swim in the arena. Two feet of muddy stinking water helps nobody. And you'll be chained onto me with a four-foot length of chain."

"Let's get our armor on, then you'd better tell me all you know. Perhaps we can work out a plan of campaign."

As he picked up the combined breastplate and shoulder guard, Awn untied her belt and lifted her dress over her head. Underneath she wore only a ragged pair of white briefs. She commenced to take those off.

Javlin stared at her with surprise—and pleasure. It had been years since he had been within hailing distance of a woman. This one—yes, this one was a beauty.

"What are you doing that for?" he asked. He hardly recognized his own voice.

"The less we have on the better in that water. Aren't you going to take your clothes off?"

He shook his head. Embarrassed, he fumbled on the rest of his kit. At least she wouldn't look so startling with her breastplate and skirt armor on. He checked his long and shortswords, clipping the one into the left belt clip, the other into the right. They were good swords, made by redul armorers to Terrestrial specifications. When he turned back to Awn, she was fully accoutered.

Nodding in approval, he offered her a seat on the bench beside him. They clattered against each other and smiled.

Another bout had ended in the arena. The cheers and chirrups drifted through the bars to them.

"I'm sorry you're involved in this," he said with care.

"I was lucky to be involved in it with you." Her voice was not entirely steady, but she controlled it in a minute. "Can't I hear water?"

He had already heard it. An unnatural silence radiated from the great inhuman crowd in the circus as they watched the stuff pour in. It would have great emotional significance for them, no doubt, since they had all lived in water for some years in their previous life stage.

"They have wide-bore hoses," he said. His own voice had an irritating tremor. "The arena fills quite rapidly."

"Let's formulate some sort of plan of attack then. These things, these yillibeeth must have some weaknesses."

"And some strengths! That's what you have to watch for."

"I don't see that. You attack their weak points."

"We shall be too busy looking out for their strong ones. They have long segmented gray bodies—about twenty segments, I think. Each segment is of chitin or something tough. Each segment bears two legs equipped with razor combs. At tail end and top end they have legs that work like sort of buzz saws, cut through anything they touch. And there are their jaws, of course."

The keeper was back. His antennae flopped through the grating and then he unbolted the door and came in. He bore a length of chain as long as the cell was wide. Javlin and Awn did not resist as he locked them together, fitting the bracelets onto Javlin's right arm and Awn's left.

"So." She stared at the chain. "The yillibeeth don't sound to have many weak points. They could cut through our swords with their buzz saws?"

"Correct."

"Then they could cut through this chain. Get it severed near one of our wrists, and the other has a better long-distance weapon than a sword. A blow over the head with the end of the chain won't improve their speed. How fast are they?"

"The buzz saw takes up most of their speed. They're nothing like as fast as the reduls. No, you could say they were pretty sluggish in movement. And the fact that the two of them will also be chained together should help us."

"Where are they chained?"

"By the middle legs."

"That gives them a smaller arc of destruction than if they were chained by back or front legs. We are going to slay these beasts yet, Javlin! What a murderous genus it must be to put its offspring in the arena for the public sport."

He laughed.

"Would you feel sentimental about your offspring if you had a million babies?"

"I'll tell you that when I've had the first of them. I mean, if I have the first of them."

He put his hand over hers.

"No if. We'll kill the bloody larvae OK."

"Get the chain severed, then one of us with the longest bit of chain goes in for the nearest head, the other fends off the other brute. Right?"

"Right."

There was a worker redul at the outer door now, the door that led to the arena. He flung it open and stood there with a flaming torch, ready to drive them out if they did not emerge.

"We've—come to it then," she said. Suddenly she clung to him.

"Let's take it at a run, love," he said.

Together, balancing the chain between them, they ran toward the arena. The two yillibeeth were coming out from the far side, wallowing and splashing. The crowd stretched up toward the blue sky of Earth, whistling their heads off. They didn't know what a man and a woman could do in combination. Now they were going to learn.

ALL THE WORLD'S TEARS

If you could collect up all the tears that have fallen in the history of the world, you would have not only a vast sheet of water: you would have the history of the world.

Some such reflection as this occurred to J. Smithlao, the psychodynamician, as he stood in the 139th sector of Ing Land watching the brief and tragic love of the wild man and Charles Gunpat's daughter. Hidden behind a beech tree, Smithlao saw the wild man walking warily across the terrace; Gunpat's daughter, Ployploy, stood at the far end of the terrace, waiting for him.

It was the last day of summer in the last year of the Forty-Fourth Century. The wind that rustled Ployploy's dress breathed leaves against her; it sighed around the fantastic and desolate garden like fate at a christening, ruining the last of the roses. Later, the tumbling pattern of petals would be sucked from paths, lawn, and patio by the steel gardener. Now, it made a tiny tide around the wild man's feet as he stretched out his hand, momentously, to touch Ployploy.

Then it was that the tear glittered in her eyes.

Hidden, fascinated, Smithlao the psychodynamician saw that tear. Except perhaps for a stupid robot, he was the only one who saw it, the only one who saw the whole episode. And although he was shallow and hard by the standards of other ages, he was human enough to sense that here—here on the graying terrace—was a little charade that marked the end of all that man had been.

After the tear, of course, came the explosion. Just for a minute, a new wind lived among the winds of Earth.

Only by accident was Smithlao walking in Charles Gunpat's
estate. He had come on the routine errand, as Gunpat's
psychodynamician, of administering a hate-brace to the old
man. Oddly enough, as he swept in for a landing, leafing
his vane down from the stratosphere, Smithlao had caught a
glimpse of the wild man approaching Gunpat's estate.

Under the slowing vane, the landscape was as neat as a
blueprint. The impoverished fields made impeccable rectangles.
Here and there, one robot machine or another kept nature
to its own functional image; not a pea podded without cyber-
netic supervision; not a bee bumbled among stamens without
radar check being kept of its course. Every bird had a number
and a call sign, while among every tribe of ants marched the
metallic teller ants, tell-taling the secrets of the nest back to
base. The old, comfortable world of random factors had vanished under the pressure of hunger.

Nothing living lived without control. The countless popu-
lations of previous centuries had exhausted the soil. Only
the severest parsimony, coupled with fierce regimentation,
produced enough nourishment for the present sparse population. The billions had died of starvation; the hundreds who
remained lived on starvation's brink.

In the sterile neatness of the landscape, Gunpat's estate
looked like an insult. Covering five acres, it was a little island
of wilderness. Tall and unkempt elms fenced the perimeter,
encroaching on the lawns and house. The house itself, the
chief one in Sector 139, was built of massive stone blocks. It
had to be strong to bear the weight of the servomechanisms
which, apart from Gunpat and his daughter, Ployploy, were
its only occupants.

It was just as Smithlao dropped below tree-level that he
thought he saw a human figure plodding toward the estate.
For a multitude of reasons, this was very unlikely. The great
material wealth of the world being now shared among comparatively few people, nobody was poor enough to have to
walk anywhere. Man's increasing hatred of Nature, spurred
by the notion it had betrayed him, would make such a walk
purgatory—unless the human were insane, like Ployploy.

Dismissing the figure from his thoughts, Smithlao dropped
the vane onto a stretch of stone. He was glad to get down:
it was a gusty day, and the piled cumulus through which he
had descended had been full of air pockets. Gunpat's house,
with its sightless windows, its towers, its endless terraces, its
unnecessary ornamentation, its massive porch, lowered at him
like a forsaken wedding cake.

There was activity at once. Three wheeled robots approached from different directions, swiveling light atomic weapons at him as they drew near.

Nobody, Smithlao thought, could get in here uninvited. Gunpat was not a friendly man, even by the unfriendly standards of his time.

"Say who you are," demanded the leading machine. It was ugly and flat, vaguely resembling a toad.

"I am J. Smithlao, psychodynamician to Charles Gunpat," Smithlao replied; he had to go through this procedure every visit. As he spoke, he revealed his face to the machine. It grunted to itself, checking picture and information with its memory. Finally it said, "You are J. Smithlao, psychodynamician to Charles Gunpat. What do you want?"

Cursing its monstrous slowness, Smithlao told the robot, "I have an appointment with Charles Gunpat at ten hours," and waited while that was digested.

"You have an appointment with Charles Gunpat at ten hours," the robot finally confirmed. "Come this way."

It wheeled about with surprising grace, speaking to the other two robots, reassuring them, repeating mechanically to them. "This is J. Smithlao, psychodynamician to Charles Gunpat. He has an appointment with Charles Gunpat at ten hours," in case they had not grasped these facts.

Meanwhile, Smithlao spoke to his vane. A part of the cabin, with him in it, detached itself from the rest and lowered wheels to the ground, becoming a mobile sedan. Carrying Smithlao, it followed the other robots.

Automatic screens came up, covering the windows, as Smithlao moved into the presence of other humans. He could only see and be seen via telescreens. Such was the hatred (equals fear) man bore for his fellow man, he could not tolerate them regarding him direct.

One following another, the machines climbed along the terraces, through the great porch, where they were covered in a mist of disinfectant, along a labyrinth of corridors, and so into the presence of Charles Gunpat.

Gunpat's dark face on the screen of his sedan showed only the mildest distaste for the sight of his psychodynamician. He was usually as self-controlled as this: it told against him at his business meetings, where the idea was to cow one's opponents by splendid displays of rage. For this reason, Smithlao was always summoned to administer a hate-brace when something important loomed on the day's agenda.

Smithlao's machine maneuvered him within a yard of his

patient's image, much closer than courtesy required.

"I'm late," Smithlao began, matter-of-factly, "because I could not bear to drag myself into your offensive presence one minute sooner. I hoped that if I left it long enough, some happy accident might have removed that stupid nose from your—what shall I call it?—*face*. Alas, it's still there, with its two nostrils sweeping like rat-holes into your skull. I've often wondered, Gunpat, don't you ever catch your big feet in those holes and fall over?"

Observing his patient's face carefully, Smithlao saw only the faintest stir of irritation. No doubt about it, Gunpat was a hard man to rouse. Fortunately, Smithlao was an expert in his profession; he proceeded to try the insult subtle.

"But of course you would never fall over," he proceeded, "because you are too depressingly ignorant to know up from down. You don't even know how many robots make five. Why, when it was your turn to go to the capital to the Mating Center, you didn't even realize that was the one time a man has to come out from behind his screen. You thought you could make love by tele! And what was the result? One dotty daughter . . . one dotty daughter, Gunpat! Think how your rivals at Automotion must titter at that, sunny boy. 'Potty Gunpat and his dotty daughter,' they'll be saying. 'Can't control your genes,' they'll be saying."

The taunts were having their desired effect. A flush spread over the image of Gunpat's face.

"There's nothing wrong with Ployploy except that she's a recessive—you said that yourself!" he snapped.

He was beginning to answer back; that was a good sign. His daughter was always a soft spot in his armor.

"A recessive!" Smithlao sneered. "How far back can you recede? She's *gentle*, do you hear me, you with the hair in your ears? She wants to *love*!" He bellowed with ironic laughter. "Oh, it's obscene, Gunnyboy! She couldn't hate to save her life. She's no better than a savage. She's worse than a savage, she's mad!"

"She's not mad,' Gunpat said, gripping both sides of his screen. At this rate, he would be primed for the conference in ten more minutes.

"Not mad?" the psychodynamician asked, his voice assuming a bantering note. "No, Ployploy's not mad; the Mating Center only refused her the right even to breed, that's all. Imperial Government only refused her the right to a tele-vote, that's all. United Traders only refused her a Consumption Rating, that's all. Education Inc. only restricted her to beta recreations, that's all. She's a prisoner here because she's a genius, is that it? You're crazy, Gunpat, if you don't think that girl's stark, staring loony. You'll be telling me next, out of that grotesque, flapping mouth, that she hasn't got a white face."

Gunpat made gobbling sounds.

"You dare to mention that!" he gasped. "And what if her face is—that color?"

"You ask such fool questions, it's hardly worthwhile bothering with you," Smithlao said mildly. "Your trouble, Gunpat, is that your big bone head is totally incapable of absorbing one single simple historical fact. Ployploy is white because she is a dirty little throwback. Our ancient enemies were white. They occupied this part of the globe, Ing Land and You-Rohp, until the Twenty-Fourth Century, when our ancestors rose from the East and took from them the ancient privileges they had so long enjoyed at our expense. Our ancestors intermarried with such of the defeated that survived.

"In a few generations, the white strain was obliterated, diluted, lost. A white face has not been seen on Earth since before the terrible Age of Overpopulation: fifteen hundred years, let's say. And *then*—then little lord recessive Gunpat throws one up neat as you please. What did they give you at Mating Center, sunny boy, a *cavewoman*?"

Gunpat exploded in fury, shaking his fist at the screen.

"You're sacked, Smithlao," he snarled. "This time you've gone too far, even for a dirty, rotten psycho! Get out! Go on, get, and never come back again!"

Abruptly, he bellowed to his auto-operator to switch him over to the conference. He was just in a ripe mood to deal with Automotion and its fellow crooks.

As Gunpat's irate image faded from the screen, Smithlao sighed and relaxed. The hate-brace was accomplished. It was the supreme compliment in his profession to be dismissed by a patient at the end of a session; Gunpat would be all the keener to reengage him next time. All the same, Smithlao felt no triumph. In his calling, a thorough exploration of human psychology was needed; he had to know exactly the sorest points in a man's makeup. By playing on those points deftly enough, he could rouse the man to action.

Without being roused, men were helpless prey to lethargy, bundles of rag carried around by machines. The ancient drives had died and left them.

Smithlao sat where he was, gazing into both past and future.

In exhausting the soil, man had exhausted himself. The psyche and a vitiated topsoil could not exist simultaneously; it was as simple and as logical as that.

Only the failing tides of hate and anger lent man enough impetus to continue at all. Else, he was just a dead hand across his mechanized world.

So this is how a species becomes extinct thought Smithlao, and wondered if anyone else had thought it. Perhaps Imperial Government knew all about it, but was powerless to do anything; after all, what more could you do than was being done?

Smithlao was a shallow man—inevitably in a caste-bound society so weak that it could not face itself. Having discovered the terrifying problem, he set himself to forget it, to evade its impact, to dodge any personal implications it might have. With a grunt to his sedan, he turned about and ordered himself home.

Since Gunpat's robot had already left, Smithlao traveled back alone the way he had come. He was trundled outside and back to the vane, standing silent below the elms.

Before the sedan incorporated itself back into the vane, a movement caught Smithlao's eye. Half concealed by a verandah, Ployploy stood against a corner of the house. With a sudden impulse of curiosity, Smithlao got out of the sedan. The open air, besides being in motion, stank of roses and clouds and green things turning dark with the thought of autumn. It was frightening for Smithlao, but an adventurous impulse made him go on.

The girl was not looking in his direction; she peered toward the barricade of trees which cut her off from the world. As Smithlao approached, she moved around to the rear of the house, still staring intently. He followed with caution, taking advantage of the cover afforded by a small plantation. A metal gardener nearby continued to wield shears along a grass verge, unaware of his existence.

Ployploy now stood at the back of the house. Here a rococo fancy of ancient Italy had mingled with a Chinese genius for fantastic portal and roof. Balustrades rose and fell, stairs marched through circular arches, gray and azure eaves swept almost to the ground. But all was sadly neglected; Virginia creeper, already hinting at its glory to come, strove to pull down the marble statuary; troughs of rose petals clogged every sweeping staircase. And all this formed the ideal background for the forlorn figure of Ployploy.

Except for her delicate pink lips, her face was utterly

pale. Her hair was utterly black; it hung straight, secured only once, at the back of her head, and then falling in a tail to her waist. She looked mad indeed, her melancholy eyes peering toward the great elms as if they would scorch down everything in their line of vision. Smithlao turned to see what she stared at so compellingly.

The wild man was just breaking through the thickets around the elm boles.

A sudden shower came down, rattling among the dry leaves of the shrubbery. Like a spring shower, it was over in a flash; during the momentary downpour, Ployploy never shifted her position, the wild man never looked up. Then the sun burst through, cascading a pattern of elm shadow over the house, and every flower wore a jewel of rain.

Smithlao thought of what he had thought in Gunpat's room. Now he added this rider: it would be so easy for Nature, when parasite man was extinct, to begin again.

He waited tensely, knowing a fragment of drama was about to take place before his eyes. Across the sparkling lawn, a tiny tracked thing scuttled, pogo-ing itself up steps and out of sight through an arch. It was a perimeter guard, off to give the alarm.

In a minute it returned. Four big robots accompanied it; one of them Smithlao recognized as the toad-like machine that had challenged his arrival. They threaded their way purposefully among the rose bushes, five different-shaped menaces. The metal gardener muttered to itself, abandoned its clipping, and joined the procession toward the wild man.

"He hasn't a dog's chance," Smithlao said to himself. The phrase held significance: all dogs, declared redundant, had long since been exterminated.

By now the wild man had broken through the barrier of the thicket and come to the lawn's edge. He broke off a leafy branchlet and stuck it into his shirt so that it partially obscured his face; he tucked another branch in his trousers. As the robots drew nearer, he raised his arms above his head, a third branch clasped in his hands.

The six machines encircled him.

The toad robot clicked, as if deciding on what it should do next.

"Say who you are," it demanded.

"I am a rose tree," the wild man said.

"Rose trees bear roses. You do not bear roses. You are not a rose tree," the steel toad said. Its biggest, highest gun came level with the wild man's chest.

"My roses are dead already," the wild man said, "but I have leaves still. Ask the gardener if you do not know what leaves are."

"This thing is a thing with leaves," the gardener said at once in a deep voice.

"I know what leaves are. I have no need to ask the gardener. Leaves are the foliage of trees and plants which give them their green appearance," the toad said.

"This thing is a thing with leaves," the gardener repeated, adding, to clarify the matter, "The leaves give it a green appearance."

"I know what leaves are. I have no need to ask you, gardener."

It looked as if an interesting, if limited, argument would break out between the two robots, but at this moment one of the other machines spoke.

"This rose tree can speak," it said.

"Rose trees cannot speak," the toad said at once. Having produced this pearl, it was silent, probably mulling over the strangeness of life. Then it said, slowly, "Therefore either this rose tree is not a rose tree or this rose tree did not speak."

"This thing is a thing with leaves," began the gardener again. "But it is not a rose tree. Rose trees have stipules. This thing has no stipules. It is a breaking buckthorn. The breaking buckthorn is also known as the berry-bearing alder."

This specialized knowledge extended beyond the vocabulary of the toad. A strained silence ensued.

"I am a breaking buckthorn," the wild man said, still holding his pose. "I cannot speak."

At this, all the machines began to talk at once, lumbering around him for better sightings as they did so, and barging into each other in the process. Finally, the toad's voice broke above the metallic babble.

"Whatever this thing with leaves is, we must uproot it. We must kill it," it said.

"You may not uproot it. That is only a job for gardeners," the gardener said. Setting its shears rotating, telescoping out a mighty scythe, it charged at the toad.

Its crude weapons were ineffectual against the toad's armor. The latter, however, realized that they had reached a deadlock in their investigations.

"We will retire to ask Charles Gunpat what we shall do," it said. "Come this way."

"Charles Gunpat is in conference," the scout robot said.

"Charles Gunpat must not be disturbed in conference. There-fore we must not disturb Charles Gunpat."

"Therefore we must wait for Charles Gunpat," said the metal toad imperturbably. He led the way close by where Smithlao stood; they all climbed the steps and disappeared into the house.

Smithlao could only marvel at the wild man's coolness. It was a miracle he still survived. Had he attempted to run, he would have been killed instantly; that was a situation the robots had been taught to cope with. Nor would his double talk, inspired as it was, have saved him had he been faced with only one robot, for a robot is a single-minded creature. In company, however, they suffer from a trouble which often afflicts human gatherings to a lesser extent: a tendency to show off their logic at the expense of the object of the meeting.

Logic! That was the trouble. It was all robots had to go by. Man had logic and intelligence. he got along better than his robots. Nevertheless, he was losing the battle against Nature. And Nature, like the robots, used only logic. It was a para-dox against which man could not prevail.

Directly the file of machines had disappeared into the house the wild man ran across the lawn and climbed the first flight of steps, working toward the motionless girl. Smithlao slid behind a beech tree to be nearer to them; he felt like a per-vert, watching them without an interposed screen, but could not tear himself away. The wild man was approaching Ploy-ploy now, moving slowly across the terrace as if hypnotized.

"You were resourceful," she said to him. Her white face carried pink in its cheeks now.

"I have been resourceful for a whole year to get to you," he said. Now his resources had brought him face to face with her, they failed, and left him standing helplessly. He was a thin young man, thin and sinewy, his clothes worn, his beard unkempt.

"How did you find me?" Ployploy asked. Her voice, un-like the wild man's, barely reached Smithlao. A haunting look, as fitful as the autumn, played on her face.

"It was a sort of instinct—as if I heard you calling," the wild man said. "Everything that could possibly be wrong with the world is wrong. . . . Perhaps you are the only woman in the world who loves; perhaps I am the only man who could answer. So I came. It was natural: I could not help myself."

"I always dreamed someone would come," she said. "And

for weeks I have felt—*known*—you were coming. Oh, my darling. . . ."

"We must be quick, my sweet," he said. "I once worked with robots—perhaps you could see I knew them. When we get away from here, I have a robot plane that will take us right away—anywhere: an island, perhaps, where things are not so desperate. But we must go before your father's machines return."

He took a step toward Ployploy.

She held up her hand.

"Wait!" she implored him. "It's not so simple. You must know something. . . . The—Mating Center refused me the right to breed. You ought not to touch me."

"I hate the Mating Center!" the wild man said. "I hate everything to do with the ruling regime. Nothing they have done can affect us now."

Ployploy had clenched her hands behind her back. The color had left her cheeks. A fresh shower of dead rose petals blew against her dress, mocking her.

"It's so hopeless," she said. "You don't understand. . . ."

His wildness was humbled now.

"I threw up everything to come to you," he said. "I only desire to take you into my arms."

"Is that all, really all, all you want in the world?" she asked.

"I swear it," he said simply.

"Then come and touch me," Ployploy said.

That was the moment at which Smithlao saw the tear glint in her eye.

The hand the wild man extended to her was lifted to her cheek. She stood unflinching on the gray terrace, her head high. And so the loving hand gently brushed her countenance. The explosion was almost instantaneous.

Almost. It took the traitorous nerves in Ployploy's epidermis only a fraction of a second to analyze the touch as belonging to another human being and convey their findings to the nerve center; there, the neurological block implanted by the Mating Center in all mating rejects, to guard against such a contingency, went into action at once. Every cell in Ployploy's body yielded up its energy in one consuming gasp. It was so successful that the wild man was also killed by the detonation.

Yes, thought Smithlao, you had to admit it was neat. And, again, logical. In a world on the brink of starvation, how else stop undesirables from breeding? Logic against logic, man's pitted against Nature's: that was what caused all the tears of the world.

He made off through the dripping plantation, heading back for the vane, anxious to be away before the robots reappeared. The shattered figures on the terrace were still, already half covered with leaves and petals. The wind roared like a great triumphant sea in the treetops. It was hardly odd that the wild man did not know about the neurological trigger: few people did, bar psychodynamicians and the Mating Council—and, of course, the rejects themselves. Yes, Ployploy knew what would happen. She had chosen deliberately to die like that.

"Always said she was mad!" Smithlao told himself. He chuckled as he climbed into his machine, shaking his head over her lunacy.

It would be a wonderful point to rile Charles Gunpat with next time he needed a hate-brace.

AMEN AND OUT

~~~~~~

The day had begun mightily, showering sunshine over the city, when Jaybert Darkling rose from his bed. He tucked his feet into slippers and went over to the shrine by the window,

As he approached, the curtains that normally concealed the shrine slid back, the altar began to glow. Darkling bowed his head once and said, "Almighty Gods, I come before you at the start of another day dedicated to your purposes. Grant that I may in every way fulfill myself by acting according to your law and walking in your ways. Amen."

From the altar came an answering voice, thin, high, remote.

"Grant that you may indeed. But try to remember how you offered the same prayer yesterday, and then spent your day pleasing yourself."

"I will do differently today, Almighty Gods. I will spend the day working at the project, which is surely dedicated to your ends."

"Excellent, son, especially as that is what the governors employ you for. And while you work, reflect in your inner heart on your hypocrisy, which is great."

"Your will be done."

The light died, the curtains drew together.

Darkling stood there for a moment, licking his lips. There was no doubt in his mind that the Gods had him taped; he was a hypocrite.

He shuffled across to the window and peered out. Although, as a human, he played a not unimportant role in the city, it was primarily a city of machines. It stretched to the

115

horizon, and most of it moved. The machines willed it that way. Most of the giant building structures had never been entered by man, and they moved because it was convenient they moved.

The walls of the project gleamed brightly. Inside there, Darkling's immortals were imprisoned. Thank Gods that building did not move!

Hypocrite, eh? Well, he had faced the terror and glory of the idea since he was a lad. The Gods had seen to that.

Undressing, he walked toward the shower, and looked at his watch as he went. In seventy minutes, he could be at the project; today he surely would try to be a better man and live a better life. There was no doubt it paid.

He cursed himself for his double thoughts, but they were the only kind he knew.

Zee Stone was also late in getting up. He did not approach the shrine in his small room. Instead, as he staggered across to the bathroom, he called, "I suppose I'm due for my usual bawling out!"

The voice of the Gods came from the unlit shrine, deep, paternal, but on the chilly side. "You wenched and fornicated yesterday night: in consequence, you will be late on the project today. You do not need us to tell you, you were in sin."

"You know everything—you know why it was. I'm trying to write a story. I want to be a writer. But whenever I begin, even if I have it all planned out, it turns into a different story. You're doing it, aren't you?"

"All that happens within you, you try to blame on things outside. That way, you will never prosper."

"To hell with that!" He turned the shower on. He was young, independent. He was going to make good at the project and with his writing—and with that brunette with yellow eyes. All the same, there was a lot in what the Gods said; inside, outside, he hardly knew the difference. His hated boss, Darkling; maybe much of Darkling's nastiness existed only in Stone's imagination.

His thoughts drifted. As he splashed under the warm water, his mind returned to his current story. The Gods had more control over him than he had over his characters.

Dean Cusak got up early enough. What delayed him was the quarrel with his wife. The morning was fresh and sweet; the quarrel was foul and stale.

"We're never going to make that little farm," Edith Cusak grumbled as she dressed. "You were going to save and we were going to go to the country. How many years ago was that? I notice you've still got your moldy ill-paid job as doorman at the project!"

"It's a very responsible job," Dean squeaked.

"How come it's so ill-paid then?"

"Promotion just didn't come my way." He got his voice a tone lower and went into the bathroom to brush his teeth. He hated Edith's discontent because he still cared for her; her complaints were justified. He had held out the vision of a little farm when they got married. But he'd always—admit it, he'd always been so subservient that the powers-that-be at the project found it easy to ignore his existence.

She followed him into the bathroom and took up the argument precisely at the point to which his thoughts had delivered it.

"What are you, for Gods' sake? Are you going to be a yes-man all your life? Stand up for yourself! Don't be a mere order-taker! Throw your weight about down there, then maybe they'll notice you."

"That's your philosophy, I know," he muttered.

When she had gone into the kitchen to dial breakfast, Cusak hurried back into the bedroom and knelt before the bedside shrine. As the light came on behind the altar, he clasped his hands and said, "Almighty Gods, help me. I'm a terrible worm, she's right, a terrible worm! You know me, you know what I am. Help me—it's not that I haven't struggled, you know I've struggled, but things are going from bad to worse. I've always served you, tried to do your will, Gods, don't let me down!"

A fatherly voice filled the air, saying, "Reforms are sometimes best performed piecemeal, Cusak. You must build your own self-confidence bit by bit."

"Yes, Gods, thanks, I will, I will, I'll do exactly as you say—but . . . how?"

"Resolve to use your own judgment at least once today, Cusak."

He begged humbly for further instructions, but the Gods cut off; they were notoriously untalkative. At last, the doorman rose to his feet, struggled into his brown uniform jacket, brushed his hair, and slouched toward the kitchen.

"Even the Gods call me by my surname," he mumbled.

Unlike Dean Cusak, who had a wife to keep him in check,

unlike Jaybert Darkling and Zee Stone, whose lives were secure, who showered most mornings, who enjoyed the fruits and blondes of late Twenty-Second Century civilization, Otto Jack Pommy was an itinerant. He possessed practically nothing but the shrine on his back.

It had been a bad night for Otto, wandering the automated city, and only when dawn had broken did he find a comfortable deserted house in which to sleep. He roused to find the sun shining through a dirty pane onto the stained mattress on which he lay, and remained for a long time angrily entranced—he was an acid head and had taken his last ration of LSD only a week ago—by the conjunction of stains, stripes, and fly specks there, which seemed to epitomize so much of the universe.

At length, Otto rolled over and snapped open his portable shrine. The light failed to glow behind the altar.

"What's matter? You lot feeling dim too? Expecting me to pray when you can't even light up like you used to? Gods?! I spit 'em!"

"Son, you know you sold your good shrine for this poor cheap one that has never worked properly. But as we come to you through an imperfect instrument, so you are the imperfect instrument for the performance of our will."

"Hell, I know, I sinned! Look, you know me, Gods, not the best of men but not the worst either. Leave me alone, can't you? Did I ever exploit anyone? Remember what it used to say in the pre-Gods book: 'Blessed are the meek, for they shall inherit the Earth.' How about that, then?"

The Gods made a noise not unlike a human snort. "Meek! Otto Pommy, you are the most conceited old man that ever inflicted prayer upon us! Try to behave a little less arrogantly today."

"OK, OK, but all I want is to go and see Father at the project. Amen."

"And buy a new battery for this altar. Have you no reverence?"

"Amen, I said; Amen and out."

The Immortality Investigation Project occupied a few acres in the center of the city. This contrast with the spacestations, which were always situated outside the cities, was one on which Jaybert Darkling had dilated at length to some of the governors of the project.

"It's symbolic, isn't it?" he had said pleasantly. "Man forges outward, ever outward—at least, our machines do—but the important things lie inward. As one of the sages of the Twentieth Century put it, we need to explore inner space. It's a sign of that need that although our precious space-stations lie on the outskirts of town, we find room for this great, this metaphysical project, right at the center of things."

Right or not, he said it often enough to silence most of the governors.

Before getting down to his paper work on this fine morning, Darkling went briskly on a tour of inspection. Robots and machines had care over most things here, but the housing and guarding of the immortals was his responsibility. As he walked through into the first Wethouse, he saw some dis-approval that young Zee Stone was on duty and flirting with a slight blonde secretary.

"Stone!"

"Sir!"

They walked together into the antechamber of the Wet-house, pulling on boots and oilskins.

In the Wethouse itself basked the immortals. The project housed thousands of them. This first hall contained perhaps twenty, most of them unmoving.

The temperature was maintained at a rigid seventy-two degrees Fahrenheit. From the high ceiling, showers spouted. Around the walls, taps gushed, their waters running across the tiles into a pool that occupied half of the floor space. In the center of the pool, fountains played. Cool jets of air, hurtling in at ceiling level, made tiny localized clouds and random cloudbursts that played hydropic variations in the chamber.

Statuesquely, the immortals stood or lay in the water torents. Many slumped half-submerged on the sloping edges of the pool, their eyes unblinkingly looking at some distant scene. The waters, beaten to a broth by the downpour, lapped around their limbs.

Yet they themselves conveyed an impression of drought. Not a man or woman here was less than one hundred and eighty years old. They resembled planed wood planks with the grain standing out strongly, so covered were their skins with the strange whorls and markings that represented hall-marks of immortality. From the time when they first took the series of three ROA5 injections, they had been plunged into the extreme throes of old age; their skin had wrinkled and dried, their hair thinned, their marrows shriveled. They developed the appearance and postures of extreme old age.

That phase had passed. Gradually, they penetrated the

senility barrier. Their skin flattened again, smoothed curiously, became as patterned and strange as oak planking.

These were external signs only. Inside, the changes were infinitely greater.

"What are you thinking about this morning, Palmer?" Darkling asked of one reclining figure that lay wallowing at the pool's edge. He squatted in his oilskins, putting his face down to Palmer's, with its great brown and black whorls as if time had set a thumbprint over it.

It took a brief while for Palmer to begin to answer, rather as if the message had to travel to Mars and back before reaching his brain.

"I am pursuing a line of thought that preoccupied me some sixty or so years ago. Not so much a line as a nexus of thought."

Since he then fell silent, Darkling had to prompt. "And the thought is. . . ?"

"I couldn't say in words. It is less a thought than . . . than a shade. Some of us here discussed the idea of a language of color. If we had a language of color, I could tell you precisely about what I was thinking."

"The idea of a color language was aired and dismissed long before I took over here," Darkling said firmly. "The consensus of opinion was—and you immortals agreed—that colors were far more limiting than words: fewer in number, for that matter."

Palmer thrust his face into a jet of water and let it play gently on his nose. Between gasps, he said, "Many more colors exist than you know of. It is simply a matter of registering them. And my idea is of a supplementary rather than a substitute language. If this other business the group was talking about, a way in which an eye could project as well as absorb light, comes to anything, the color language may have a future."

"Well, let me know if you think of anything."

"OK, director."

As they padded away through the rain, Stone said, "Does that sound like a fruitful idea to you?"

Darkling said, "There I must keep my own counsel, my boy. To the untrained mind, even their fuzziest ideas can be dangerous—like slow depth-charges, you know. It takes an expert to evaluate their real worth." He remembered what the Gods had said that very morning and added, with an effort, "Still, off the cuff, I'd say it sounded like an unfruitful idea."

The two men walked among the wallowing bodies, ex-changing a word here and there. One or two of the immortals had something fresh to offer, which Darkling noted on a waterproof slate for one of the trained interrogators to follow up later. Most of the ideas they gleaned here were not prac-ticable in terms of man's society; just a few had revolution-ized it.

The immortality project was a failure in its origins: this protraction of life proved too eccentric for anyone to volun-teer to become an immy. Nevertheless, by preserving these strange old failures, the project was skimming off a useful by-product: ideas, and rearrangements of old ideas. The immies now represented a great capital investment—as the governors were aware.

At last the morning round was finished and Darkling and Stone made their way to less humid quarters, where they removed their boots and oilskins.

"Don't seem to be earning their keep much, these days, do they?" Stone commented. "We ought to ginger them up a bit, cut off their water supply or something."

"What an immoral idea!—Useless, too, because it was tried many, many years ago. No, we have to face it, Stone, they are different from us, very different."

He toweled his face vigorously, and continued, "The im-mortals have been cut off from man's root drives. For obvious reasons, the only drives we can inherit are those that mani-fest themselves before reproduction. It was argued in times past, quite dogmatically, that there were no other drives. Well, we see differently now. We see that once through the senility barrier, man is no longer a doing creature but a thinking creature. Vice versa, we see that we on the green side of the senility barrier are doing rather than thinking creatures—another idea that would have upset our ancestors. Our thinking is just embryo thinking. These immortals are our brains. Frankly, in this star-going age, we can't afford to be without them."

Stone had switched off several sentences ago. Hearing his boss's voice die, he said, in a vague tone of agreement, "Yeh, well, we ought to ginger them up or something."

He was thinking of his story. What he needed was new characters—young ones, who wouldn't have to think at all.

"We cannot ginger them up!" In Darkling's voice was a sudden rasp that shook Stone to full attention. His superior had swung on to him, his little moustache twitching, as if with a malevolent life of its own.

"Your trouble is, Stone, you don't listen to what's being said. The immortals are merely given care here, you know—this isn't a prison, it's a refuge from the complex world outside."

He had never liked Darkling; that went for his moustache too. Putting on a calm and insulting drawl, he said, "Oh come now, sir, let's not pretend they aren't prisoners. That's a bit hypocritical, isn't it?"

Perhaps it was the word "hypocritical." Darkling's face went very red. "You watch your step, Stone! Don't think I don't know of your activities with Miss Roberts when you should be on duty. If one of the immortals wished to leave us—which never has happened and never could happen, because they live here in ideal conditions—they would be free to. And I'd back their decision against the governors."

They looked at each other in helpless antagonism.

"I still think it would be a miracle if one got away," Stone said.

As he left the room, Darkling reached for his pocket shrine. There was something about Zee Stone that put him in need of spiritual comfort.

When Otto Pommy arrived at the project, he was in a fine ecstatic mood of resignation. Resignation filled him, and he executed every gesture with pugnacious resignation.

While he completed the questionnaires it was vital he fill in before speaking to an immy, while he was undergoing a medical examination, while he was having his retinal pattern checked, he concentrated on a number of absorbing arrangements in space-time that served to keep his mood one of substantial mellowness. In particular, he dug a number of universals out of the toecap of his left boot or, more particularly, the hinge between the toecap and the rest of the boot. By the time he was allowed in to see his relation in the Wethouse, Otto had decided that for one skilled in the art, it would be possible to read from the creases in the hinge a complete history of all the journeys he had undertaken in this particular pair of boots. The right boot seemed somehow altogether more evasive about its history.

"Hullo, Father Palmer! Old Acid Head come to see you again. Remember me? It's been two years!"

The generations were a little mixed. Otto, in fact, was nothing less than great-great-great-great-grandson to Palmer Pommy's long-dead brother, and the title "Father" he used was therefore part honorary, part derisory. Despite his two hundred years and his zebra-striped senility effect, Palmer looked younger than the shaggy, whiskery Otto. Only in his voice was there a suggestion that he basked on considerably remoter shores than Otto would ever attain.

"You are my closest living relation, descended by six generations from my brother. Your name is Otto Jack Pommy. You have shaved since I saw you last."

Otto broke into affectionate laughter. "Only you'd be able to detect it!" He stretched forth a hand and gripped Palmer's; it had a blubbery feel and was cold, but Otto did not flinch. "I love you damned old immies—you're so funny!—I wonder why the hell I don't come to see you more often."

"You're more faithful to the principle of inconsistency than to any individual, that's why. Also, you don't like the climate of the Wethouse."

"Yeah, that's a consideration—though it's not one I had considered." He stopped talking, absorbed in meditation on Palmer's face. It was a cartographic face, he came to the conclusion. Once the marks of senility, the wrinkles and pits and folds, had been as real as irregularities in hilly ground; now they were abstracts merely, like contours. "You got a cartographic face," he said.

"It is not a map of me: I don't wear my heart on my face."

"Of time, then? Marked out in isobars or secobars or something?" His attention was wandering. He knew why everyone hated the immortals, why nobody wanted to become immortals, although their great contributions to life were so obvious. The immies were too different, strange to look at, strange to talk to—except that *he* did not find them so. He loved them: or he loved Palmer.

It was the Wethouse he could not bear, with its continual gouts of water. Otto was an anti-water man. He and Palmer were talking now—or staring at each other in a dream, as was their custom—in one of the guest rooms, where no water was in evidence. Palmer was garbed in a wraparound toweling robe from which his ancient tattooed head and striped legs protruded like afterthoughts. He was smiling; over the last hundred years, he had smiled as widely perhaps once every six years; he liked Otto because Otto amused him. It made him proud of his long-dead brother to look at his great-great-great-great-grandson.

"Are you managing this session pretty painlessly without water?" Otto asked.

"It doesn't hurt for a while. The hurt doesn't hurt for a while."

"I've never understood your whole water-orientation—or for that matter whether you immies yourselves understood it."

Palmer had momentarily lost contact. "Difference between hurt and harm. A term should be inserted between them meaning 'benevolent pain stimulus.' "

"Water-orientation, Father."

"No, that doesn't . . . oh, water-orientation. . . . Well, it depends what you mean by understanding, Otto. Life renews itself in wetness and slime. The central facts of existence— at least until my kind arrived—were bathed in moisture. The vagina, semen, womb—goodness me, I've almost forgotten the realities those terms represent. . . . Mankind comes from the sea, is conceived and born amid salty liquid, dissolves not into dust and ashes but slimes and salts. Except, that is, for us immortals. We're up past our bedtimes and it seems to give us a terrible neurosis for water and the irreplaceable liquids that once belonged to our natural state."

"Up past bedtime? Never thought of the grave as satisfying any particular craving of mine. . . ."

"Longevity is a nodal zone where thirsts partly metaphysical supplant most other desires." He closed his ancient eyes, the better to survey the desert of nondeath across which his kind journeyed.

"You talk as if you were dried up inside. Your blood still circulates as surely as the oceans of the world, doesn't it?"

"The blood still circulates, Otto. . . . It's below that level that the dryness starts. We need something we haven't got. It may not be extinction but it reveals itself as ever-rushing waters."

"Water, that's all you see! You need a change of scenery."

"I've forgotten your world, Otto, with its crowds and change and speed."

Otto grew excited. He began to snap his fingers and a curious twitch developed in the region of his left cheek.

"Palmer, Palmer, you idiot, that's not my goddamned world any more than it's yours. I've opted out from the machine culture just as thoroughly as you. I'm an acid head —I know that rush of dark waters you mention pretty well myself. I love you, Palmer, I want to get you out of here. This place is like a damned prison."

Palmer screwed up his eyes and looked slowly around the

room, beginning to shudder, as if an ancient engine had started within his frame.

"I'm a captive," he whispered.

"Only because you think there's nowhere to go. I've got a place for you, Father! Perfect place, no more than twenty miles away. Some friends of mine—bangers, every one of them, hopped high but gentle, I swear—we got hold of an old swimming pool. Indoor. Works fine. We bunk in the cubicles. You could be in the shallow end. You'd be at home. Real home! People to talk to'd understand you. New faces, new ideas. Whole setup built for you. I'll take you. Go right now!"

"Otto, you're mad! I'm a captive here!"

"But would you? Would you like to?"

His eyes were sometimes all surface and meaningless, like a patterned carpet; now they looked out and lived. "Even if only for a little while. . . . To be away. . . ."

"Let's go then! You need nothing else!"

Palmer caught his hand pitifully "I keep telling you, I'm a captive. They'd never let us go."

"The bosses? It's in the constitution! You're free to walk out whenever you want. The government pays. You don't owe anyone a damned thing."

"In a century and a half, no immortal ever walked out of the project. It would be a miracle."

"We'll pray for a miracle!"

Shaking his head to show he would listen to not one more word of protest, Otto unstrapped his old secondhand shrine from his back and set it up before him on the table. He opened it, struck it when the altar light refused to glow, shrugged and assumed what Palmer took for a gesture of reverence. He began to pray.

"O Gods, sorry to bother you twice in one day! This is your old friend and troublemaker Otto Jack Pommy in a proper fit of reverence. You'll recollect that when I was on to you first thing this morning, you were saying how arrogant I was. Remember?"

No answer came. Otto nodded in understanding. "They have no small talk in heaven. Very proper. Of course you remember. Well, I'm never going to be arrogant again, and in exchange I beg of you, Almighty Gods, just one small miracle."

From the darkness behind the altar, a level voice said, "The Gods do not bargain."

Otto cleared his throat and pointed an eyebrow at Palmer

to indicate that this might be difficult. "Quite right. Understandable in your position, O Gods. O Gods, I therefore pray you do me one small miracle without strings attached—wait, let me tell you—"

"There are no miracles, only favorable conjunctions of circumstances."

"Very well put, O great Gods, in which case I pray you for one small favorable conjunction of circumstances, to wit, letting me get my dear old Father here out of this lousy project. That's all! That's all! And in return, I swear I will remain humble all the days of my life. Hear my prayer, O Gods, for thine is the power and the glory and we are in a genuine fix, forever and ever. Amen."

The Gods said, "If you wish to remove the immortal, then the time to go is now."

"Ah!" Otto grabbed his shrine in both hands and fervently kissed the altar. "You're lovely people to treat an old acid head so, and I swear I'll declare the miracle abroad and walk in truth and righteousness all the days of my life and get a new battery for the altar light. Amen in the highest, amen and out!"

Turning to Palmer with his eyes gleaming, he strapped the shrine back over his shoulder.

"There! What do you think of that? When the Gods work in our favor, there's nothing Twenty-Second Century civilization can do to stop us! Come on, daddy-o, and I'll look after you like a child."

He pulled the immortal to his feet and led him from the room. In confused excitement, Palmer in turn protested that he could not go and longed to leave. One arguing, one encouraging, they made their way down the extensive corridors of the project. Nobody stopped them, although several officials stared and looked hard after their eccentric progress.

It was when they got to the main door that their way was blocked. Dean Cusak, imposing in his brown uniform, popped forward like a dummy and asked for their passes.

Otto showed his visitor's pass and said, "As you'll probably recognize, this is one of the immortals, Mr. Palmer Pommy. He is leaving with me. He has no pass. He has lived here for the past one hundred and fifty years."

This was Cusak's big moment, and he painfully recognized it as such. Never having been face to face with an immortal before, he felt, as many another man had done, the stunning impact of that encounter, which was invariably followed by a shockwave of envy, fear, and other emotions: for here was a being already four times as old as himself, and due to go on living long after all the present generation was subsumed into ashes.

Cusak's voice came reedily. "I can't let nobody through here without a pass, sir. It's the rules."

"For the Gods' sake, man, what are you? Are you going to be someone else's yes-man all your life?—A mere taker-of-orders? Look on this immortal and then ask yourself if you have any right to offend his wishes!"

Cusak's eyes met Palmer's, and then dropped. It could have been that he was not even thinking of this present moment at all, or of these persons, but of some other time when someone else held the stage and a shriller voice made the same demands of him.

When he looked up, he said, "You're quite right, sir. I pleases myself who I lets through here. I don't exist just to carry out Mr. Darkling's orders. I'm my own man, and one day I'm going to run my own little farm. Carry on, gentlemen!"

He saluted as they went by.

Directly the two men were gone, Cusak began to suffer qualms. He dialed his superior, Zee Stone, and told him that one of the immortals had left the project.

"I'll deal with it, Cusak," Stone said, snapping off the doorman's flow of apology. He sat for a moment staring into vacancy, wondering what to do with this interesting piece of news. It was his only for a while; by evening, if he let the immy go, it would be all over the planet. The news value was colossal; no immortal had ever dared leave the project before. Certainly the news would bring the project under close investigation and no doubt a number of secrets would come to light.

In particular, it would bring Jaybert Darkling under investigation. He would probably get the sack. So, for that matter, might Zee Stone.

"I don't care!" he said. "I'd be free to write, to suffer as a writer should. . . ."

The old vision was back with renewed strength. Only he could not quite get it in focus. It wasn't fiction exactly he wanted to write—the characters were too difficult in fiction. It was . . . it was . . .

Well, he could settle that later Meanwhile, he could settle the hash of his beloved boss, Darkling, if he played his cards right.

Darkling's moustache twitched as Stone entered.

"I won't detain you a minute, sir. A little matter has just arisen that I'm sure you can deal with."

His tone was so unusually pleasant that Darkling knew something horrible was about to emerge.

"I'm expecting a call from the Extrapolation Board at any second, so you'd better be brief."

"Oh, I will be brief. You were telling me this morning, sir—I was very interested in what you said—about how you disapproved of the policy of the board of governors of this project."

"I hardly think I am likely to make such a comment to my subordinates, Stone."

"Oh, but you did, sir. I mean, we all know how the project exists to milk the immortals of their strange ideas and turn them into practical applications for the benefit of mankind. Only it also happens to benefit the governors as well, and so although the immortals began as free men here, the project merely providing an ideal environment, they've come to be no more than prisoners."

"I said—"

"And you said that if one of them escaped, you'd back him against the governors."

"Well, yes, maybe I did say something like that."

"Sir, I wish to report that one of the immortals has just escaped."

Darkling was on his fet in an instant, his fingers on the nearest buzzer.

"You fool, Stone, why shilly-shally? We must get him back at once! Think of the publicity. . . ." His face was white. He faltered to a stop.

"But, sir, you just said—"

Darkling cut him off. "Circumstances alter cases."

"Then this *is* a prison, sir."

Darkling rushed at him, arms waving. "You crafty little bastard, Stone, get out of my office! You're trying to trick me, aren't you? I know your kind—"

"It was just what we were saying about hypocrisy—"

"Get out! Get out at once and never come in here again!"

He slammed the door after Stone's retreating back. Then he leaned on the door, trembling, and rubbed the palm of his hand over his forehead. He knew the Gods were looking down on him; he knew that they, in their infinite cunning, had sent Stone to him for a scourge. This was his time of testing. For once he would have to stand by what he had represented to be his own true feelings, or else be forever damned in his own eyes.

If he let the immy go, the governors would surely have his blood. If he hauled the immy back—and the matter was urgent, or he would be lost in the city—Stone would see he was morally discredited, perhaps even with the governors. Either way, he was in trouble; his only policy was to stand by what he had said—said more than once, he recalled faintly.

From somewhere came an unwonted memory of someone jokingly defending hypocrisy in his presence by saying, "Hypocrites may be scoundrels, but by their nature they sometimes have to live up to the fine feelings to which they pretend." Darkling had wanted to tell the idiot that he failed to understand the essential thing about a hypocrite: that their nature was genuinely mixed, that the fine feelings were there all right, that it was the will that was weak . . . well, now the will was trapped by circumstance.

He would have to let the immy go.

"You win, Gods!" he cried. "I've been a better man today, and it'll probably ruin me!"

Shakily, he went around to his desk. As he sat down, a bright idea came to him. A smile that Stone might have recognized as sly and dangerous played on his face. There was, after all, a way in which he could defend himself from the wrath of the governors—by enlisting the big battalions on his side.

His eyes went momentarily upwards, in silent thanks for the hope of release.

Pressing the secretarial button on his desk, he said crisply, "Get me World Press on the line. I wish to tell them why I have seen fit to release an immortal from this institution."

He occupied the time pleasantly, while waiting for the call to come through, in summoning the doorman, Cusak, to make financial arrangements with him for his cooperation, and in dropping Stone a note demanding his resignation.

By the side of the old swimming pool, a crowd gathered. A few women sprawled among the men, their hair as lank and uncombed as their mates'. Such garments as were worn were nondescript; some of the younger men went naked. Everyone moved in a gentle, bemused manner.

Palmer Pommy did not move. He lay on a couch erected in the shallow end of the pool so that his striped body was awash. Some of the shower equipment had been reassembled so that he was perpetually sprayed with warm water. He was laughing as he had not done for many decades.

"You bangers are on my wavelength," he said. "We immies can't take the thoughts of ordinary short-span people—they're too banal. But you lot think as daft as me."

"We take a shot of immortality occasionally," one of the crowd said. "But you're as good as a dose, Palmer—the impact of meeting you lops me double, like a miracle."

"Gods sure sent him," another said.

"Hey, what do you mean, Gods sent him? *I* brought him," Otto said. He was lounging by the poolside in an old chair while one of the more repellent girls stroked his neck. "Besides, Palmer don't believe in Gods, do you, Father?"

"I invented them."

They all lauged. A blonde girl said, "I invented sex." They turned it into a game.

"I invented feet."

"I invented kneecaps."

"I invented Pommy Palmer."

"I invented inventions."

"I invented me."

"I invented dreams."

"I invented you all—now I disinvent you!"

"I invented the Gods," Palmer repeated. He was smiling but serious now. "Before any of you were alive, or your parents. That's what we immies are for, thinking up crazy ideas because our minds aren't lumbering with ordinary thoughts, else they'd kill us off because the immortality project didn't turn out as they hoped—it wasn't fit for all and sundry.

"The Gods were more or less in existence. Vast computers were running everything, comsats supplied instantaneous communication, beamed power was possible, psychology was a strict science. Mankind had always regarded computers half prayerfully, right from their inception. All I did was think of hooking them all up, giving everyone a free communicator or shrine, and there was a new power in the world: the Gods. It worked at once, thanks to the ancient human need for gods—which never died even in scientific societies like ours."

"Not mine, dad-o!" one of the men cried. "I'm no robot-bugger! And say, if you invented the Gods, who invented the theology to go with them? Did you serve that too?"

"No. That came naturally. When the computers spoke, each of the old religions fell into step and adapted their forms. They had to survive: like none of them ever could stand up against personalized answer to prayers. Cranky notion . . . but war's died since the Gods ruled."

"Who's Waugh?" someone asked.

"That was a miracle. There've been others. Ask Otto. He claims that getting me out of the project was a miracle."

Otto wriggled and removed his nose from the repellent girl's navel.

"I don't know about that. I mean I'm not so sure," he said, scratching his chest. "It was just that old fool doorman was bluffed into letting us out. No, I did it—I'm the miracle worker."

"You told me different," Palmer said, looking searchingly from the pool.

"You think I'm being arrogant. You could be right. But I reckon what I really feel, Father, is that there isn't any such thing as a miracle—just favorable conjunctions of circumstances, that's all."

There was a scraggy girl in the crowd who leaned forward anxiously and tapped Palmer's zebra arm.

"If you've really handed us over into the power of the machines, isn't there a danger they will end by ruling us completely?"

Palmer looked slowly about the echoing chamber before deciding what to reply. He loked at the lounging group about him, most of whom had already recovered from the novelty of his presence and were interesting themselves in each other. He looked long at Otto, who had unstrapped his old shrine for comfort and was now cuddling the repellent girl in a purposeful way. Then his face crinkled into a grin.

"Don't wory, girlies! Men always cheat their gods," he said.

THE SOFT PREDICAMENT
> "Calculate thyself within, seek not thyself in
> the Moon, but in thine own Orb or Microcosmical
> Circumference. Let celestial aspects admonish
> and advise, not conclude and determine thy ways."
> Sir Thomas Browne: *Christian Morals*

THE SOFT PREDICAMENT

~~~~~~

I. JUPITER. With increasing familiarity, he saw that the slow writhings were not inconsequential movement but ponderous and deliberate gesture.

Ian Ezard was no longer aware of himself. The panorama entirely absorbed him.

What had been at first a meaningless blur had resolved into an array of lights, gently drifting. The lights now took on pattern, became luminous wings or phosphorescent backbones or incandescent limbs. As they passed, the labored working of those pinions ceased to look random and assumed every appearance of deliberation—of plan—of consciousness! Nor was the stew in which the patterns moved a chaos any longer; as Ezard's senses adjusted to the scene, he became aware of an environment as much governed by its own laws as the environment into which he had been born.

With the decline of his first terror and horror, he could observe more acutely. He saw that the organisms of light moved over and among—what would you call them? Bulwarks? Fortifications? Cloud formations? They were no more clearly defined than sandbanks shrouded in fog; but he was haunted by a feeling of intricate detail slightly beyond his retinal powers of resolution, as if he were gazing at flotillas of baroque cathedrals, sunk just too deep below translucent seas.

He thought with unexpected kinship of Lowell, the astronomer, catching imaginary glimpses of Martial canals—but his own vantage point was much the more privileged.

The scale of the grand gay solemn procession parading

before his vision gave him trouble. He caught himself trying to interpret the unknown in terms of the known. These organisms reminded him of the starry skeletons of Terrestrial cities by night, glimpsed from the stratosphere, or of clusters of diatoms floating in a drop of water. It was hard to remember that the living geometries he was scanning were each the size of a large island—perhaps a couple of hundred miles across.

Terror still lurked. Ezard knew he had only to adjust the infrared scanners to look miles deeper down into Jupiter's atmosphere and find—life?—images?—of a different kind. To date, the Jupiter Expedition had resolved six levels of life-images, each level separated from the others almost as markedly as sea was separated from air, by pressure gradients that entailed different chemical compositions.

Layer on layer, down they went, stirring slowly, right down far beyond detection into the sludgy heart of the protosun! Were all layers full of at least the traces and chimeras of life?

"It's like peering down into the human mind!" Ian Ezard exclaimed; perhaps he thought of the mind of Jerry Wharton, his mixed-up brother-in-law. Vast pressures, vast darknesses, terrible wisdoms, age-long electric storms—the parallel between Jupiter's atmospheric depths and the mind was too disconcerting. He sat up and pushed the viewing helmet back on its swivel.

The observation room closed in on him again, unchanging, wearily familiar.

"My god!" he said, feebly wiping his face. "My god!" And after a moment, "By Jove!" in honor of the monstrous protosun riding like a whale beneath their ship. Sweat ran from him.

"It's a spectacle right enough," Captain Dudintsev said, handing him a towel. "And each of the six layers we have surveyed is over one hundred times the area of Earth. We are recording most of it on tape. Some of the findings are being relayed back to Earth now."

"They'll flip!"

"Life on Jupiter—what else can you call it but life? This is going to hit Russia and America and the whole of Westciv harder than any scientific discovery since reproduction!"

Looking at his wristputer, Ezard noted that he had been under the viewer for eighty-six minutes. "Oh, it's consciousness there right enough. It stands all our thinking upside down. Not only does Jupiter contain most of the inorganic material of the system, the sun apart—it contains almost all the life as well. Swarming, superabundant life. . . . Not an amoeba smaller than Long Island. . . . It makes Earth just a rocky outpost on a far shore. That's a big idea to adjust to!"

"The White World will adjust, as we adjusted to Darwinism. We always do adjust."

"And who cares about the Black World. . . ."

Dudintsev laughed. "What about your sister's husband that you're always complaining about? He'd care!"

"Oh, yes, he'd care. Jerry'd like to see the other half of the globe wiped out entirely."

"Well, he's surely not the only one."

With his head still full of baffling luminescent gestures, Ezard went forward to shower.

II. LUNA. Near the deep midnight in Rainbow Bay City. Standing under Main Dome at the top of one of the view-towers. The universe out there before us, close to the panes; stars like flaming fat, distorted by the dome's curvature, Earth like a chilled fingernail clipping. Chief Dream-Technician Wace and I talking sporadically, killing time until we went back on duty to what my daughter Ri calls "the big old black thing" over in Plato.

"Specialization—it's a wonderful thing, Jerry!" Wace said. "Here we are, part-way to Jupiter and I don't even know where in the sky to look for it! The exterior world has never been my province."

He was a neat little dry man, in his mid-thirties and already wizened. His province was the infinitely complex state of being of sleep. I had gained a lot of my interest in psychology from Johnnie Wace. Like him, I would not have been standing where I was were it not for the CUFL project, on which we were both working. And that big old black thing would not have been established inconveniently on the Moon had not the elusive hypnoid states between waking and sleeping which we were investigating been most easily sustained in the light-gravity condition of Luna.

I gave up the search for Jupiter. I knew where it was no more than Wace did. Besides, slight condensation was hatching drops off the aluminum bars overhead; the drafts of the dome brought the drops down slantingly at us. Tension was returning to me as the time to go on shift drew near— tension we were not allowed to blunt with drink. Soon I would be plugged in between life and death, letting CUFL suck up my psyche. As we turned away, I looked outside at an auxiliary dome under which cactus grew in the fertile Lunar soil, sheltered only slightly from external rigors.

"That's the way we keep pushing on, Johnnie," I said, indicating the cacti. "We're always extending the margins of experience—now the Trans-Jupiter Expedition has discovered that life exists out there. Where does the West get its dynamism from, while the rest of the world—the Third World—still sits on its haunches?"

Wace gave me an odd look.

"I know, I'm on my old hobbyhorse! You tell me, Johnnie, you're a clever man, how is it that in an age of progress half the globe won't progress?"

"Jerry, I don't feel about the Blacks as you do. You're such an essential part of CUFL because your basic symbols are confused."

He noticed that the remark angered me. Yet I saw the truth as I stated it. Westciv, comprising most of the Northern Hemisphere and little else bar Australia, was a big armed camp, guarding enormously long frontiers with the stagnating Black or Third World, and occasionally making a quick raid into South America or Africa to quell threatening power build-ups. All the time that we were trying to move forward, the rest of the overcrowded world was dragging us back.

"You know my views, Johnnie—they may be unpopular but I've never tried to hide them." I told him, letting my expression grow dark. "I'd wipe the slate of the useless Third World clean and begin over, if I had my way. What have we got to lose? No confusion in my symbols there, is there?"

"Once a soldier, always a soldier. . . ." He said no more until we were entering the elevator. Then he added, in his quiet way, "We can all of us be mistaken, Jerry. We now know that the freshly-charted ypsilon-areas of the brain make no distinction between waking reality and dream. They deal only with altering time-scales, and form the gateway to the unconscious. My personal theory is that Western man, with his haste for progress, may have somehow closed that gate and lost touch with something that is basic to his psychic well-being."

"Meaning the Blacks are still in touch?"

"Don't sneer! The history of the West is nothing to be particularly proud of: You know that our CUFL project is in trouble and may be closed down. Sure, we progress astonishingly on the material plane, we have stations orbiting the Sun and inner planets and Jupiter—yet we remain at odds with ourselves. CUFL is intended to be to the psyche what the computer is to knowledge, yet it consistently rejects our data. The fault is not in the machine. Draw your own conclusions."

I shrugged. "Let's get on shift!"

We reached the surface and climbed out, walking in the direction of the tube where a shuttle for Plato would be ready. The big old black thing would be sitting waiting by the crater terminus and, under the care of Johnnie Wace's team, I and the other feeds would be plugged in. Sometimes I felt lost in the whole tenuous world that Wace found so congenial, and in all the clever talk about what was dream, what was reality—though I used it myself sometimes, in self-defense.

As we made for the subway, the curve of the dome distorted the cacti beyond. Frail though they were, great arms of prickly pear grew and extended and seemed to wrap themselves around the dome, before being washed out by floods of reflected electroluminescence. Until the problem of cutting down glare at night was beaten, tempers in Main Dome would stay edgy.

In the subway, still partly unfinished, Wace and I moved past the parade of fire-fighting equipment and emergency suits and climbed into the train. The rest of the team were already in their seats, chattering eagerly about the ambiguous states of mind that CUFL encouraged; they greeted Johnnie eagerly, and he joined in their conversation. I longed to be back with my family—such as it was—or playing a quiet game of chess with Ted Greaves, simple old soldier Ted Greaves. Maybe I should have stayed a simple old soldier myself, helping to quell riots in the overcrowded lanes of Eastern Seaboard, or cutting a quick swathe through Brazil.

"I didn't mean to rub you up the wrong way, Jerry," Wace said as the doors closed. His little face wrinkled with concern.

"Forget it. I jumped at you. These days, life's too complex."

"That from you, the apostle of progress!"

"It's no good talking. . . . Look, we've found life on Jupiter. That's great. I'm really glad, glad for Ezard out there, glad for everyone. But what are we going to do about it? Where does it get us? We haven't even licked the problem of life on Earth yet!"

"We will," he said.
We began to roll into the dark tunnel.

III. RI. One of the many complications of life on Earth was
the dreams of my daughter. They beguiled me greatly: so
much that I believe they often became entangled with my
fantasies as I lay relaxed on Wace's couch under the encepha-
lometers and the rest of the CUFL gear. But they worried
me even as they enchanted me. The child is so persistently
friendly that I don't always have time for her; but her dreams
are a different matter.

In the way that Ri told them, the dreams had a peculiar
lucidity. Perhaps they were scenes from a world I wanted to
be in, a toy world—a simplified world that hardly seemed
to contain other people.

Ri was the fruit of my third-decade marriage. My fourth-
decade wife, Natalie, also liked to hear Ri's prattle; but
Natalie is a patient woman, both with Ri and me; more with
Ri, maybe, since she likes to show me her temper.

A certain quality to Ri's dreams made Natalie and me
keep them private to ourselves. We never mentioned them to
our friends, almost as if they were little shared guilty secrets.
Nor did I ever speak of them to my buddies sweating on the
CUFL project, or to Wace or the mind-wizards in the Lunar
Psyche Lab. For that matter, Natalie and I avoided dis-
cussing them between ourselves, partly because we sensed
Ri's own reverence for her nocturnal images.

Then my whole pleasure at the child's dreams was turned
into disquiet by a casual remark that Ted Greaves dropped.

This is how it came about.

I had returned from Luna on the leave-shuttle only the
previous day, more exhausted than usual. The hops between
Kennedy and Eastern and Eastern and Eurocen were becoming more crowded than ever, despite the extra jumbos
operating; the news of the discovery of life on Jupiter—even
the enormous telecasts of my brother-in-law's face burning
over every Westciv city—seemed to have stirred up the
ants' heap considerably. What people thought they could do
about it was beyond computation, but Wall Street was registering a tidal wave of optimism.

So with one thing and another, I arrived home exhausted.
Ri was asleep. Yes, still wetting her bed, Natalie admitted.
I took a sauna and fell asleep in my wife's arms. The world

turned. Next thing I knew, it was morning and I was roused by Ri's approach to our bedside.

Small girls of three have a ponderous tread; they weigh as much as baby elephants. I can walk across our bedroom floor without making a sound, but this tot sets up vibrations.

"I thought you were still on the Moon feeding the Clective Unctious, Daddy," she said. The "Clective Unctious" is her inspired mispronunciation of the Collective Unconscious; wisely, she makes no attempt at all at the Free-Living tail of CUFL.

"The Unctious has given me a week's leave, Ri. Now let me sleep! Go and read your book!"

I watched her through one half open eye. She put her head on one side and smiled at me, scratching her behind.

"Then that big old black thing is a lot clevererer and kinder than I thought it was."

From her side of the bed, Natalie laughed. "Why, that's the whole idea of the Clective Unctious, Ri—to be kinder and wiser than one person can imagine."

"I can imagine *lots* of kindness," she said. She was not to be weaned of her picture of the Unctious as a big black thing.

Climbing onto the bed, she began to heave herself between Natalie and me. She had brought along a big plastic talkie-picture-book of traditional design tucked under one arm. As she rolled over me, she swung the book and a corner of it caught me painfully on the cheek. I yelled.

"You clumsy little horror! Get off me!"

"Daddy, I didn't mean to do it, really! It was an acciment!"

"I don't care what it was! Get out! Go on! Move! Go back to your own bed!"

I tugged at her arm and dragged her across me. She burst into tears.

Natalie sat up angrily. "For god's sake, leave the kid alone! You're always bullying her!"

"You keep quiet—she didn't catch you in the eye! And she's peed her bed again, the dirty little tyke!"

That was how that row started. I'm ashamed to relate how it went on. There were the tears from the child and tears from Natalie. Only after breakfast did everyone simmer down. Oh, I can be fairly objective now in this confession, and record my failings and what other people thought of me. Believe me, if it isn't art, it's therapy!

It's strange to recall now how often we used to quarrel over breakfast. . . . Yet that was one of the calmest rooms, with the crimson carpet spread over the floor-tiles, and the white walls and dark Italian furniture. We had old-fashioned two-dimensional oil painting, nonmobile, on the walls, and no holoscreen. In one corner, half-hidden behind a vase of flowers from the courtyard, stood Jannick, our robot housemaid; but Natalie, preferring not to use her, kept her switched off. Jannick was off on this occasion. Peace reigned. Yet we quarreled.

As Natalie and I were drinking a last cup of coffee, Ri trotted around to me and said, "Would you like to hear my dream now, Daddy, if you're really not savage anymore?"

I pulled her onto my knee. "Let's hear it then, if we must. Was it the one about warm pools of water again?"

She shook her head in a dignified manner.

"This dream came around three in the morning," she said. "I know what the time was because a huge black bird like a starving crow came and pecked at my window as if it wanted to get in and wake us all up."

"That was all a part of the dream, then. There aren't any crows in this stretch of Italy."

"Perhaps you're right, because the house was sort of dirtier than it really is. . . . So I sat up and immediately I began dreaming I was fat and heavy and carrying a big fat heavy talkie-book up the hill. It was a much bigger book than any I got here. I could hardly breathe because there was hardly any air up the hillside. It was a very *plain* sort of dream."

"And what happened in it?"

"Nothing."

"Nothing at all?"

"Nothing except just one thing. Do you know what? I saw there was one of those new Japanese cars rushing down the hill toward me—you know, the kind where the body's inside the wheel and the big wheel goes all around the body."

"She must mean the Toyota Monocar," Natalie said.

"Yes, that's right, Natalie, the Toyta Moggacar. It was like a big flaming wheel and it rolled right past me and went out."

"Out where?"

"I don't know. Where do things go out to? I didn't even know where it came from! In my dream I was puzzled about that, so I looked all around and by the roadside there was a big drop. It just went down and down! And it was guarded by eight posts protecting it, little round white posts like teeth, and the Moggacar must have come from there."

Natalie and I sat over the table thinking about the dream after Ri had slipped out into the courtyard to play; she had some flame- and apricot-colored finches in cages which she loved.

I was on her small imaginary hillside, where the air was thin and the colors pale, and the isolated figure of the child stood clutching its volume and watched the car go past like a flame. A sun-symbol, the wheel on which Ixion was crucified, image of our civilization maybe, Tantric sign of sympathetic fires. . . . All those things, and the first unmanned stations now orbiting the sun—one of the great achievements of Westciv, and itself a symbol awakening great smoldering responses in man. Was that response reverberating through the psyches of all small children, changing them, charging them further along the trajectory the White World follows? What would the news from Jupiter bring on? What sort of role would Uncle Ian, the life-finder, play in the primitive theaters of Ri's mind?

I asked the question of myself only idly. I enjoyed popping the big questions, on the principle that if they were big enough they were sufficient in themselves and did not require answers. Answers never worried me in those days. I was no thinker. My job in Plato concerned feelings, and for that they paid me. Answers were for Johnnie Wace and his cronies.

"We'd better be moving," Natalie said, collecting my coffee cup. "Since you've got a free day, make the most of it. You're on frontier duty with Greaves again tomorrow."

"I know that without being reminded, thanks."

"I wasn't really reminding you—just stating a fact."

As she passed me to go into the kitchen, I said, "I know this house is archaic—just a peasant's home. But if I hadn't volunteered for irregular frontier service during my off-duty spells, we wouldn't be here. We'd be stuck in Eastern or some other enormous city-complex, such as the one you spent your miserable childhood in. Then you'd complain even more!"

She continued into the kitchen with the cups and plates. It was true the house had been built for and by peasants, or little better; its stone walls, a meter thick, kept out the heat of summer; and the brief chill of winter when it rolled around. Natalie was silent and then she said, so quietly that I could scarcely hear her where I sat in the living room, "I was not complaining, Jerry, not daring to complain. . . ."

I marched in to her. She was standing by the sink, more or less as I imagined her, her dark wings of hair drawn into place by a rubber band at the nape of her neck. I loved her, but she could make me mad!

"What's that meant to mean—'not daring to complain'?"

"Please don't quarrel with me, Jerry. I can't take much more."

"Was I quarreling? I thought I was simply asking you what you meant by what you said!"

"Please don't get worked up!" She came and stood against me, putting her arms around my waist and looking up at me. I stiffened myself and would not return her gaze. "I mean no harm, Jerry. It's terrible the way we row just like everyone else—I know you're upset!"

"Of course I'm upset! Who wouldn't be upset at the state of the world? Your marvelous brother and his buddies have discovered life on Jupiter! Does that affect us? *My* project, CUFL, that will have to close down unless we start getting results. Then there's all the disturbance in the universities— I don't know what the younger generation thinks it's doing! Unless we're strong, the Thirdies are going to invade and take over—"

She was growing annoyed herself now. "Oh yes, that's really why we came to live down here in the back of beyond, isn't it?—Just so that you could get an occasional crack at the enemy. It wasn't for any care about where I might want to live."

"Unlike some people, I care about doing my duty by my country!"

She broke away from me. "It's no part of your duty to be incessantly beastly to Ri and me, is it? Is it? You don't care about us one bit!"

It was an old tune she played.

"Don't start bringing that up again, woman! If I didn't care, why did I buy you that robot standing idle in the next room? You never use it, you prefer to hire a fat old woman to come in instead! I should have saved my money! And you have the brass nerve to talk about not caring!"

Her eyes were wild now. She looked glorious standing there.

"You don't care! You don't care! You hurt your poor little daughter, you neglect me! You're always off to the Moon, or at the frontier, or else here bullying us. Even your stupid friend Ted Greaves has more sense than you! You hate us! You hate everyone!"

Running forward, I grabbed her arm and shook her.

"You're always making a noise. Not much longer till the end of the decade and then I'm rid of you! I can't wait!"

I strode through the house and slammed out of the door

into the street. Thank the stars it was frontier duty the next day! People greeted me but I ignored hem. The sun was already high in he South Italian sky; I sweated as I walked, and rejoiced in the discomfort.

It was not true that I bullied them. Natalie might have suffered as a child, but so had I! There had been a war in progress then, the first of the Westciv-Third wars, although we had not thought of it in quite those terms at the time, before the Cap-Com treaty. I had been drafted, at an age when others were cutting a figure in universities. I had been scared, I had suffered, been hungry, been wounded, been lost in the jungle for a couple of days before the chopper patrol picked me up. And I'd killed off a few Thirdies. Even Natalie would not claim I had *enjoyed* doing that. It was all over long ago. Yet it was still with me. In my mind, it never grew fainter. The Earth revolved; the lights on that old stage never went dim.

Now I was among the hills above our village. I sat under the shade of an olive tree and looked back. It's strange how you find yourself thinking things that have nothing to do with your daily life.

It was no use getting upset over a husband-wife quarrel. Natalie was OK; just a little hasty-tempered. My watch said close to ten o'clock. Ted Greaves would be turning up at the house for a game of chess before long. I would sit where I was for a moment, breathe deep, and then stroll back. Act naturally. There was nothing to be afraid of.

IV. GREAVES. Ted Greaves arrived at the house at about ten-fifty. He was a tall fair-haired man, dogged by ill-luck most of his military career and somewhat soured toward society. He enjoyed playing the role of bluff soldier. After many years in the service, he was now Exile Officer commanding our sector of the southern frontier between Westciv and the Blacks. As such, he would be my superior tomorrow, when I went on duty. Today, we were just buddies and I got the chess board out.

"I feel too much like a pawn myself to play well today," he said, as we settled down by the window. "Spent all the last twenty-four hours in the office filling in photoforms. We're sinking under forms! The famine situation in North Africa is now reinforced by a cholera epidemic."

"The Third's problems are nothing to do with us!"

"Unfortunately we're more connected than appears on the

surface. The authorities are afraid that the cholera won't respect frontiers. We've got to let some refugees through tomorrow, and they could be carriers. An emergency isolation ward is being set up. It's Westciv's fault—we should have given aid to Africa from the start."

On the Rainbow-Kennedy flight, I had bought a can of bourbon at a duty-free price. Greaves and I broached it now. But he was in a dark mood, and was soon launched on an old topic of his, the responsibility of the States for the White-Black confrontation. I did not accept his diagnosis for one minute, and he knew I didn't; but that did not stop him rambling on about the evils of our consumer society, and how it was all based on jealousy, and the shame of the Negro Solution—though how we could have avoided the Solution, he did not say. Since we had been mere children at the time of the Solution, I could not see why he needed to feel guilt about it. In any case, I believed that the colored races of Third were undeveloped because they lacked the intellect and moral fiber of Westciv, their hated Pinkyland.

So I let Greaves give vent to his feelings over the iced bourbon while I gazed out through the window to our inner courtyard.

The central stone path, flanked by a colonnade on which bougainvillea rioted, led to a little statue of Diana, executed in Carrara marble, standing against the far wall. All the walls of the courtyard were plastered in yellow. On the left-hand side, Ri's collection of finches chirped and flitted in their cages. In the beds, orange and lemon trees grew. Above the far wall, the mountains of Calabria rose.

I never tired of the peace of that view. But what chiefly drew my eyes was the sight of Natalie in her simple green dress. I had loved her in many forms, I thought, and at the end of the decade it would not come too hard to exchange her for another—better anyhow than being stuck with one woman a life long, as under the old system—but either I was growing older or there was something particular about Natalie. She was playing with Ri and talking to the Calabrian servant. I couldn't hear a word they said, though the windows were open to let in warmth and fragrance; only the murmur of their voices reached me.

Yes, she had to be exchanged. You had to let things go. That was what kept the world revolving. Planned obsolescence as a social dynamic, in human relationships as in consumer goods. When Ri was ten, she would have to go to the appropriate Integration Center, to learn to become a functioning member of society—just as my other daughter, Melisande, had left the year before, on her tenth birthday.

Melisande, who wept so much at the parting . . . a sad indication of how much she needed integration. We were all required to make sacrifices; otherwise the standard of living would go down. Partings one grew hardened to. I scarcely thought of Melisande nowadays.

And when I'd first known Natalie. Natalie Ezard. That was before the integration laws. "Space travel nourishes our deepest and most bizarre wishes." Against mental states of maximum alertness float extravagant hypnoid states which color the outer darkness crimson and jade, and make unshapely things march to the very margins of the eye. Maybe it is because at the very heart of the richness of metal-bound space travel lies sensory deprivation. For all its promise of renaissance, vacuum-flight is life's death, and only the completely schizoid are immune to its terrors. I was never happy, even on the Kennedy-Rainbow trip.

Between planets, our most outré desires become fecund. Space travel nourishes our deepest and most bizarre wishes. "Awful things can happen!" Natalie had cried, in our early days, flinging herself into my returning arms. And while I was away, Westciv passed its integration laws, separating parents from children, bestowing on ten-year-olds the honorable orphanage of the state, to be trained as citizens.

It all took place again before the backdrop of our sunlit courtyard, where Natalie Wharton now stood. She was thinner and sharper than she had been once, her hair less black. Some day, we would have to take the offensive and wipe out every single Black in the Black-and-White World. To my mind, only the fear of what neutral China might do had prevented us taking such a necessary step already.

"You see how old it is out there!" Ted Greaves said, misreading my gaze as he gestured into the courtyard. "Look at that damned vine, that statue! Apart from lovely little Natalie and your daughter, there's not a thing that hasn't been in place for a couple of hundred years. Over in the States, it's all new, new, everything has to be the latest. As soon as roots begin forming, we tear them up and start over. The result—no touchstones! How long's this house been standing? Three centuries? In the States, it would have been swept away long ago. Here, loving care keeps it going, so that it's as good as new. Good as new! See how I'm victim of my own clichés! It's better than fucking new, it's as good as old!"

"You're a sentimentalist, Ted. It isn't things but other people that matter. People are old, worlds are old. The Russo-American ships now forging around the System are bringing home to us just how old we are, how familiar we are to ourselves. Our roots are in ourselves."

We enjoyed philosophizing, that's true.

He grunted and lit a flash-cigar. "That comes well from you, when you're building this Free-Living Collective Unconscious. Isn't that just another American project to externalize evil and prune our roots?"

"Certainly not! CUFL will be an emotions-bank, a computer if you like, which will store—not the fruits of the human intellect—but the fruits of the psyche. Now that there are too many people around and our lives have to be regimented, CUFL will restore us to the freedom of our imaginations."

"If it works!"

"Sure, if it works," I agreed. "As yet, we can get nothing out of our big old black thing but primitive archetypal patterns. It's a question of keeping on feeding it." I always spoke more cheerfully than I felt with Greaves: to counteract his vein of pessimism, I suppose.

He stood up and stared out of the window. "Well, I'm just a glorified soldier—and without much glory. I don't understand emotion banks. But maybe you overfed your big black thing and it is dying of overnourishment, just like Westciv itself. Certain archetypal dreams—the human young get them, so why not your newborn machine? The young get them especially when they are going to die young."

Death was one of his grand themes: "The peace that passeth all standing," he called it once.

"What sort of dreams?" I asked, unthinking.

"To the nervous system, dream imagery is received just like sensory stimuli. There are prodromic dreams, dreams that foretell of death. We don't know what wakefulness is, do we, until we know what dreams are. Maybe the whole Black-White struggle is a super-dream, like a blackbird rapping on a windowpane."

Conversation springs hidden thoughts. I'd been listening, but more actively I'd wondered at the way he didn't answer questions quite directly, just as most people fail to. Someone told me that it was the effect of holovision, split attention. All this I was going through when he came up with the remark about blackbirds tapping on windows, and it brought to mind the start of Ri's latest dream, when she was unsure whether she woke or slept.

"What's that to do with dying?"

"Let's take a walk in the sun before it gets too stinking hot. Some children are too ethereal for life. Christ, Jerry, a kid's close to the primal state, to the original psychological world; they're the ones to come through with uncanny prognoses. If they aren't going to make it to maturity, their psyches know about it and have no drive to gear themselves onto the next stage of being."

"Let's go out in the sun," I said. I felt ill. The poinsettias were in flower, spreading their scarlet tongues. A lizard lay along a carob branch. That sun disappearing down Ri's hill —death? And the eight teeth or posts or what the hell they were, on the edge of nothing—her years? The finches hopped from perch to perch, restless in their captivity.

V. SICILY. Almost before daybreak next morning, I was flying over Calabria and the toe of Italy. Military installations glittered below. This was one of the southern points of Europe which marked the frontier between the two worlds. It was manned by task forces of Americans, Europeans, and Russians. I had left before Ri woke. Natalie, with her wings of dark hair, had risen to wave me good-bye. Good-bye, it was always good-bye. And what was the meaning of the big black book Ri had been carrying in her dream? It couldn't be true.

The Straits of Messina flashed below our wingless fuselage. Air, water, earth, fire, the original elements. The fifth, space, had been waiting. God alone knew what it did in the hearts and minds of man, what aboriginal reaction was in process. Maybe once we finished off the Thirdies, the Clective Unctious would give us time to sort things out. There was never time to sort things out. Even the finches in their long imprisonment never had enough time. And the bird at her window? Which side of the window was in, which out?

We were coming down toward Sicily, toward its tan mountains. I could see Greaves's head and shoulders in the driver's seat.

Sicily was semineutral ground. White and Black World met in its eroded valleys. My breakfast had been half a grapefruit, culled fresh from the garden, and a cup of bitter black coffee. Voluntary regulation of intake. The other side

of the looming frontier, starvation would have made my
snack seem a fine repast.

Somewhere south, a last glimpse of sea and the smudged
distant smoke of Malta, still burning after ten years. Then
up came Etna and the stunned interior, and we settled for
a landing.

This barren land looked like machine-land itself. Sicily—
the northern, Westciv half—had as big a payload of robots
on it as the Moon itself. All worked in mindless unison in
case the lesser breeds in the southern half did anything desperate. I grabbed up my gas-cannon and climbed out into
the heat as a flight of steps snapped itself into position.

Side by side, Greaves and I jumped into proffered pogo-
armor and bounded off across the field in thirty-foot kan-
garoo-steps.

The White boundary was marked by saucers standing on
poles at ten-meter intervals; between saucers, the force barrier shimmered, carrying its flair for hallucination right up
into the sky.

The Black World had its boundary too. It stood beyond
our force field—stood, I say! It lurched across Sicily, a ragged
wall of stone. Much of the stone came from dismembered
towns and villages and churches. Every now and again, a
native would steal some of the stone back, in order to build
his family a hovel to live in. Indignant Black officials would
demolish the hovel and restore the stone. They should have
worried! I could have pogoed over their wall with ease!
And a wall of eight posts. . . .

We strode across the crowded field to the forward gate.
Sunlight and gravity. We were massive men, nine feet high
or more; boots two feet high; over our heads, umbrella-
helmets over a foot high. Our megavoices could carry over
a land-mile. We might have been evil machine-men from
the ragged dreams of Blacks. At the forward gate, we entered in and shed the armor in magnetized recesses.

Up in the tower, Greaves took over from the auto-controls
and opened his link with Palermo and the comsats high overhead. I checked with Immigration and Isolation to see that
they were functioning.

From here, we could look well into the hated enemy territory, over the tops of their wooden towers, into the miserable stone villages, from which hordes of people were already
emerging, although fifty minutes had yet to elapse before
we lowered the force-screens to let any of them through.

Beyond the crowds, the mountains crumbling into their thwarted valleys, fly-specked with bushes. No fit habitation. If we took over the island—as I always held we should—we would raise desalination-plants on the coast, import topsoil and fertilizer and the new plus-crops, and make the whole place flow with riches in five years. With the present status quo, the next five would bring nothing but starvation and religion; that was all they had there. A massive cholera epidemic, with deaths counted in hundreds of thousands, was raging through Africa already, after moving westward from Calcutta, its traditional capital.

"The bastards!" I said. "One day, there will be a law all over the world forbidding people to live like vermin!"

"And a law forbidding people to make capital out of it," Greaves said. His remark meant nothing to me. I guessed it had something to do with his cranky theory that Westciv profited by the poor world's poverty by raising import tariffs against it. Greaves did not explain, nor did I ask him to.

At the auxiliary control panel, I sent out an invisible scanner to watch one of the enemy villages. Although it might register on the antiquated radar screens of the Blacks, they could only rave at the breach of international regulations without ever being able to intercept it.

The eye hovered over a group of shacks and adjusted its focus. Three-dimensionally, the holograph of hatred traveled toward me in the cube.

Against doorways, up on balconies decked with ragged flowers, along alleys, stood groups of Blacks. They would be Arabs, refugee Maltese, branded Sicilians, renegades from the White camp; ethnic groups were indistinguishable beneath dirt and tan and old nonsynthetic clothes. I centered on a swarthy young woman standing in a tavern doorway with one hand on a small boy's shoulder. As Natalie stood in the courtyard under the poinsettias, what had I thought to myself? That once we might have propagated love between ourselves?

Before the world had grown too difficult, there had been a sure way of multiplying and sharing love. We would have bred and raised children for the sensuous reward of having them, of helping them grow up sane and strong. From their bowels also, health would have radiated.

But the Thirdies coveted Westciv's riches without accepting its disciplines. They bred. Indiscriminately and prodigally. The world was too full of children and people, just as the emptiness of space was stuffed with lurid dreams. Only the weak and helpless and starved could cast children onto the world unregulated. Their weak and helpless and starved progeny clogged the graves and wombs of the world. That laughing dark girl on my screen deserved only the bursting seed of cannonfire.

"Call that scanner back, Jerry!" Greaves said, coming toward me.

"What's that?"

"Call your scanner back."

"I'm giving the Wogs the once-over."

"Call it back in, I told you. As long as no emergency's in force, you are contravening regulations."

"Who cares!"

"I care," he said. He looked very nasty. "I care, and I'm Exile Officer."

As I guided the eye back in, I said, "You were rough all yesterday too. You played a bum game of chess. What's got into you?"

But as soon as I had asked the question, I could answer it myself. He was a bag of nerves because he must have had word that his son was coming back from the wastes of the Third World.

"You're on the hook about your anarchist son Pete, aren't you?"

It was then he flung himself at me.

In the dark tavern, Pete Greaves was buying his friends one last round of drinks. He had been almost three weeks in the seedy little town, waiting for the day the frontier opened; in that time, he had got to know just about everyone in the place. All of them—not just Max Spineri who had traveled all the way from Alexandria with him—swore eternal friendship on this parting day.

"And a plague on King Cholera!" Pete said, lifting his glass.

"Better get back to the West before King Cholera visits Sicily!" a mule-driver said.

The drink was strong. Pete felt moved to make a short speech.

"I came here a stupid prig, full of all the propaganda of the West," he said. "I'm going back with open eyes. I've become a man in my year in Africa and Sicily, and back home I shall apply what I've learned."

"Here's your home now, Pete," Antonio the Barman said. "Don't go back to Pinkyland or you'll become a machine like the others there. We're your friends—stay with your friends!" But Pete noticed the crafty old devil shortchanged him.

"I've got to go back, Antonio—Max will tell you. I want to stir people up, make them listen to the truth. There's got to be change, got to be, even if we wreck the whole present setup to get it. All over Pinkyland, take my word, there are thousands—millions—of men and girls my age who hate the way things are run."

"It's the same as here!" a peasant laughed.

"Sure, but in the West, it's different. The young are tired of the pretense that we have some say in government, tired of bureaucracy, tired of a technocracy that simply reinforces the powers of the politicians. Who cares about finding life on Jupiter when life here just gets lousier!"

He saw—it had never ceased to amaze him all his time in Blackyland—that they were cool to such talk. He was on their side, as he kept telling them. Yet at best their attitude to the Whites was ambivalent: a mixture of envy and contempt for nations that they saw as slaves to consumer goods and machines.

He tried again, telling them about Student Power and the Underground, but Max interrupted him. "You have to go soon, Pete. We know how you feel. Take it easy—your people find it so hard to take it easy. Look, I've got a parting gift for you. . . ."

Drawing Pete back into a corner, he produced a gun and thrust it into his friend's hand. Examining it, Pete saw it was an ancient British Enfield revolver, well-maintained. "I can't accept this, Max!"

"Yes, you can! It's not from me but from the Organization. To help you in your revolution. It's loaded with six bullets! You'll have to hide it, because they will search you when you cross the frontier."

He clasped Max's hand. "Every bullet will count, Max!"

He trembled. Perhaps it was mainly fear of himself.

When he was far from the heat and flies and dust and his ragged unwashed friends, he would hold this present brave image of himself, and draw courage from it.

He moved out into the sun, to where Roberta Arneri stood watching the convoy assembling for the short drive to the frontier gate. He took her hand.

"You know why I have to go, Roberta?"

"You go for lots of reasons."

It was true enough. He stared into the harsh sunlight and

tried to remember. Though hatred stood between the two worlds, there were areas of weakness where they relied on each other. Beneath the hatred were ambiguities almost like love. Though a state of war existed, some trade continued. And the young could not be pent in. Every year, young Whites—"anarchists" to their seniors—slipped over the frontier with ambulances and medical supplies. And the supplies were paid for by their seniors. It was conscience money. Or hate money. A token, a symbol—nobody knew for what, though it was felt to be important, as a dream is felt to be important even when it is not comprehended.

Now he was going back. Antonio could be right. He would probably never return to the Third World; his own world would most likely make him into a machine.

But he had to bear witness. He was sixteen years old.

"Life without plumbing, life with a half full belly," he had to go home and say. "It has a savor to it. It's a positive quality. It doesn't make you less a human being. There's no particular virtue in being white of skin and fat of gut and crapping into a nice china bowl every time the laxatives take hold."

He wondered how convincing he could make it sound, back in the immense hygienic warrens of Westciv—particularly when he still longed in his inner heart for all the conveniences and privileges, and a shower every morning before a sit-down breakfast. It had all been fun, but enough was enough. More than enough, when you remembered what the plague was doing.

"You go to see again your father," Roberta diagnosed.

"Maybe. In America, we are trying to sever the ties of family. After you get through with religion you destroy the sacredness of the family. It encourages people to move to other planets, to go where they're told."

He was ashamed of saying it—and yet half proud.

"That's why you all are so nervous and want to go to war all the time. You don't get enough kisses as little kids, eh?"

"Oh, we're all one-man isolation units! Life isn't as bad as you think, up there among the wheels of progress, Roberta," he said bitterly. He kissed her, and her lips tasted of garlic.

Max slapped him on his shoulder.

"Cut all that out, fellow—you're going home! Get aboard!"

Pete climbed onto the donkey cart with another anarchist White who had recently sailed across to the island from Tunisia. Pete had arrived in the mysterious Third World driving a truck full of supplies. The truck had been stolen in Nubia, when he was down with malaria and dysentery. He was going back empty-handed. But the palms of those hands were soft no longer.

He shook Max's hand now. They looked at each other wordlessly as the cart driver goaded his animal into movement. There was affection there, yes—undying in its way, for Max was also a would-be extremist; but there was also the implacable two-way enmity that sprang up willy-nilly between Haves and Have-nots. An enmity stronger than men, incurable by men. They both dropped their gaze.

Hiding his embarrassment, Pete looked about him. In his days of waiting, the village had become absolutely familiar, from the church at one end of the broken-down bursts of cactus in between. He had savored too the pace of life here, geared to the slowest and most stupid, so that the slowest and most stupid could survive. Over the frontier, time passed in overdrive.

Across the drab stones, the hooves of the donkey made little noise. Other carts were moving forward, with dogs following, keeping close to the walls. There was a feeling— desperate and exhilarating—that they were leaving the shelter of history, and heading toward where the powerhouse of the world began.

Pete waved to Max and Roberta and the others, and squinted toward the fortifications of his own sector. The frontier stood distant but clear in the pale air. As he looked, he saw a giant comic-terror figure, twice as high as a grown man, man-plus-machine, bound across the plain toward him. Bellowing with an obscene anger as it charged, the monster appeared to burn in the sun.

It came toward him like a flaming wheel rushing down a steep hill, all-devouring.

VI. EGO. Ted Greaves was my friend of long standing. I don't know why he flung himself on me in hatred just because I taunted him about his son. For that matter, I don't know why anger suddenly blazed up in me as it did.

My last spell on CUFL had left me in relatively poor shape, but fury lent me strength. I ducked away from his first blow and chopped him hard below the heart. As he doubled forward, grunting with pain, I struck him again, this time on the jaw. He brought his right fist up and grazed my chin, but by then I was hitting him again and again. He went down.

These fits had come over me before, but not for many years. When I was aware of myself again, I was jumping into the pogo-armor, with only the vaguest recollections of what I had done to Greaves. I could recall I had let the force barrier down.

I went leaping forward toward the hated land. I could hear the gyros straining, hear my voice bellowing before me like a spinnaker.

"You killed my daughter! You killed my daughter! You shan't get in! You shan't even look in!"

I didn't know what I was about.

There were animals scattering. I overturned a cart. I was almost at the first village.

It felt as if I were running at a hundred miles an hour. Yet when the shot rang out, I stopped at once. How beautiful the hills were if one's eyes never opened and closed again. Pigeons wheeling white above tawdry roofs. People immobile. One day they would be ours, and we would take over the whole world. The whole world shook with the noise of my falling armament, and dust spinning like the fury of galaxies.

Better pain than our eternal soft predicament. . . .

I was looking at a pale-faced boy on a cart, he was staggering off the cart, the cart was going from him. People were shouting and fluttering everywhere like rags. My gaze was fixed only on him. His eyes were only on me. He had a smoking revolver in his hand.

Wonderingly, I wondered how I knew he was an American. An American who had seized Ted Greaves's face and tugged it from inside until all the wrinkles were gone from it and it looked obscenely young again. My executioner wore a mask.

A gyro labored by my head as if choked with blood. I could only look up at that mask. Something had to be said to it as it came nearer.

"It's like a Western. . . ." Trying to laugh?

Death came down from the Black hills till only his stolen eyes were left, like wounds in the universe.

They disappeared.

When the drugs revived me from my hypnoid trance, I was still plugged to CUFL, along with the eleven other members of my shift, the other slaves of the Clective Unctious.

To the medicos bending over me, I said, "I died again."

They nodded. They had been watching the monitor screens.

"Take it easy," one of them said. As my eyes pulled into focus, I saw it was Wace.

I was used to instructions. I worked at taking it easy. I was still in the front line, where individuality fought with the old nameless tribal consciousness. "I died again," I groaned.

"Relax, Jerry," Wace said. "It was just a hypnoid dream like you always get."

"But I died again. Why do I always have to die?"

Tommy Wace. His first name was Tommy. Data got mislaid.

Distantly, he tried to administer comfort and express compassion on his dried-up face. "Dreams are mythologies, part-individual, part-universal. Both de-programming dreams and prognostic-type dreams are natural functions of the self-regulating psychic system. There's nothing unnatural about dreaming of dying."

"But I died again. . . . And I was split into two people. . . ."

"The perfect defense in a split world. A form of adaptation."

You could never convey personal agony to these people, although they had watched it all on the monitors. Wearily, I passed a hand over my face. My chin felt like cactus.

"So much self-hatred, Tommy. . . . Where does it all come from?"

"Johnnie. At least you're working it out of your system. Now, here's something to drink."

I sat up. "CUFL will have to close down, Johnnie," I said. I hardly knew what I said. I was back in the real world, in the abrasive lunar laboratory under Plato—and suddenly I saw that I could distinguish true from false.

For years and years—*I'd been mistaken!*

I had been externalizing my self-hatred. The dream showed me that I feared to become whole again in case becoming whole destroyed me.

Gasping, I pushed Wace's drink aside. I was seeing visions. The White World had shed religion. Shed religion, you shed other hope-structures; family life disintegrates. You are launched to the greater structure of science. That was the Westciv way. We had made an ugly start but we were going ahead. There was no going back. The rest of the world had to follow. No—had to be led. Not shunned, but bullied. Led. Revelation!

Part of our soft predicament is that we can never entirely grasp what the predicament is.

"Johnnie, I don't always have to die," I said. "It's my mistake, our mistake!" I found I was weeping and couldn't stop. Something was dissolving. "The Black-and-White are one, not two! We are fighting ourselves. I was fighting myself. Plug me back in again!"

"End of shift," Wace said, advancing the drink again. "You've done more than your stint. Let's get you into Psych Lab for a checkup and then you're due for leave back on Earth."

"But do you see——" I gave up and accepted his beastly drink.

Natalie, Ri . . . I too have my troubled dreams, little darling. . . .

My bed is wetted and my mattress soaked with blood.

John Wace got one of the nurses to help me to my feet. Once I was moving, I could get to Psych Lab under my own power.

"You're doing fine, Jerry!" Wace called. "Next time you're back on Luna, I'll have Jupiter pinpointed for you!"

Doing fine!—I'd only just had all my strongest and most emotionally-held opinions switched through one hundred and eighty degrees!

In the Psych Lab, I was so full of tension that I couldn't let them talk. "You know what it's like, moving indistinguishably from hypnoid to dream state—like sinking down through layers of cloud. I began by reliving my last rest period with Natalie and Ri. It all came back true and sweet, without distortion, from the reservoirs of memory! Distortion only set in when I recollected landing in Sicily. What happened in reality was that Ted Greaves and I let his son back through the frontier with the other White anarchists. I found the revolver he was trying to smuggle in—he had tucked it into his boot-top.

"That revolver was the symbol that triggered my nightmare. Our lives revolve through different aspects like the phases of the Moon. I identified entirely with Pete. And at his age, I too was a revolutionary, I too wanted to change the world, I too would have wished to kill my present self!"

"At Pete Greaves's age, you were fighting *for* Westciv, not against it, Wharton," one of the psychiatrists reminded me.

"Yes," I said. "I was in Asia, and handy with a gun. I carved up a whole gang of Thirdies. That was about the time when the Russians threw in their lot with us." I didn't want to go on. I could see it all clearly. They didn't need a true confession.

"The guilt you felt in Asia was natural enough," the psychiatrist said. "To suppress it was equally natural—suppressed guilt causes most of the mental and physical sickness in the country. Since then, it has gone stale and turned to hate."

"I'll try to be a good boy in the future," I said, smiling and mock-meek. At the time, the ramifications of my remark were not apparent to me, as they were to the psychiatrist.

"You've graduated, Wharton," he said. "You're due a vacation on Earth right now."

VII. CLECTIVE. The globe, in its endless revolution, was carrying us into shade. In the courtyard, the line of the sun was high up our wall. Natalie had set a mosquito-coil burning; its fragrance came to us where we sat at the table with our beers. We bought the mosquito-coils in the local village store; they were smuggled in from the Third World, and had "Made in Cairo" stamped on the packet.

Ri was busy at one end of the courtyard with a couple of earthenware pots. She played quietly, aware that it was after her bedtime. Ted Greaves and Pete sat with us, drinking beer and smoking. Pete had not spoken a word since they arrived. At that time I could make no contact with him. Did not care to. The ice flows were still melting and smashing.

As Natalie brought out another jar and set it on the rough wood table, Greaves told her, "We're going to have a hero on our hands if your brother flies over to see you when he gets back from Jupiter. Do you think he'll show up here?"

"Sure to! Ian hates Eastern Seaboard as much as most people."

"Sounds like he found Jupiter as crowded as Eastern Seaboard!"

"We'll have the Clective Unctious working by the time he arrives," I said.

"I thought you were predicting it would close down?" Greaves said.

"That was when it was choked with hate."

"You're joking! How do you choke a machine with hate?"

"Input equals output. CUFL is a reactive store—you feed in hate, so you get out hate."

"Same applies to human beings and human groups," Pete Greaves broke in, rubbing his thumbnail along the grain of the table.

I looked at him. I couldn't feel sweet about him. He was right in what he said but I couldn't agree with him. He had killed me—though it was me masquerading as him—though it had been a hypnoid illusion.

I forced myself to say, "It's a paradox how a man can hate people he doesn't know and hasn't even seen. You can easily hate people you know—people like yourself."

Pete made no answer and wouldn't look up.

"It would be a tragedy if we started hating these creatures on Jupiter just because they are there."

I said it challengingly, but he merely shrugged. Natalie sipped her beer and watched me.

I asked him, "Do you think some of your wild friends from over the frontier would come along and feed their archetypes into CUFL? Think they could stand the pace and the journey?"

Both he and his father stared at me as if they had been struck.

Before the kid spoke, I knew I had got through to him. He would not have to go quietly schizoid. He would talk to Natalie and me eventually, and we would hear of his travels at firsthand. Just a few defensive layers had to come down first. Mine and his.

"You have to be joking!" he said.

Suddenly, I laughed. Everyone thought I was joking. Depending on your definition of a joke, I felt I had at last ceased joking after many a year. I turned suddenly from the table, to hide a burning of my eyes.

Taking Natalie by the arm, I said, "Come on, we must get Ri to bed. She thinks we've forgotten about her."

As we walked down the path, Natalie said, "Was your suggestion serious?"

"I think I can work it. I'll speak to Wace. Things have to change. CUFL is unbalanced." The finches fluttered in their cages. The line of sun was over the wall now. All was shadow among our orange trees, and the first bat was flying. I loomed over Ri before she noticed me. Startled, she stared up at me and burst into tears. Many things had to change.

I picked her up in my arms and kissed her cheeks.

Many things had to change. The human condition remained enduringly the same, but many things had to change.

Even the long nights on Earth were only local manifestations of the sun's eternal daylight. Even the different generations of man had archetypes in common, their slow writhings not merely inconsequential movement but ponderous and deliberate gesture.

So I carried her into the dim house to sleep.

AS FOR OUR
FATAL CONTINUITY...

~~~~~~~~

DAYLING, Orton Gausset (1972-1999).

In a brief transmission, scant justice can be done to this great and still controversial artist. The accompanying holograms will convey Dayling's outstanding qualities better than words.

Illusion and dissolution mark the stamp of his mind. During the last period of his life, Dayling believed himself to be alone in the world, and to have been appointed custodian of the city of Singapore, which he spoke of as one of the world's deserted cities on which the tide was fast encroaching.

His mother was the noted biophysicist, Mary May Dayling. His father was killed in a traffic accident on the day of his birth. Perhaps it was this ill chance, coupled with a peculiar cast of mind, that caused him to become obsessed with the last words of dying men. He came to them, as he came to art and love, precociously early; last words form the titles of all his creations. Once he had access to his mother's artcomputer terminal at the age of five, creation seems to have been a continuouus process with him, at least until the lost years of his middle period.

His first great work,
The Sun, My Dear, the Sun is God,
dates from 1979. Its contrapuntal sets of interwoven structures culminating in an attenuated parallelism is a gesture toward representation which seldom recurs—Dayling's is the art of a world beyond mundane perception. Although the work is not well-integrated, its daring and light remain attractive and, in its overall spiral movement, it stands as a

fitting statement on the painter Turner, whose last words
contribute the title and whose life inspired the young Dayling.
More Light, More Light

Goethe's last words, and related schematically to the item
above. More ambitious, less intense, already showing a fine
awareness for the new language Dayling was creating. It
points its way gropingly toward
Give Dayrolles a Chair

indisputably an early masterpiece, with its mobile nonrepeat-
ing series of peripheral lights and the first use of that central
darkness—speaking of radiance as well as gloom—which later
becomes a feature of Dayling's work. No reference here to
the external world, unless it be to the basic formal structures
of physical phenomena themselves. A certain delicacy about
the entire composition reminds us that the words were spoken
by the dying Lord Chesterfield.
I Have Been a Most Unconscionable Time A-Dying

This work is also known as *Open the Curtains that I May
Once More See Daylight,* apparently through some confusion
over what the last words of King Charles II actually were.
The former title is certainly to be preferred, since this
work marks the end of the first stage of Dayling's career;
like the three works preceding, it has as its theme light, and
the rioting radials suggest a variety of diffusions of light.
From now on, the works become more vigorous and coarser,
as Dayling masters his life and his medium, beginning with
the almost Rabelaisian account of
I Could Do with One of Bellamy's Meat Pies

said to be the last words of one of England's great prime
ministers, William Pitt the Younger. Dayling's amazing
tumescent forms enter for the first time, as yet not dominant,
but certainly in the ascendant. This is a large work, almost
the size of the Houses of Parliament, with which it has
sometimes jocularly been compared, and for durability
Dayling and the computer used daylite, a plastic of their own
devising with a semifluid core. With daylite, the famous
"molten look" was developed, so that in some of the later
works in this series, such as the
*I Wish the Whole Human Race Had One Neck and I Had
My Hands Around It,* based on the words of the mass-mur-
derer Carl Panzram, the *If This is Life, Roll on Germ Warfare,* of the Scottish Patriot McGuffie, and the
Of Course the Confounded Goat Was an Exaggeration of
the painter Holman Hunt, one cannot tell whether the forms
emerge from obscurity and formlessness or are being pressed

back into obscurity and formlessness. Perhaps it is because of this sense of what one critic, Andre Prederast, has called "cellular oppression" that Dayling has been spoken of as a latter-day Rodin; but Rodin dominated his sculpture; the tentative statement of
As to Which End of the Bed is Which . . . would be beyond him. Dayling's morbid preoccupation with death and his sense of humor combined, are complementary, and force him to work always on the verge of disintegration, at the point at which being becomes nonbeing. Although his approach could scarcely be called scientific, the extent to which he was conversant with current scientific theory is generally apparent, not least in *As to Which End of the Bed is Which. . .* , where the strange tumescent forms of *Bellamy's Meat Pies* have transformed themselves into clouds of virus, life and nonlife, fitting symbols of this terminal art.

No artist's art stands apart from his life. At this period, Dayling's love-group broke dramatically apart. The three males and two females who comprised the group had lived in equipoise for some eight years. Dayling suddenly found himself alone.

Now follow the somewhat mysterious years of wandering, when little is known of Dayling's life beyond the facts that he subjected himself to the hallucinatory drug DXB and underwent five years in suspended animation in a clinic in Canton. For the rest, he appeared not to have gone near a computer terminal. His only work from these lost years* is *I've Had Eighteen Straight Whiskies—I Think that's the Record* registered from a monastery in the Sanjak in Yugoslavia. Based on the last words of the Welsh poet Dylan Thomas, this small block shows no development and generally marks a return to the more formal tone of *Give Dayrolles a Chair*.

Only in 1995 did Dayling emerge again; he had but four years to live. He was in his twenty-third year and had had both legs and one arm amputated, the better, he said, to concentrate on his art. He settled in Bombay, under the firm impression that it was Singapore. Despite such delusions, his mind was creatively clear enough, and he set to again wholeheartedly, living in a deserted government office, the complete solitary, though in an overpopulated city, seen only when he made an occasional midnight march on cybolegs to

---

*The once accepted *Madame, Please Remove Your Lipstick, I Can Hardly Hear You* is now known to be a forgery.

stare out over the sea, which he believed to be moving in over the land.

His method of work was now more brutal than before. He worked on the daylite himself, leaving the computer to copy the results, to change and eradicate according to open programming. Thus, he was working not with light but with the material itself—a reversion in technique, perhaps, but one which yielded its own unique results. There may always be an area of discussion centering on these last desperate works. Was this reversion a sign of Dayling's failure to adjust to himself and his times? Or is the reversion merely to be regarded as a substitution, remembering that Dayling is the great transition figure, the last major artist spanning the days of the biological revolution, the last major artist to work in inorganic material?

However we answer such questions, there is no disputing the maimed vigor of Dayling's output in his final years: *One World at a Time; On the Whole, I'd Rather Be in Philadelphia; Make My Skin into Drumheads for the Bohemian Cause;* and *As for Our Fatal Continuity.* . . . These are small works, small, dense, and ruinous. All of them speak of fatal discontinuities. All of them have formed the basis since for countless experiments into the new media of semi-sentience.

It may be, as Torner Mallard has claimed, that these final works of Dayling's mark the demise of a too-long sustained system of aesthetics going back as far as Classical Greece, and the beginning of a new and more biologically-based structure; certainly we can see that, in the Dadaist titles, as well as in the works themselves, Dayling was undergoing a pre-post-modernist purgation of outworn attitudes, and carrying art forward from the aesthetic arena of balance and proportion to the knife-edge between existence and nonexistence.

In his reckless sweeping away of all the inessential props of life, Dayling—by which of course we mean Dayling-And-Art-Computer—takes the bone-bare universe of Samuel Beckett a stage further; humor and death contemplate each other across a tumbled void. Only the grin of the Cheshire Cat is left, fading above Valhalla.

From *Sculpting Your Own Semi-Sentients:* A Primer for Boys and Girls. By Gutrud Slayne Laboratories.

SEND HER VICTORIOUS

OR,

THE WAR AGAINST THE VICTORIANS, 2000 A.D.

The news hit New York in time to feature in the afternoon editions. No editor splashed it very large, but there it was, clear enough on the front pages:

MANY DEATHS IN CASTLE CATASTROPHE

and

QUEEN'S HOME GONE

and

BRITIAN'S ENEMIES STRIKE?

Douglas Tredeager Utrect bought two papers as he fought his way to the Lexington Advanced Alienation Hospital, where he was currently engaged as Chief Advisor. The news did not tell him as much as he wished to know, which he found was generally the way with news. In particular, it did not mention his English friend, Bob Hoggart.

All that was said was that, during the early afternoon, a tremendous explosion which might be the work of hostile foreign powers had obliterated the grounds of the royal park of Windsor, Berkshire, England, and carried away most of Windsor Castle at the same time. Fortunately, the Queen was not in residence. Fifty-seven people were missing, believed killed, and the death roll was mounting. The Army was mobilizing and the British Cabinet was meeting to discuss the situation.

Utrect had no time to worry over the matter, deeply though it concerned him. As soon as he entered his office in the Advanced Alienation Hospital, he was buttonholed by Dr. Froding.

"Ah, Utrect, there you are! Your severe dissociation case, Burton. He attacked the nurse! Quite inexplicable in such a quiet patient—rather, only explicable as anima-hostility, which hardly fits with his other behavior. Will you come to see him?"

Utrect was always reluctant to see Burton. It alarmed him to discover how attracted he was by the patient's psychotic fantasy world. But Froding was not only a specialist on the anima; he was a forceful man. Nodding, Utrect followed him along the corridor, thrusting his moody reindeer's face forward as if scenting guilt and danger.

Burton sat huddled in one corner of his room—a characteristic pose. He was a pale slight man with a beard. This appeared to be one of the days when his attention was directed to the real world; his gestures toward it were courtly, and included the weariness which is so often a part of courtliness, although here it seemed more, Utrect thought, as if the man were beckoning distantly, and part of him issuing fading calls for help. Don't we all? he thought.

"We are pleased to receive your majesty," Burton said, indicating the chair, secured to the floor, on which Utrect might sit. "And how is the Empress today?"

"She is away at present," Utrect said. He nodded toward Froding, who nodded back and disappeared.

"Ah, absent, is she? Absent at present. Traveling again, I suppose. A beautiful woman, the Empress, your majesty, but we must recognize that all her traveling is in the nature of a compulsion."

"Surely, Herr Freud; but, if we may, I would much rather discuss your own case. In particular, I would like to know why you attacked your nurse."

Burton looked conspiratorial. "This Vienna of ours, your majesty, is full of revolutionaries these days. You must know that. Croats, Magyars, Bohemians—there is no end to them. This nurse girl was hoping to get at your majesty through me. She was in the pay of Serbian assassins."

He was convinced that he was Sigmund Freud, although, with his small stature and little copper-colored beard, he looked more like Algernon Charles Swinburne, the Victorian poet. He was convinced that Utrect was the Emperor Franz Josef of Austria. This confused mental state alternated with periods of almost complete catatonia. Year by year, the world's mental illnesses were growing more complex, spiraling toward ultimate uterine mindlessness, as the ever-expanding population radiated high dosages of psychic interference on all sides.

Although Burton's case was only one among many, its fascination-repulsion for Utrect was unique, and connected, directly but at a subrational level, with the commission on which he had sent Bob Hoggart to London, England. Many were the nights he had sat with Burton, humoring the man in his role, listening to his account of life in Vienna in the Nineteenth Century.

As a result, Utrect knew Vienna well. Without effort, he could hear the clatter of coaches in the streets, could visit the opera or the little coffee houses, could feel the crosscurrents that drifted through the capital of the Habsburgs from all corners of Europe. In particular, he could enter the houses, the homes. There was one home he loved, where he had seen a beautiful girl with a peacock feather; there, the walls were clear-colored and plain, and the rooms light with dark-polished pieces of furniture. But he knew also the crowded homes of Freud's acquaintances, had made his way toward overstuffed horsehair sofas, knocking a Turkish rug from an occasional table, brushed past potted palms and ferns. He had sat and stared at dim volumes, too heavy to hold, which contained steel engravings of customs in the Bavarian Alps or scenes from the Khedive's Egypt. He had seen Johannes Brahms at a reception, listened to recitals of the Abbé Liszt and the waltzes of Johann Strauss. He knew —seemed to know—Elizabeth of Austria, Franz Josef's beautiful but unhappy wife, and occasionally found himself identifying her with his own doomed wife, Karen. He felt himself entirely at home in that distant Victorian world—far more at home than an alienist with an international reputation in the year 2000 should be.

This afternoon, as Burton rambled on about treason and conspiracies at court, Franz Josef's attention wandered. He had an illusion much greater than one man's madness to diagnose. He knew that he, his companions, his ailing wife, the great bustling world, faced imminent disaster. But he continued to dispense automatic reassurance, while sustaining the role of the Emperor.

As he left Burton at last, Froding happened to be passing along the corridor. "Does he seem disturbed?"

"I cannot make sense of the fellow," Utrect said. Then he recalled himself. He was not the Emperor, and must not talk like him. "Er—he is quiet at present, probably moving toward withdrawal. Pulse rate normal. See that he is monitored on 'A' Alert tonight."

Dismissing Froding rather curtly, he hurried to his office. He could catch a news bulletin in four minutes. He flicked on the desk 3V and opened up his wrisputer, feeding it the nugatory data contained in the paper report on Windsor Castle. He added to the little computer, "More details when the newscast comes up. Meanwhile, Burton. He attacked his nurse, Phyllis. In his Freud persona, he claims that she was a revolutionary. Revolution seems to be dominating his thinking these days. He also claims an anti-Semitic conspiracy against him at the university. Multi-psychotic complex of persecution-theme. Indications his mental condition is deteriorating."

Switching off for a moment, Utrect swallowed a pacifier. Everyone's mental condition was deteriorating as the environment deteriorated. Burton had simply been cheated out of the presidency of a little tin-pot society he had founded; that had been enough to topple him over the brink. Utrect dismissed the man from his mind.

He ignored the adverts scampering across the 3V screen and glanced over the routine daily bulletins of the hospital piled on his desk. Under the new Dimpsey Brain Pressure ratings, the figures in all wards were up at least .05 over the previous day. They had been increasing steadily, unnervingly, for a couple of years, but this was the biggest jump yet. The World Normality Norm had been exceeded once more; it would have to be bumped up officially again before alarm spread. By the standards of the early nineties, the whole world was crazy; by the standards of the seventies, it was one big madhouse. There were guys now running banking houses, armies, even major industries, who were proven around the bend in one or more (generally many more) of three thousand two hundred and six Dimpsey ways. Society was doing its best to come to terms with its own madness: more than one type of paranoia was held to be an inescapable qualification for promotion in many business organizations.

The oily voice seeping from the 3V screen asked, "Ever feel this busy world is too much for you? Ever want to scream in the middle of a crowd? Ever want to murder everyone else in your apartment building? Just jab a Draculin. . . . Suddenly, you're all alone. . . ! Just jab a Draculin. . . . Remember, when you're feeling overpopulated, just jab a Draculin. . . . Suddenly, you're all alone!" Drug-induced catatonia was worth its weight in gold these days.

Struggling under all his responsibilities, acknowledged or secret, Utrect could admit to the fascination of that oily siren voice. He was burdened with too many roles. Part of his morbid attraction to the Burton case lay in the fact that he liked being Franz Josef, married to the beautiful Elizabeth. It was the most restful part of his existence!

The oily voice died, the news flared. Utrect switched on his wrisputer to record. A picture of Windsor Castle as it had been intumesced from the 3V confronted Utrect. He stared tensely, omitting to blink, as shots of the disaster came up. There was very little left of the residence of the anachronistic British sovereigns, except for one round tower. The demolition was amazing and complete. No rubble was left, no dust: just level ground where the building and part of the town had been.

The commentator said, "The historic castle was only on the fringe of a wide area of destruction. Never before has one blow destroyed so much of the precious British heritage. Historic Eton College, for centuries the breeding ground of future aristocrats, has been decimated. Shrine of world-famous historic Nineteenth Century Queen Victoria, at Frogmore, situated one mile southeast of the castle, was wiped out completely."

Bob Hoggart! I sent you to your death! Utrect told himself. He switched off, unwilling to listen to the fruitless discussion about which enemy nation might have knocked off the castle; *he* knew what had wrought the terrible destruction.

"Hoggart," he said to the wrisputer. "You have a record of his probable movements at the time when disaster struck Windsor. What are your findings?"

The little machine said, "Hoggart was scheduled to spend day working at Royal Mausoleum and—to cover his main activity—investigating nearby cemetery adjoining mausoleum, in which lesser royalties are buried. At time destruction happened, Hoggart may have been actually at Royal Mausoleum. Prediction of probability of death, based on partial data: fifty-six point nine percent."

Burying his face in his hands, Utrect said, "Bob's dead, then. . . . My fault. . . . My guilt, my eternal damned guilt. . . . A murderer—worse than a murderer! Hoggart was just a simple but courageous little shrine-restorer, no more. Yet subconsciously I maneuvered him into a position where he was certain to meet his death. Why? Why? Why do I actually hate a man I thought I really liked? Some unconscious homosexual tendencies maybe, which had to be killed?" He sat up. "Pull yourself together, Douglas! You are slumping into algolagnic depression, accentuated by that recurrent guilt syndrome of yours. Hoggart was a brave man, yes; you ordered him to go to Windsor, yes; but you in turn had your orders from the PINCS. There is no blame. These are desperate times. Hoggart died for the world—as the rest of us will probably do. Besides, he may not be dead after all. I must inform PINCS. Immediately."

One thing at least was clear, one thing at least stood out in fearful and uncompromising hues: the universe lay nearer to the brink of disaster than ever before. The dreaded Queen Victoria had struck and might be about to strike again.

The United States, in the year 2000, was riddled with small and semi-secret societies. All of its four hundred million inhabitants belonged to at least one such society; big societies like the Anti-Procreation League; small ones, like the Sons of Alfred Bester Incarnate; crazy ones, like the Ypslanti Horse-Hooves-and-All-Eating Enclave; dedicated ones, like the Get Staft; religious ones, like the Man's Dignity and Mulattodom Shouting Church; sinister ones, like the Impossible Smile; semi-scholarly ones, like the Freud in His Madness Believers, which the insane Burton had founded; save-the-world ones, like All's Done In Oh One Brotherhood.

It was in the last category that the Philadelphia Institute for Nineteenth Century Studies belonged. Behind the calm and donnish front of PINCS, a secret committee worked, a committee comprising only a dozen men drawn from the highest and most influential ranks of cosmopolitan society. Douglas Tredeager Utrect was the humblest member of this committee; the humblest, and yet his aim was theirs, his desire burned as fiercely as theirs: to unmask and if possible annihilate the real Queen Victoria.

Committee members had their own means of communication. Utrect left the Advanced Alienation Hospital and headed for the nearest call booth, plunging through the crowded streets, blindly pushing forward. He was wearing his elbow guards but, even so, the sidewalk was almost unendurable. The numbers of unemployed in New York City were so great, and the space in their overcrowded flats and rooms so pronounced, that half the family at any one time found life more tolerable just padding around the streets.

To Utrect's disgust, a married couple, the woman with an eighteen-month-old child still being breast-fed, had moved into the call booth; they were employees of the phone company and had evidence of legal residence. However, since Utrect could show that this was an hour when he could legitimately make a call, they had to turn out while he dialed.

He got three wrong numbers before Disraeli spoke on the other end. The visiscreen remained blank; it was in any case obscured by a urine-soaked child's nightshirt. Disraeli was a PINCS' code name; Utrect did not know the man's real one. Sometimes, he suspected it was none other than the President of the United States himself.

"Florence Nightingale here." Utrect said, identifying himself, and said no more. He had already primed his wrisputer. It uttered a scream lasting point six of a second.

A moment's silence. A scream came back from Disraeli's end. Utrect hung up and fled, leaving the family to take possession again.

To get himself home fast, he called a rickshaw. Automobiles had been banned from the city center for a decade now; rickshaws provided more work for more people. Of course, you had to be Caucasian Protestant to qualify for one of the coveted rickshaw-puller's licenses.

He was lucky to qualify for a luxury flat. He and his wife, Karen, had three rooms on the twenty-fifth floor of the Hiram Bucklefeather Building—high enough to evade some of the stink and noise of the streets. The elevator generally functioned, too. Only the central heating had failed; and that would have been no bother in mild fall weather had not Karen been cyanosis-prone.

She was sitting reading, huddled in an old fur coat, as Utrect entered the flat.

"Darling, I love you!" she said dimly, glancing up, but marking her place on the page with a bluish fingertip. "I've missed you so."

"And me you." He went to wash his hands at the basin, but the water was off.

"Have a busy day, darling?" At least she pretended to be interested.

"Sure." She was already deep back in—he saw the title because she, as undeviatingly intellectual now as the day he married her, held it so that he might see—*Symbolic Vectors in Neurasthenic Emotional Stimuli.* He made a gesture toward kissing the limp hair on her skull.

"Good book?"

"Mm. Absorbing." Invalidism had sapped her ability to tell genuine from false. Maybe the only real thing about us is our pretenses, Utrect thought. He patted Karen's shoulder; she smiled without looking up.

Cathie was in the service-room-cum-bedroom, sluggishly preparing an anemic-looking piece of meat for their supper. She was no more substantial than Karen, but there was a toughness, a masculine core, about her, emphasized by her dark skin and slight, downy moustache. Occasionally, she showed a sense of humor. Utrect patted her backside; it was routine.

She smiled. "Meat stinks of stilbestrol these days."

"I didn't think stilbestrol had any odor."

"Maybe it's the stilbestrol stinks of meat."

They'd done OK, he thought as he locked himself in the bathroom-toilet. They'd done OK. With his two sons, Caspar and Nero, they were a household of five, minimum number in relation to floor space enforced by the housing regulations. Karen and Cathie had enjoyed a Lesbian relationship since graduate days, so it was natural to have Cathie move in with them. Give her her due, she integrated well. She was an asset. Nor was she adverse to letting Utrect explore her hard little body now and then.

He dismissed such sympathetic thoughts and turned his attention to the wrisputer, which slowed Disraeli's phoned scream and retransmitted it as a comprehensible message.

"Whetther or not Robert Hoggart managed to fulfill his mission at the Windsor mausoleum is immaterial. Its sudden destruction is conclusive proof that he, and we, were on the right track with our Victoria hypothesis. We now operate under Highest Emergency conditions. Secret PINCS messengers are already informing Pentagon in Washington and our allies in the Kremlin in Moscow. Now that the entity known as Queen Victoria has revealed her hand like this, she will not hesitate to distort the natural order again. The fact that she has not struck until this minute seems to indicate that she is not omniscient, so we stand a chance. But clearly PINCS is doomed if she has discovered our secret. You will stand by for action, pending word from Washington and Moscow. Stay at home and await orders. Out."

As he switched off, Utrect was trembling. He switched on again, getting the wrisputer to launch into a further episode of the interminable pornographic story it had been spinning

Utrect for years; it was a great balance-restorer; but at that moment there was a banging at the toilet door, and he was forced to retreat.

He was a man alone. The Draculin situation, he thought wryly. Alone, and hunted. He looked up at the seamed ceiling apprehensively. That terrible entity they called Queen Victoria could strike through there, at any time.

The sons came home from work, Caspar first, thin, strawy, colorless save for the acne rotting his cheeks. Even his teeth looked gray. He was silent and nervous. Nero came in, two years the younger, as pallid as his brother, blackheads and adolescent pimples rising like old burial mounds from the landscape of his face. He was as talkative as Caspar was silent. Grimly, Utrect ignored them. He had some thinking to do. Eventually, he retreated into the shower, sitting on the cold tiles. Queen Victoria might not see him there.

The evening dragged by. He was waiting for something and did not know what, although he fancied it was the end of the world.

The doomed life of the place slithered past. Utrect wondered why most of the tenants of the Hiram Bucklefeather Building had harsh voices. He could hear them through the walls, calling, swearing, suffering. Cathie and Karen were playing cards. At least the Utrect apartment preserved reasonable quiet.

Utrect's sons, heads together, indulged in their new hobby. They had joined the Shakespeare-Spelling Society. Their subscription entitled them to a kit. They had built the kit into an elaborate rat-educator. Two rats lived in the educator; they had been caught in the corridor. The rats had electrodes implanted in the pleasure centers of their brains. They were desperate for this pleasure and switched on the current themselves; when it was on, the happy creatures fed themsleves up to seven shocks a second, their pink paws working the switches in a frenzy of delight.

But the current was available only when the rats spelled the name SHAKESPEARE correctly. For each of the eleven letters the rats had a choice of six letters on a faceted drum. The letters they chose were flashed onto a little screen outside the educator. The rats knew what they were doing, but, in their haste to get the coveted shock, they generally misspelled, particularly toward the end of the word. Caspar and Nero tittered together as the mistakes flashed up.

THAMEZPEGPE

SHAKESPUNKY

SRAKISDOARI

The Utrect tribe ate their stilbestrol steak. Since the water supply was on, Karen washed up, wearing her coat still. Utrect had thought he might take a walk when the pedestrians thinned a little, despite PINCS' orders, but it was too late now. The hoods were out there, making the night unsafe even for each other. Every eight days, New York City needed one new hospital, just to cope with night injuries, said the statistics.

MHAKERPEGRE

SHAKESPEAVL

Utrect could have screamed. The rats played on his latent claustrophobia. Yet he was diverted despite himself, abandoning thought, watching the crazy words stumble across the screen. He thought as he had often thought: supposing man did not run the goddamned rats? Supposing the goddamned rats ran men? There were reckoned to be between three and four million people already in the Shakespeare-Spelling Society. Supposing the rats were secretly working away down there to make men mad, beaming these crazy messages at men which men were forced to read and try to make some sort of meaning of? When everyone was mad, the rats would take over. They were taking over already, enjoying their own population explosion, disease-transmitting but disease-resistant. As it was, the rats had fewer illusions than the boys. Caspar and Nero had a rat-educator; therefore they believed they were educating rats.

SIMKYSPMNVE

SHAKESPEARE

The Bard's name stayed up in lights when the rodents hit the current-jackpot and went on a pleasure binge, squealing with pleasure, rolling on their backs showing little white thighs as the current struck home. Utrect refused to deflect his thoughts as Cathie and the boys crowded around to watch. Even if these rats were under man's surveillance, they were not interfered with by man once the experiment was set up. The food that appeared in their hoppers must seem to do so by natural law to them, just as the food thrusting out of the ground came by a natural law to mankind. Supposing man's relationship to Queen Victoria was analogous to the rats' relationship to man? Could they possibly devise some system to drive *her* crazy, until she lost control of her experiment?

CLUKYZPEGPY

Pleasure was brief, sorrow long, in this vale of rodential tears. Now the creatures had to pick up the pieces and begin again. They had always forgotten after the pleasure-bout.

DRALBUCEEVE

The family all slept in the same room since Utrect had caught the boys indulging in forbidden activity together. Their two hammocks now swung high over the bed in which the women slept. Utrect had his folding bunk by the door, against the cooker. Often, he did not sleep well, and could escape into the living room. Tonight, he knew, he would not sleep.

He dreamed he was in the Advanced Alienation Hospital. He was going to see Burton, pushing through the potted palms to get to the patient. An elderly man was sitting with Burton; Burton introduced him as his superior, Professor Krafft-Ebing of Vienna University.

"Delighted," Utrect murmured.

"Clukyzpegpy," said the professor. "And dralbuceeve."

What a thing to say to an Emperor!

Groaning, Utrect awoke. These crazy dreams! Maybe he was going mad; he knew his Dimpseys were already pushing the normality norm. Suddenly it occurred to him that the whole idea of Queen Victoria's being a hostile entity in a different dimension was possibly an extended delusion, in which the other members of PINCS conspired. A mother-fear orgy. A multiple mother-fear orgy—induced by the maternal guilt aspects of overpopulation. He lay there, trying to sort fantasy from reality, although convinced that no man had ever managed the task to date. Well, Jesus, maybe; but if the Queen Victoria hypothesis was correct, then Jesus never existed. All was uncertain. One thing was clear, the inevitable chain of events. If the hypothesis was correct, then it could never have been guessed earlier in the century, when normality norms were lower. Overpopulation had brought universal neurosis; only under such conditions could men reasonably work on so untenable a theory.

The Cheyne-Stokes breathing of his wife came to him, now laboring heavily and noisily, now dying away altogether. Poor dear woman, he thought; she had never been entirely well; even now, she was not entirely ill. In somewhat the same way, he had never loved her wholeheartedly; but even now, he had not ceased to love her entirely.

174 Brian W. Aldiss

Tired though he was, her frightening variations of breathing
would not let him rest. He got up, wrapped a blanket around
himself, and padded into the next room. The rats were still at
work. He looked down at them.

SLALEUPEAKE

SLAKBUDDDVS

Sometimes, he tried to fathom how their sick little brains
were working. The Shakespeare-Spelling Society issued a
monthly journal, full of columns of misspellings of the Bard's
name sent in by readers; Utrect pored over them, looking for
secret messages directed at him. Sometimes the rodents in their
educator seemed to work relaxedly, as if they knew the desired word was bound to come up after a certain time. On
other occasions, they threw up a bit of wild nonsense, as if
they were not trying, or were trying to cure themselves of
the pleasure habit.

DOAKERUGAPE

FISMERAMNIS

Yes, like that, you little wretches, he thought.
The success of the Shakespeare-Spelling Society had led
to imitations, the All-American-Spelling, the Rat-Thesaurus-
Race, the Anal-Oriented-Spelling, and even the Disestablish-
mentarianism-Spelling Society. Rats were at work everywhere,
ineffectually trying to communicate with man. The deluxe
kits had chimps instead of rats.

SHAPESCUNRI

SISEYSPEGRE

Tiredly, Utrect wondered if Disraeli might signal to him
through the tiny screen.

DISPRUPEARS

The exotic words flickered above his head. He slept, skull
resting on folded arms, folded arms resting on table.
Burton was back as Freud, no longer disconsolate as the
sacked president of the Freud in His Madness Believers but
arrogant as the arch-diagnoser of private weaknesses. Utrect
sat with him, smoking in a smoking jacket on a scarlet plush
sofa. It was uncertain whether or not he was Franz Josef.
There were velvet curtains everywhere, and the closed sweet
atmosphere of a high-class brothel. A trio played sugary
music; a woman with an immense bust came and sang a

poem of Grillparzer's. It was Vienna again, in the fictitious Nineteenth Century.

Burton/Freud said, "You are sick, Doctor Utrect, or else why should you visit this church?"

"It's not a church." He got up to prove his point, and commenced to peer behind the thick curtains. Behind each one, naked couples were copulating, though the act seemed curiously indistinct and not as Utrect had visualized it. Each act diminished him; he grew smaller and smaller. "You're shrinking because you think they are your parents," Burton/Freud said superciliously.

"Nonsense," Utrect said loudly, now only a foot high. "That could only be so if your famous theory of psychoanalysis were true."

"If it isn't true, then why are you secretly in love with Elizabeth of Austria?"

"She's dead, stabbed in Geneva by a mad assassin. You'll be saying next I wish I'd stabbed my mother, or similar nonsense."

"You said it—I didn't!"

"Your theories only confuse matters."

An argument developed. He was no higher than Freud's toecap now. He wanted to pop behind a pillar and check to see if he was not also changing sex.

"There is no such thing as the subconscious," he declared. Freud was regarding him now through pink reflecting glasses, just like the ones Utrect's father had worn. Indeed, it came as no surprise to see that Freud, now sitting astride a gigantic smiling sow, *was* his father. Far from being nonplussed, the manikin pressed his argument even more vigorously.

"We have no subconscious. The Nineteenth Century is our subconscious, and you stand as our guardian to it. The Nineteenth Century ended in 1901 with the death of Queen Victoria. And of course it did not really exist, or all the past ages in which we have been made to believe. They are memories grafted on, supported by fake evidence. The world was invented by the Queen in 1901—as she has us call that moment of time."

Since he had managed to tell the truth in his dream, he began to grow again. But the hairy creature before him said, "If the Nineteenth Century is your subconscious, what acts as the subconscious of the Victorians?"

Utrect looked about among the potted palms, and whispered. "As *we* had to invent mental science, *you* had to invent the prehistoric past—that's your subconscious, with its great bumping monsters!"

And Burton was nodding and saying, "He's quite right, you know. It's all a rather clumsy pack of lies."

But Utrect had seen that the potted palms were in fact growing out of the thick carpets, and that behind the curtains stalked great unmentionable things. The velvet drapes bulged ominously. A great stegosaurus, lumbering, and rounder than he could have imagined, plodded out from behind the sofa. He ran for his life, hearing its breathing rasp behind him. Everything faded, leaving only the breathing, that painful symptom of anemia, the Cheyne-Stokes exhalations of his wife in the next room. Utrect sprawled in his chair, tranquil after the truth-bringing nightmare, thinking that they (Queen Victoria) had not worked skillfully enough. The mental theories of 2000 were organized around making sense of the mad straggle of contradiction in the human brain. In fact, only the Queen Victoria hypothesis accounted for the contradictions. They were the scars left when the entirely artificial setup of the world was commenced at the moment they perforce called 1901. Mankind was not what it seemed; it was a brood of rats with faked memories, working in some gigantic educator experiment.

SHAKESPEGRL

SHAKERPEAVE

Like the rats, he felt himself near to the correct solution. Yes! Yes, by God! He stood up, almost guilty, smiling, clutching the blanket to his chest. Obviously, analytic theory, following the clues in the scarred mind, could lead to the correct solution, once one had detected the 1901 barrier. And he saw! He knew! They were all cavemen, stone age men, primitive creatures, trying to learn—what?—for the terrible woman in charge of this particular experiment. Didn't all mental theory stress the primitive side of the mind? Well, they *were* primitive! As primitive and out of place as a stegosaurus in a smoking room.

SHAKESPEARL

Shakespearls before swine, he thought. He must cast his findings before PINCS before *She* erased him from the experiment. Now that he *knew,* the Queen would try to kill him as she had Hoggart.

There it was again. . . . He went to the outer door. He had detected a slight sound. Someone was outside the flat, listening, waiting. Utrect's mind pictured many horrible things. The stegosaurus was lying in wait, maybe.

"Douglas?" Dinosaurs didn't talk.

"Who is it?" They were whispering through the hinge.

"Me. Bob, Bob Hoggart!"

Shaking, Utrect opened up. Momentary glimpse of dim-lit corridor with homeless people snoozing in corners, then Hoggart was in. He looked tired and dirty. He staggered over to the table and sat down, his shoulders slumping. The polished restorations expert looked like a fugitive from justice.

SHAMIND

Utrect cut off the rats' source of light.

"You shouldn't have come here!" he said. "She'll destroy this building—maybe the whole of New York!"

Hoggart read the hostility and fear in Utrect's expression.

"I had to come, Florence Nightingale! I jumped a jumbojet from London. I had to bring the news home personally."

"We thought you were dead. PINCS thinks you're dead."

"I very nearly am dead. What I saw . . . give me a drink, for God's sake! What's that noise?"

"Quiet! It's my wife breathing. Don't rouse her. She suffers from hemoglobin-deficiency with some other factors that haven't yet been diagnosed. One of these new diseases they can't pin down—"

"I didn't ask for a case history. Where's that drink?" Hoggart had lost his English calm. He looked every inch a man that death had marked.

"What have you found?"

"Never mind that now! Give me a drink."

As he drank the alcohol-and-water that Utrect brought him, Hoggart said, "You heard she blasted the mausoleum and half Windsor out of existence? That was a panic move on her part—proves she's human, in her emotions at least. She was after me, of course."

"The tomb, man—what did you find?"

"By luck, one of the guards happened to recognize me from an occasion when I was restoring another bit of architecture where he had worked before. So he left me in peace, on my own. I managed to open Queen Victoria's tomb, as we planned."

"Yes! And?"

"As we thought!"

"Empty?"

"Empty! Nothing. So we have our proof that the Queen, as history knows her—our fake history—does not exist."

"Another of her botches, eh? Like the Piltdown Man and the Doppler Shift and the tangle of nonsense we call Relativity. Obvious frauds! So she's clever, but not all that clever. Look, Bob, I want to get you out of here. I'm afraid this place will be struck out like Windsor at any minute. I must think of my wife."

"OK. You know where we must go, don't you?" He stood up, straightening his shoulders.

"I shall phone Disraeli and await instructions. One thing— how come you escaped the Windsor blast?"

"That I can't really understand. Different time scales possibly, between her world and ours? Directly I saw the evidence of the tomb, I ran for it, got into my car, drove like hell. The blast struck almost exactly an hour after I opened the tomb. I was well clear of the area by then. Funny she was so unpunctual. I've been expecting another blast ever since."

Utrect was prey to terrible anxiety. His fingers trembled convulsively as he switched off his wrisputer, in which this conversation was now recorded. Before this building was destroyed, with Karen and all the innocent people in it, he had to get Hoggart and himself away. Grabbing his clothes, he dressed silently, nodding a silent good-bye to his wife. She slept with her mouth open, respiration now very faint. Soon, he was propelling Hoggart into the stinking corridor and down into the night. It was two-thirty in the morning, the time when human resistance was lowest. He instinctively searched the sky for a monstrous regal figure.

Strange night cries and calls sounded in the canyons of the streets. Every shadow seemed to contain movement. Poverty and the moral illness of poverty settled over everything, could almost be felt; the city was an analogue of a sick subconscious. Whatever her big experiment was, Utrect thought, it sure as hell failed. The cavemen were trying to make this noble city as much like home territory as they could. Their sickness (could be it was just homesickness?) hung in the soiled air.

By walking shoulder-to-shoulder, flick-knives at the alert, Utrect and Hoggart reached the nearby call booth without incident.

"Night emergency!" Utrect said, flinging open the door. The little family were sleeping in papoose hammocks, hooked up behind their shoulder blades, arms to their sides, like three great chrysalids. They turned out, sleepy and protesting. The child began to howl as its parents dragged it onto the chilly sidewalk.

Hoggart prepared a wrisputer report as Utrect dialed Disraeli. When his superior's throaty voice came up—again no vision—Hoggart let him have the scream. After a pause for encoding, another scream came from the other end. The wrisputer decoded it. They had to state present situation. When they had done this, a further scream came back. The matter was highest priority. They would be picked up outside the booth in a couple of minutes.

"Can we come back in, mister? The kid's sick!"

Utrect knew how the man felt.

As they bundled in, Utrect asked, "When are you getting a real place?"

"Any year now, they say. But the company's agreed to heat the booth this winter, so it won't be so bad."

We all have blessings to count, Utrect thought. Until the experiment is called off. . . .

He and Hoggart stood outside, back to back. A dark shape loomed overhead. A package was lowered. It contained two face masks. Quickly, they put them on. Gas flooded down, blanketing the street. A whirler lowered itself and they hurried aboard, immune from attacks by hoods, to whom a whirler would be a valuable prize. They lifted without delay.

Dr. Randolph Froding's lips were a thin pale scarlet. As he laughed, little bubbles formed on them, and a thin spray settled on the glass of the television screen.

"This next part of my experiment will be very interesting, you'll see, Controller," he said, glancing up, twinkling, at Prestige Normandi, Controller of the Advanced Alienation Hospital, a bald, plump man currently trying to look rather gaunt. Normandi did not like Dr. Froding, who constantly schemed for the controllership. He watched with a jaundiced eye as, on Froding's spy screen, the whirler carried Hoggart and Chief Adviser Utrect over the seamy artery of the Hudson.

"I can hardly watch any longer, Froding," he said, peering at his wrisputer. "I have other appointments. Besides, I do not see you have proved your point."

Froding tugged his sleeve in an irritating way.

"Just wait and watch this next part, Controller. This is where you'll see how Dimpsey Utrect really is." He mopped the screen with a Kleenex, gesturing lordly with it as if to say, "Be my guest, look your fill!"

Normandi fidgeted and looked; Froding was a forceful man.

They both stared as, in the 3V, the whirler could be seen to land on a bleak wharf, where guards met Utrect and Hoggart and escorted them into a warehouse. The screen blanked for a

moment and then Froding's spy flipped on again, showing
Utrect and Hoggard climbing out of an elevator and into a
heavily-guarded room, where a bulky man sat at a desk.

"I'm Disraeli," the bulky man said.

Froding nudged the Controller. "This is the interesting part,
Controller! See this new character? Notice anything funny
about him? Watch this next bit and you'll see what I'm getting
at."

On the screen, Disraeli was shaking hands with Hoggart and
Utrect. He wore the uniform and insignia of a general. He led
the two newcomers into an adjoining room, where ten men
stood stiffly around a table.

Bowing, Disraeli said, "These are the other members of our
secret committee. My I introduce Dickens, Thackeray, Gordon,
Palmerston, Gladstone, Livingstone, Landseer, Ruskin, Rag-
lan, and Prince Albert, from whom we all take our orders."

As Utrect and Hoggart moved solidly around the group,
shaking hands and making the secret sign, distant Machiavellian
Dr. Froding chuckled and sprayed the screen again.

"At last I'm proving to you, Controller, what I've been saying around the Lexington for years—Utrect is clean Dimpsey."

"He looks normal enough to me." Dirty little Froding; so
clearly after Utrect's job as well as Normandi's own.

"But observe the others, Prince Albert, Disraeli and the rest!
They aren't real people, you know, Controller. You didn't
think they were real people, did you? Utrect thinks they are
real people, but in fact they are dummies, mechanical dummies,
and Utrect is talking to them as if they were real people. That
proves his insanity, I think?"

Taken aback, Normandi said, ". . . Uh . . . I really have to go
now, Froding." Horrified by this glimpse into Froding's mentality, Normandi excused himself and almost ran from the
room.

Froding shook his head as the Controller hurried away. "He
too, poor schmuck, he too is near his upper limit. He will not
last long. It's all this overcrowding, of course, general deterior-
ation of the environment. The mentality also deteriorates."

He had his own method of safeguarding his own sanity.
That was why he had become a member of the Knights of
the Magnificent Microcosm. Although, as a bachelor, he was
allowed only this one small room with shared conveniences
with the specialist next door, he had rigged up internal 3V
circuits in it so as to enlarge his vistas enormously. Leaning
back, Froding could look at a bank of three unblinking
screens, each showing various parts of the room in which he

sat. One showed a high view of the room from above the autogrill, looking down on Froding from the front and depicting also the worn carpet and part of the rear wall where there hung a gray picture executed by a victim of anima-hostility. One showed a view across the length of the room from behind the door, with the carpet, part of the table, part of the folding bed, and the corner in which Froding's small personal library, together with his voluminous intimate personal dream diary, was housed in stacked tangerine crates. One showed a view from a corner, with the carpet, the more comfortable armchair, and the back of Froding's head as he sat in the chair, plus the three screens on which he was watching the three views of his room which included a view of him watching the three screens in his room on which he was watching this magnficent microcosm.

Meanwhile, at the subterranean PINCS HQ, Utrect had recognized Prince Albert; it was the Governor of New York City.

"We have a brief report of your activities in England, Hoggart," Albert said. "One question. How come you took so long to get here? You knew how vital it was to alert us."

Hoggart nodded. "I got away from Victoria's mausoleum before the destruction, as I told Nightingale and Disraeli. The information I thought I ought to reserve until I could talk to a top authority like yourself, sir, was this. Once Windsor and the Royal Mausoleum were destroyed, I believed I might be safe for an hour or two. So I went back."

"You went back to the devastated area?"

The Englishman inclined his head. "I went back to the devastated area. You see, I was curious to find out whether the Queen—as I suppose we must continue to call her—had been trying to obliterate me or the evidence. It was easy to get through the police and military cordon; it was only just going up, and the devastation covers several square miles. Finally, I got to the spot where I judged the mausoleum had stood. Sure enough, the hole under the vault was still there."

"What is so odd about this hole?" Dickens asked, leaning forward.

"It's no ordinary hole. I didn't really have time to look into it properly, but it—well, it baffles the sight. It's as if one were looking into a space—well, a space with more dimensions than ours; and that's just what I suspect it is. It's the way—a way, into Queen Victoria's world."

There was a general nodding of heads. Palmerston said in

a crisp English voice. "We'll take your word for it. Each of us bears a navel to indicate our insignificant origins. This hole you speak of may be Earth's navel. It is a not unreasonable place to expect to find it, in the circumstances, given the woman's mentality. We'd better inspect it as soon as possible. It will be guarded by now, of course."

"You can fix the guards?" Disraeli asked.

"Of course," Palmerston said.

"How about shooting a bit of hardware through the hole?"

They all consulted. The general feeling was that since they and possibly the whole world were doomed anyway, they might as well try a few H-bombs.

"No!" Utrect said. "Listen, think out the situation, gentlemen! We all have to accept the truth now. At last it is in the open. Our world, as we believed we knew it, is a fake, a fake almost from top to bottom. Everything we accept as a natural factor is a deception, mocked-up by someone—or some civilization—of almost unbelievable technological ability. Can you imagine the sheer complexity of a mind that invented human history alone? Pilgrim Fathers? Ice Age? Thirty Years' War? Charlemagne? Ancient Greece? The Albigensians? Imperial Rome? Abe Lincoln? The Civil War? All a tissue of lies— woven, maybe, by poly-progged computers.

"OK. Then we have to ask: *why?* What did they go to all the trouble for? Not just for fun! For an experiment of some kind. In some way, we must be a benefit to them. If we could see what that benefit was, then we might be in a bargaining position with—Queen Victoria."

There was a moment of silence.

"He has a point," Dickens said.

"We've no time," Disraeli said. "We want action. I'll settle for bombs."

"No, Disraeli," Albert said. "Florence Nightingale is right. We have everything to lose by hasty action. Victoria—or the Victorians—could wipe us out if they wanted. We must bargain if possible, as Nightingale says. The question is, what have we got that they need?"

Everyone started talking at once. Finally, Ruskin, who had the face of a well-known Russian statesman, said, "We know the answer to that. We have the anti-gravitational shield that is the latest Russo-American technological development. Next month, we activate it with full publicity, and shield the Earth from the moon's harmful tidal action. The shield is the greatest flowering of our Terrestrial technology. It would be invaluable even to these Victorians."

This brought a general buzz of agreement.

Utrect alone seemed unconvinced. Surely anyone who had set up a planet as an experimental environment would already have full command of gravitational effects. He said, doubtfully, "I think that psychoanalysts like myself can produce evidence to show that the Victorians' experiment is in any case nearly over. After all, experiments are generally run or financed only for a limited time. Our time's almost up."

"Very well, then," said Ruskin. "Then our anti-gravitational screen is the climax of the experiment. We hold onto it and we parley with the Victorians."

It seemed that the PINCS committee members would adopt this plan. Disraeli, Utrect, and Hoggart were to fly to Britain, meet Palmerston there, and put it into action. The three of them snatched a quick meal while the rest of the committee continued its discussion. Hoggart took a shower and a Draculin.

"Guess you were right to adopt a more gentle approach to Victoria," Disraeli told Utrect. "I'm just a dog-rough Army man myself, but I can take a hint. We can't expect to kill her. She's safe in her own dimension."

"I feel no animosity toward Victoria," Utrect said. "We still survive, don't we? Perhaps it is not her intention to kill us."

"You're changing your mind, aren't you?" Hoggart said.

"Could be. You and I are still alive, Bob! Maybe the object of the experiment was to see if we could work out the truth for ourselves. If we are actually of a primitive cave-dwelling race, maybe we've now proved ourselves worthy of Victoria's assistance. She just could be kind and gentle."

The other two laughed, but Utrect said, "I'd like to meet her. And I have an idea how we can get in contact with her —an idea I got from some rats. Let me draw you a sketch, Disraeli, and then your engineers can rig it for us in a couple of hours."

Disraeli looked strangely at him. "Rats? You get ideas off rats?"

"Plenty." And then he started trembling again. Could Victoria really be kind when she had them all in a vast rat-educator, or did he just *hope* she was, for his own and Karen's sake?

When Disraeli was studying the sketch Utrect made, Hoggart said confidentially in the latter's ear, "This Disraeli and all the other committee members—you don't see anything funny about them?"

"Funny? In what way?"

"They are real people, aren't they, I suppose? I mean, they couldn't be dummies, animated dummies, could they?" He looked at Utrect very chill and frightened.

Utrect threw back his head and laughed. "Come on, Bob! You're suggesting that Queen Victoria could have some sort of power over our minds to deceive us utterly—so that, for instance, when we get to England we shall not really have left the States at all! So that these people are just dummies and this is all some sort of paranoid episode without objective reality! Absolute nonsense!"

"It didn't happen. It was a phantasm of my tired over-crowded brain, without objective reality. Senior members of my staff do not spy on each other."

Thus spake Prestige Normandi, Controller of the Advanced Alienation Hospital to himself, as he strode away from Frod-ing's room down the crowded corridor toward his office. He was trying not to believe that Froding really had a bug ray on Utrect; it was against all ethics.

Yet what were ethics? It was only by slowly jettisoning them and other principles that people could live in such densities as Central New York; something had to give; their rather stuffy fathers back in the sixties would have found this city uninhabitable. Under the sheer psychic pressure of popu-lation, what was an odd hallucination now and again?

A case in point. The woman coming toward him along the corridor, that regal air, those grand old-fashioned clothes . . . Normandi had a distinct impression that this was some old-time sovereign, Queen Victoria or the Empress Elizabeth of Austria. He wasn't well up in history. She sailed by, seemed to shoot him a significant glance, and was gone.

Impressed, he thought, She really might have been there. Maybe it was a nurse going off duty, member of some odd society or other. Normandi disapproved of all these societies, believing they tended to encourage fantasies and neuroses, and was himself President of the Society for the Suppression of Societies. All the same, he was impressed enough by the regal apparition to pause at Burton's cell; Burton would know what to think, it was in his line.

But he was too tired for the Freud act. With his hand on the door knob, he paused, then he turned away and pushed through the mob which always jostled along the corridor, toward his own little haven.

Safely there, he sat at his desk and rested his eyes for a minute. Froding was scheming against Utrect. Of course

Utrect was probably spying against someone else. It was really deplorable, the state they had come to. Sadly, he slid open a secret drawer in his deck, switched on the power, and clicked switches. Then he sat forward, shading his eyes, to watch the disgusting Froding spying on Utrect.

Utrect and Hoggart were half comatose, eyes shaded against the bilious light inside the plane as it hurtled eastward across the Atlantic, England-bound.

The communications equipment Utrect had specified had been built and was stowed in the cargo hatch. Not until they were landing at Londonport in a rainy early afternoon did the news come through. Gripping Utrect's shoulder, Disraeli handed him a message from the PINCS undersea headquarters.

It read: "Regret to report that the Hiram Bucklefeather Building on Three Hundredth at Fifteenth was obliterated at seven-thirty this morning. All the occupants, estimated at upward of five thousand, were immediately annihilated. It is certain this was the work of the entity known as Queen Victoria."

"Your place?" Disraeli asked.

"Yes." He thought of Karen with her cyanosis and her tragic breathing. He thought of the two unhappy lads, dying a few feet apart. He thought of Cathie, a patient woman. He even recalled the two rats, slaving over their spelling. But above all, he thought of Karen, so keen to seem intellectual, so hopeless at being anything, her very psyche sapped by the pulsating life about her. He had always done too little for her. He closed his eyes, too late to trap a tear. His wife, his girl.

Lovely Elizabeth of Austria, murdered needlessly on a deserted quay beside her lady-in-waiting—an irrelevant tableau slipping in to perplex his grief. All sweet things dying.

As they hurried across the wet runway, Hoggart said shakily, "Victoria was after *me*, the bitch! She's a bitch! A bloody cow of a bitch, Douglas! Think of it—think of the way she built herself into the experiment as a sort of mother figure! Queen of England—sixty glorious years. Empress of India. She even named the age after herself. The Victorian Age. God Almighty! Began the experiment with her own supposed funeral, just for a laugh! What a cosmic bitch! By God . . ." He choked on his own anger.

Palmerston was there to meet them in a military car. He

shook Utrect's hand. He had heard the news. "You have my deepest sympathy."

"Why did she—what I can't understand—why did she destroy the building five hours after we had left?" Utrect asked painfully, as they whizzed from the airport, their apparatus stowed in the back of the car.

"I've worked that out," Hoggart said. "She missed me by an hour at Windsor, didn't she? It's British Summer Time here—the clocks go forward an hour. In New York, she missed us by five hours. She can't be all-knowing! She's going by Greenwich Mean Time. If she'd gone by local time, she'd have nailed us dead on both occasions."

"Ingenious," Disraeli admitted. "But if she can see us, then how could she make such a mistake?"

"I told you I thought there might be different dimensions down this hole we are going to investigate. Obviously, *time* is a little scrambled as well as the space between her world and ours, and it doesn't help her to be as effective as otherwise she might be. That could work to our advantage again."

"God knows, we need every advantage we can get," Palmerston said.

Alone in his little office, Controller Prestige Normandi sat shading his eyes and suffering the crowded woes of the world, but always watching his tiny secret screen, on which Dr. Froding, in his room, sat scanning the exploits of Utrect on his tiny screen. Psychic overcrowding with a vengeance, the Controller thought; and all the events that Utrect was now undergoing: were they real or, as Froding claimed, a paranoid episode without objective reality, enacted by dummies? Froding crouched motionless watching in his chair; Normandi did the same.

A knock at the door.

Quickly sliding the spy screen away in the secret door of his desk, Normandi rapped out an official order to enter.

Froding stepped in, closing the door behind him.

Suddenly atremble, Normandi clutched his throat. "Good Dimpsey! You're not really there. Froding, you're just a paranoic delusion! I must get away for a few days' rest! I know you're really down in your room, watching Utrect, sitting comfortably in your chair."

Swelling two inches all around, Froding stamped his foot. "I will not be referred to as a paranoic delusion, Controller! That is a dummy sitting in my chair; it has taken over and will not leave when asked. So I have wrung from you a confession that you spy on your staff! You have not heard the end of this, by any means, nor even the beginning."

"Let's be reasonable, Froding. Have a calmer with me." Hurriedly, Normandi went to a secret cupboard and brought out pills and a jug of chlorinated water. "We are reasonable men; let us discuss the situation reasonably. It boils down to the old question of what is reality, does it not? As I see it, improved means of communication have paradoxically taken mankind further from reality. We are all so near to each other that we seek to keep apart by interposing electronic circuits between us. Only psychic messages get through, but those we still prefer not to recognize officially. Can I believe anything I see Utrect doing when he is removed from me by so many scientifico-artistic systems? The trouble is, our minds identify television, even at its best, with the phantasms of inner vision—wait! I must write a paper on the subject!" He picked up a laserpen and scrawled a note on his writing screen. "So, contemporary history, which we experience through all these scientifico-artistic media, becomes as much a vehicle for fantasy as does past history, which comes filtered through the medium of past-time. What's real, Froding, tell me that, what is real?"

"Which reminds me," Froding said coldly. "I came in to tell you that Burton/Freud has escaped within the last few minutes."

"We can't let him get away! He's our star patient, nets us a fortune on the weekly 'Find the Mind' show!"

"I feel he is better free. We cannot help him at Lexington."

"He's *safer* confined here."

Froding raised an eyebrow loaded with irony. "You think so?"

"How did he get away?"

"His nurse Phyllis again, poor Phyllis. He attacked her, tied her up, and left his cell disguised as a woman, some say as Queen Victoria."

Effortlessly, Normandi made anti-life noises with his throat. "I saw her—him. She—he—passed me in the corridor. He—she—shot me a significant glance, as the writer says. . . . What are we to do?"

"You're the Controller. . . ." But not for so much longer, Froding thought. Events were rolling triumphantly in his direction. Utrect was as good as defeated; now Normandi also was on his way out. All he had to do now was get rid of that damned dummy sitting in his armchair.

Undisturbed by the gale of psychic distortion blowing about him, the dummy sat uncomfortably in Dr. Froding's chair and stared at the 3V screen.

In it, he could see Palmerston's large military car slowing as it reached the outskirts of Windsor. The pale face of Utrect looked out at the military barriers and machine gun posts.

Inwardly, Utrect fermented with anger at the thought of what had happened to his wife. All the hate in his unsettled nature seemed to boil to the surface. He had claimed that Victoria might be kind! He had spoken up against throwing bombs at her! Now he wished he could throw one himself.

Gradually, his emotionalism turned into something more chilly. He recalled the way poor insane Burton was lapsing back into Nineteenth Century dreams. He knew thousands of cases in New York alone. And all the little secret societies that covered America—they could be interpreted as a regression toward primitivism, as if a long hypnosis were wearing off. He recalled what they had said earlier: the big experiment was coming to an end. The various illusions were breaking up, becoming thin, transparent. Hence the widespread madness—to which, he realized bitterly, he was far from immune. He had enjoyed too deeply pretending to be the Emperor Franz Josef; now his real life Elizabeth had also been randomly assassinated.

So what was the aim of it all? Timed to run just a hundred years, only a few more weeks to go, this ghastly experiment of Victoria's had been aimed to prove *what*?

He could not believe that all mankind was set down on this temporary Earth merely to develop the Russo-American antigravitational shield. Victoria could have got away with a simpler, cheaper environmental cage than this, had she just required the development of the shield. No, the point of it all had to be something that would explain the great complexity of the teeming Terrestrial races, with all their varying degrees of accomplishment and different psychologies.

They were slogging across the wet and blasted ground of Windsor now, with two assistants dragging the communications equipment. Utrect stopped short. He had the answer!

It went through him like a toothache. He pictured the rats again. Man had carried out simple population-density experiments with rats as long ago as the Nineteen-Fifties. Those rats had been given food, water, sunlight, building material, and an environment which, initially at least, had been ideal. Then they had been left without external interference to breed and suffer the maladies resulting from subsequent over-population.

Now the experiment was being repeated—on a human scale!

It was the human population explosion—the explosion that mankind, try as it might, had never been able to control—which was being studied. Now it was breaking up because Victoria had all the data she needed. He figured that lethal interstellar gas would enfold Earth on New Year's Day 2001, a few weeks from now. Project X terminated successfully.

Unless . . .

The assistants were fixing up the communicator so that it shone down the hole. Soldiers were running up with a generator. A respectful distance away, tanks formed a perimeter, their snouts pointing inward. Each tank had a military figure standing on it, binoculars focused on the central group. A whirler hovered just above them, 3V cameras going. The rain fell sharply, bubbling into the pulverized ground.

Utrect knew what happened to rats at the end of an experiment. They never lived to a ripe old age. They were gassed or poisoned. He knew, too, where the rats came from. He had a vision of the true mankind—primitive people, on a primitive planet, scuttling like rats for shelter in their caves while the—the Victorians, the super-race, the giants, the merciless ones, the gods and goddesses, hunted them, picked them up squealing, conditioned them, dropped them into the big educator. To breed and suffer. As Karen had suffered.

Now, Disraeli and Palmerston gave the signal. Lights blazed along the facets of the communicator. Their message flashed down into the hole, one sentence changed into another and back, over and over, as the letter drums rolled.

I RECOGNIZE YOU

QUEEN VICTORIA

OFFER IDENTITY

CONSIDER PEACE

The rats were trying to parley!

For the first time, Utrect stared down into the hole that had once been hidden by the mausoleum—Earth's navel, as Palmerston had put it. The light coming from it was confusing. Not exactly too bright. Not exactly too dim. Just—wrong. Nastily and disturbingly wrong. And—yes, he swore it, something was moving down there. Where there had been emptiness, a confused shadow moved. The bitch goddess was coming to investigate!

Utrect still had his flick-knife. He did not decide what to do; he simply started doing it. The others were too late to hold him back. He was deaf to Hoggart's shout of warning. Avoiding the signaling device, he ran forward and dived head-first into the dimension hole.

It was a color he had not met before. A scent in his nostrils unknown. An air fresher, sharper, than any he had ever breathed. All reality had gone, except the precious reality of the blade in his hand. He seemed to be falling upward.

His conditioning dropped away, was ripped from his brain. He recalled then the simple and frightened peoples of the caves, living in community with some other animals, dependent mainly on the reindeer for their simple needs. There had not been many of them, comparatively speaking.

And the terrible lords of the starry mountains! Yes, he recalled them too, recalled them as being enemies whispered of in childhood before they were ever seen, striding, raying forth terrible beams of compulsion . . . lords of stars and mountains. . . .

The vision cut off as he hit dirt. He was wearing a simple skin. Grit rasped between his toes as he stood upright. He still had his knife. Scrubby bushes roundabout, a freshness like a chill. Strange cloud formations in a strange sky. *And a presence.*

She was so gigantic that momentarily he had not realized she was there. Of course I'm mad, he told himself. That guy in Vienna—he would say this was the ultimate in mother fixations! Sure enough, she was too big to fight, too horribly horribly big!

She grabbed him up between two immense pudgy fingers. She was imperious, regal, she was Queen Victoria. And she was not amused.

The dummy viewing the scene from Dr. Froding's armchair stirred uncomfortably. Some of the things one saw on 3V nowadays were really too alarming to bear.

Dr. Froding entered and pointed an accusing finger at the dummy.

"I accuse you of being the real Dr. Froding!"

"If I am the real Dr. Froding, who are you?"

"I am the real dummy."

"Let's not argue about such minor matters at a time like this! Something I have just witnessed on the box convinces me that the world, the galaxy, the whole universe as we know it —not to mention New York City—is about to be destroyed by lethal interstellar gas."

Froding jerked his head. "That's why I want to be the dummy!"

END